THE
BEST
HARDCORE
BAND IN PA

THE
BEST
HARDCORE
BAND IN PA

A NOVEL

BILL ELENBARK

Walrus Publishing | Harrisonville, MO 64701

Walrus Publishing
an imprint of Amphorae Publishing Group
Harrisonville, MO 64701

For information, contact:
Amphorae Publishing Group
117 South Lexington St., Suite 100
Harrisonville, MO 64701
www.amphoraepublishing.com

Manufactured in the United States of America
Cover Design by Kristina Blank Makansi
Cover art: IStock
Set in Adobe Caslon Pro and Battery Park
Library of Congress Control Number: 2022948577
ISBN: 9781736318232

To Mom and Dad

ONE

JEFF AND I PLAY IN A BAND. Blistering guitars and heavy drums, almost like punk but harder—hardcore—these devastating rhythms and insane screaming you can't understand on the first thirty listens, but the music builds, it builds then explodes, swift rattling beats bursting through the seams, and I can barely breathe when we're playing a song. I never listened to hardcore before Jeff, and I never thought I'd be in a band, but there isn't a music scene in Dallastown, no hardcore or raging punk, so Jeff said we should start the scene ourselves. That we should start a band.

I have a decent set of drums that I haven't practiced with enough but Jeff is good enough to cover, the way he's good at everything. Sometimes when we play, I'll drift away and imagine us on a stage, adrenaline rushing our veins, the mosh pits overflowing—filling to exploding—this massive crowd cheering for the best ever hardcore band in Pennsylvania.

"Dude, we suck," Jeff says, sweeping his hair away from his eyes. The stray strands stick to his skin. "I know it's only been a couple weeks but I figured we'd be better by now."

We've been practicing every night in his garage but we haven't gotten it down yet. We start to talk about what to play or how to play it but it's tough to describe how fast you should go or when the pauses should break, then Jeff whips out the weed and we forget what we wanted to play.

"Definitely," I say.

I get shy around Jeff sometimes, which is strange because I'm not that shy—I mean, I'm not some great conversationalist and I like to think before I speak, so maybe I am kind of shy, or people perceive me that way. But it's hard not to think about him, the way I think about him, the way the sweat glistens on his skin in the garage's flickering fluorescents, the tufted waves of brown settling over his ears.

We're friends. He's my best friend. I shouldn't want more than this.

That's what I keep telling myself.

"And we need a name. We can't get anywhere without a name," he says, wiping the sweat from his skin. The garage door is open but breezes die in August in Central P.A. "But it's got to be something cool, you know, something permanent. There's so many bands with shitty names."

"Right," I say.

"So I had this thought last night, like I'm lying in bed and I can't even sleep because I'm thinking about the band, trying to come up with names and then it hits me—what if we called ourselves Satan's Fingers. Like guitar strings?"

He tickles the strings of his ESP Viper, which is as good as a Fender, according to the guy at the York Music Shop.

"Or what about this?" He lets the guitar fall to his side and spreads his arms wide. "Young Vengeance. Or no, no, no. Velocity Fuck."

I adjust the cymbals on my swiveled seat behind the kit. We arranged his garage like a mini studio, my drum kit close to the garage door, across from a set of shelves filled with his stepfather's woodworking projects, the amp and speakers cater-cornered on the near wall.

"Dallastown Sucks My Balls?"

I laugh.

"You like that one?"

"Absolutely."

Dad got me the drum set for my thirteenth birthday because he didn't know what to get me, without Mom around to tell him, and I used to play a lot but I had stopped until Jeff suggested we start the band. So, I struggled at first. I mean, I knew how to set up the kit with the bass and the hi-hat, the snare to my left, cymbals to the right, and I knew how to grip the sticks but they kept slipping with every stroke, never the same force with each hit. And I keep striking with too much wrist, not enough rebound, this fitful movement and wasted motion, frantic stabs at forming a sound.

I'm not sure if Jeff has noticed. Sometimes he doesn't notice things.

"You ready to try again?" he says.

"Absolutely," I say.

The amp shoots out a spastic squeal and Jeff leans into it until the strings smooth into a crackling beat, his hands shifting up and down the spine, these wicked thoughts itching up and down my mind. I shouldn't think of him like that, look at him like that.

"You playing?" he says.

"Oh. Right."

I smash down on the snare, right foot on the bass, my sticks kicking up just enough to spark a series of sick rebounds, crashing cymbals ringing out like we're on a stage somehow, like we're stars now, the crowd below us roaring with the sound. Jeff's fingers float on the frets in front of me, the amp pulsing and crackling behind me, my hands straining and cracking, my foot on the bass keeping pace with his pace and we end the verse at the same time.

"That was awesome," he says, a wide bright smile spread across his lips, stepping toward my kit. "Great job, man."

"Thanks," I say. I'm not sure what to say. He sets his guitar against the wall and whips out the familiar Altoids tin from the pocket of his shorts.

"You want a break?"

The sweat is circling his skin—I can smell it on him, summer sun mixed with California beach, the scent of his Ocean Charge shampoo. I saw the bottle in his bathroom last week and I couldn't resist the urge to sniff.

"Sure." I set my sticks on the floor next to the kit.

"Oh shit, I forgot to tell you." Jeff eases onto a broken stool by the overhead door, packing the bowl with buds from the tin. "Joyce Manor is playing in Philly."

"Are you serious? When?"

"Next month. We should get tickets," he says.

"One hundred percent," I say, moving out from behind the kit to take a seat beside him on an upside-down milk crate.

Jeff is taller than me, five foot ten maybe, and not quite as thin—he has muscles where a body should have muscles, not just skin tagged tight to his bones.

"Do you think your sister could drive us?"

"She's leaving for college next week," I say.

"Damn, that's right. I missed my chance." He hands me the bowl.

"Relax."

"What? You don't think she's hot?"

"That's disgusting."

Jeff's bowl is a small glass pipe only the length of my finger, not big enough to hold too much but it fits inside the tin for easy storage. I flick on the lighter and suck in the smoke before release.

"I mean, set aside for a second that she's your sister," Jeff says, shifting on his stool as I hand him back the pipe. "And female. You can evaluate women, can't you?"

"Umm, no. Not her," I say, offended by the suggestion. Angela is nothing but an evil presence sent to torment me. "Can you tell which guys are hot?"

"Sure," he says, matter-of-fact. "I mean, I know I'm hot."

I laugh. We never talk like this.

Jeff's the only one at school who knows I'm gay. Not that I'm trying to hide, it's just I am kind of shy, and I don't have many friends other than him. After Mom died, I became the kid whose mom died, because twelve-year-olds don't know how to react to news like that. My classmates treated me like I had some rare disease they might catch if they spent too much time with me.

"Hey, so do you think your dad would mind if we practiced in your garage next time?" Jeff says.

"Oh, um. Our garage is pretty full. We've got some old furniture and my mom's clothes are packed away."

"I'm sorry," he says. "I didn't know."

"It's okay."

Mom knew. I know she knew. The way she never talked about girls or dating with me, like she talked to Angela. And I couldn't hide anything from her anyway. We were always close—Mom and me, separate from Angela and Dad—so when she died, I felt disconnected from them, like they were mourning in their own way, exchanging memories as stories that I couldn't bear to hear. It hurt too much.

"We could use the basement, I guess."

"Yeah. The acoustics are probably better there anyway."

Our basement is small and half-unfinished and the part that's finished is cramped as it is. But Jeff and I took over the space this summer, playing video games and listening to hardcore and punk on the stereo system I brought down from my bedroom.

"We're not allowed to play in here anymore?" I ask.

"No," Jeff says, handing me the bowl again. "The stepfuck told me to get our equipment out of here. Said we were 'encroaching on his space'." He air-quotes and intones like his stepfather's speaking, lowering his voice an octave or two. "We're not even in his parking spot. But God forbid we leave a stray strand of sweat in his path, the wrath of the righteous will rain down on our souls."

A group of middle-school kids bike past Jeff's front lawn, where a split-trunked maple with sprouted leaves obscures the view of the road. I take another hit as a smattering of red-and-gray finches on the maple's low branches chirp their way into our conversation.

"I can't take it, you know." Jeff stands up. "Like I finally have something I'm interested in—which he's been on me to show an interest in something—and I work all day at the Parks Department mowing lawns in the ridiculous heat to come home and have a little fun and now he says we can't even play in here anymore."

He lifts the wobbly stool he abandoned and smashes it against the floor, the splintered leg cracking across the concrete.

"Holy crap."

"I hate him, Cy," Jeff says. "Fuck his whole life."

Jeff's stepfather spends all his time at this crazy evangelical church in Red Lion, one of those places where the wife is to submit to her husband and sex outside of marriage is the unholiest of sins. My Aunt Donna says religions that focus on sex are afraid of women's sexuality, which is odd to me. I mean, I'm afraid of sex too but I would still like to have it—not with a woman, or a man, but last month on vacation in California, I met this cute boy named Cody who recognized my Joyce Manor T-shirt and we've been talking ever since.

"You know, I've been thinking about leaving," he says. "Maybe go live with my father down in Florida. Get the hell out of Dallastown for good."

Leaving Dallastown is one of our constant refrains, with so little to do and nothing ever to see and you can't get anywhere cool without a car or a license. Cody invited me to California when we spoke last night, said I could stay at his house. The heat presses into my skin.

"Have you been talking to him?" I say. "Your father?"

"No. He never reaches out," Jeff says. "And I still love my mom so I guess I'm stuck with the stepfuck until I graduate."

Jeff's father drank so much that his parents stopped talking and then they started fighting and it got so bad that his dad left—his mother and Jeff and the state behind. Jeff's pacing back and forth between our makeshift studio and the twin rows of shelving filled with shiny metal tools, paint, and glue.

"At least we have the band," Jeff says, stopping in front of me. "I would shoot myself if all I had to do is work at the Parks Department and get high."

He reaches forward like he's going for the pipe, but he brushes my elbow, his fingers on my skin. His brown hair is almost blond from all summer in the sun.

"We need to keep practicing, okay? Every day. So we could get good enough to start playing shows. High school parties at first but then we'll book gigs in town, or way out in Baltimore or Philly. Get the fuck out of this place."

He picks up the guitar and shifts into a violent riff as I watch transfixed.

Sometimes I get shy around Jeff and forget I'm supposed to speak.

TWO

"DID YOU EVER SETTLE ON A NAME?"

"We thought we did," I say, leaning back from my MacBook, set between The Drummer's Bible and several guides to reading music, half-opened and spread across my desk. "Do you know the Japandroids song, 'Lucifer's Symphony'?"

"Sure," Cody says. "The one with the long intro before they sing?"

"Yeah. That was going to be our name but last night Jeff got worried we'd get confused with classical bands so—"

"I'm not sure classical musicians are that big into Lucifer," Cody says. His hair is shorter than Jeff's, tight at the sides but fuller on top, brown at the roots and white at the tips. "I mean, they might be, but are they even in 'bands'? Isn't the symphony itself a band by proxy?"

"I'm not sure."

"I feel like we've digressed."

He smiles at me, the sun through the skylight above his head. His top teeth to the left impinge on the others and on FaceTime, he's beautiful.

"Well, I'd like to hear you play it at least. If you don't mind me being all fanboy and all," he says. "If you become famous, or when you become famous, I want it to be known I was your first fan."

"It would be my honor," I say and divert my eyes from his reaction because I'm blushing too much to look up. Cody's younger than me, only by a few months, but it's enough that we're a grade apart so I think he looks up to me. No one ever looks up to me.

"What are you up to tonight?" he says.

"We're going to a party."

"What party?"

The poster on the wall behind him is a picture of a lone surfer shrouded by the sun at the crest of a wave.

"My sister's. I mean, it's not her party, but some friends of hers."

"So, you're crashing a party?" Cody says.

"Pretty much."

My walls are littered with posters of bands, not surfing: Joyce Manor live in black-and-white with Maybe Human is Not Such a Bad Thing to Be scrawled at the base of a three-paneled print above my desk; Cloud Nothings' Here and Nowhere Else, with the photo of a European-style house in muted brown and beige above my unmade bed; Iceage's Beyondless, with the molecular blood vessel zoomed-in, red-and-white with a splash of purple on the side, on the opposite wall above my dresser.

"I've never crashed a party before. I'm quite jealous."

"Well, I'm jealous that you've already been to the beach today and I haven't even left my room."

Cody spent the morning surfing on a beach within walking distance from his house, which is such an odd concept I can't even be upset. I don't have a car or a license, so the three-hour drive to the Jersey Shore might as well be forever.

"At least you're out of bed," he says. "That's a fifty-fifty proposition when we talk."

"Relax," I say. He laughs. We've talked almost every night since we met, up close on each other's laptops, like we're in the same room. Except his room is a massive converted attic while mine is a tiny cave at the back of our house where the neighbor's overgrown oaks obscure all light through my windows. "What are your plans? Something cool and Southern California, possibly involving surfing?"

"I wish," he says. "I have to work."

"Oh, right. I'm sorry."

"Nah, it's okay," he says. "It's every Saturday night, so it's normal by now. And sometimes you happen to meet someone who makes the fact that you're not crashing parties with tu hermana worth it."

My dad travels for work all the time, lately to Southern California, and the last time he went, he extended his stay for a few extra days so I could join him in L.A., my first trip to the state. On our last night there, we stopped by Manhattan Beach and inside the ice cream shop, this olive-skinned boy behind the counter smiled and said he liked my T-shirt. A Joyce Manor shirt featuring the cover art from their latest album, Cody.

Almost like it's fate.

"Cyrus!" The scream is followed by a knock—three sharp bangs on my door. "Dad is calling for you."

Angela leans inside the room and Cody can see her over my shoulder with the way my laptop is positioned. His eyes grow wide.

"Get your ass downstairs," she says, looking around the space. "And make your bed, for fuck's sake."

She slams the door shut.

"Is that your sister?"

"Yup."

"She seems nice."

He holds his smile a second longer than usual, and my heart wrenches from the front of my chest into my throat until I don't think I can speak. In a good way.

"Well, I need to get going anyway," he says. "I have to make my brother breakfast. Same time tomorrow?"

"Absolutely," I say.

We haven't talked about dating because of the distance but it feels like something we both would want if we were closer. Dad goes back to the state next week and I thought about asking to go with him but I don't want to leave Jeff, with the band just beginning and all of the practice we're putting in.

"You going to make your bed for me tomorrow?" he says.

"For you, not my sister," I say and he laughs, his blinking eyes meeting mine on the screen.

We don't get to kiss because the technology doesn't exist to bend time and space and have us physically in the same place. But I think he wants to kiss me. I want him to kiss me. We time our goodbyes with extended smiles on each other's screens.

Angela parks her car pretty far from Tyler Brower's uncle's house, but it's a dead-end street and you can hear the party from where we parked, hip-hop blaring with bass beats pounding, students on the lawn drinking beer from silver cans. We weren't actually invited because we don't know Tyler, but he's holding a blowout for the graduating seniors who are fleeing Dallastown this week. My sister spots some friends as we walk up the driveway and abandons us at once. I stay close to Jeff.

"Do you want to head inside or stay out here?" I say.

"I want to find beer," Jeff says, curving away from the driveway across the withered brown grass, his tank top showing off the shoulders and arms that grew muscles this summer, mowing lawns for the Parks Department. He points to several cases of beer on the lawn next to the house.

"So, outside?" I say. He laughs.

While Jeff sneaks us a couple cans, I watch the football jocks doing keg stands on the porch, upperclassmen that would never speak to me at school. Or here. Not that I equate myself with the gay boys online lusting over thick muscled guys with biceps on top of biceps, but some of them look decent under the lights without shirts. Jeff spots Sharane across the lawn.

"Hey Cyrus," she says when we approach.

She's shorter than me with curly black hair that she's straightened tonight, glitter at the sides of her eyes. Some Drake song swells from the speakers at the side of the house.

"How long have you been here?" Jeff asks.

"Not long. But Mindy said she's got to get home so we need to leave soon."

"It's not even late," Jeff says.

"I know. But her mom is super strict," she says.

Sharane's voice is pitched and kind of grating and there's something in the casual way she's speaking to Jeff that's irritating. I tug on his shirt to pull him back toward the porch but he ignores.

"How's the practice going?" Sharane says.

"Not great," Jeff says.

I don't know how she knows about the band unless they've been hanging out, which he hasn't mentioned, but with the way he's reacting to her every little sentence I can tell more is happening than him just being polite. I take a breath. I get kind of crazy when he talks to girls.

"Cyrus?" Sharane says.

"Huh?"

"I said, how do you think you're doing?"

Jeff slaps me on the arm, pretty hard but with a laugh. I run my sneakers through the sticky brown grass. "We smoked earlier," he says. "I think Cy had too much."

We smoked, but that was a while ago and I'm pretty sure I'm sober. Just annoyed. He hasn't had a girlfriend in the year we've been hanging out and it could mean something or it could mean nothing, but sometimes I hope it means everything.

"What instrument do you play?" Sharane asks. She has a harsh face with square features, the chin not quite right and jutting out.

"Drums."

"He's good," Jeff says. "But I'm playing horribly. I need to get used to this new guitar and we need to start writing songs. I tried but I haven't come with anything decent and Cy's the writing talent so I'm leaving it up to him."

"I am?"

"I want two songs by Monday," he says, touching my arm again. I look down to my elbow and he pulls it away.

"Hi Cyrus," Mindy says, approaching from the side with two cups in her hands.

She's taller than Sharane and wearing a long-sleeve shirt instead of Sharane's low-cut display. And I know her better—we sat together in English class last year, exchanging cracks about Ms. Patterson's breakfast choice each morning—bacon and eggs or everything bagels, detectable from the third row.

"How's your summer been?" she says.

"Not bad," I say. "Just working."

"You're at the high school, right?"

"Yeah, Cy couldn't get enough of school so he decided to spend his summer there," Jeff says.

"I didn't decide that," I say, throwing an elbow into his side. One of Dad's poker buddies is on the Board of Education and got me the position. I've spent every week stuck inside the guidance office while Jeff is outside at the Parks Department, in the sun getting tanned. His skin shines in the half-light from the porch, a perfect shade of copper, like he's spent all summer on the beaches of California, not this wasted space in central P.A.

"What do you do at school?" Sharane asks.

"Nothing. It's mostly a time suck."

"He gets to see the records of all the students," Jeff says.

"Really?"

Mindy's eyes widen as she leans in, the four of us forming an egg-shaped circle on the lawn.

"I'm not supposed to look at them," I say, "but it's not like anyone cares if I take a glance."

"Did you see mine?" Sharane says, brushing up against Jeff's shoulder. She keeps touching him.

"No."

"Mine?" Mindy says.

I shake my head as the music plays louder—Cardi B. I think, with all the cursing, but I don't follow hip-hop so I get the artists confused.

"What are you guys drinking?" Jeff says.

"Punch," Sharane says.

"Mixed with?"

Mindy examines her cup like she's considering.

"Alcohol?"

Jeff laughs and Sharane reaches for his arm again, petting him like a dog. I hate her. He doesn't pull away.

"Did you get your schedule yet?" Mindy asks. "They have it online."

"Not yet," I say.

"I got Mr. Oates for AP History," Mindy says. "My sister said he's excellent."

Mindy's one of the top students in our class and we did a history project together last fall—a reenactment of the Gettysburg address in Claymation form that she filmed on her laptop in painstaking detail. I helped her mold a few clay figures and we both got an A. She's kind of amazing.

"I'll have to take a look," I say.

I'm a pretty good student but I keep a low profile, so none of the teachers ever notice me, except Ms. Patterson in English. She pulled me aside after class one time to tell me she likes my writing and that I should keep working at it, the way she could see the "potential" in my stories, which sounds more like criticism than praise, but it's more than any other teacher offered so I took as a good thing.

"Hold on, hold on," Mindy says. "Sharane said you guys are in a band?"

"They are," Sharane says, like she's part of our management team.

"What do you play?" Mindy says.

"Hardcore," Jeff says. "Mixed with punk. Cy is writing some songs so we can start recording next week."

He keeps saying that. I don't know why he keeps saying that.

"Awesome," Mindy says. "I'm in. When's the next practice?"

"Huh?" Jeff says.

"I'm joining your band," Mindy says. "What do you need me to play?"

"What do you play?"

"Well, I'm classically trained in piano but I know guitar and a little drums, and I've got mad skills on the violin even though I haven't taken any lessons," she says. "It's kind of insane when you think about it."

"She's super talented," Sharane says. A swarm of mosquitos emerge near my head and I almost strike her as I swat them away.

"Sorry," I say.

"Here, take down my number," Mindy says, reaching for my phone. She puts in her digits with a "Mindy" and a heart.

"Call me before your next practice." She hands me back the phone and latches onto my forearm. "I'm serious."

"Okay," I say.

I'm not sure what to say. I don't have any female friends, none that I'm close with. I like that it's just Jeff and me.

"You want this?" Mindy hands me her drink, still full because she didn't take a sip. "We need to leave."

"Now?" Sharane says.

"I'm sorry, I suck. But my mom is not aware I'm at a party. Nor will she ever find out." Mindy turns to Jeff. "Snitches get stitches, okay?"

Sharane and Jeff laugh at the same time and she promises to text him when she gets home. I blink and take a lengthy drink from Mindy's cup, double-fisting it with my beer. Jeff heads over to get another can from the random 12-pack on the lawn as more students spill outside, outlines of bodies stumbling into the field at the edge of the house, zombies seeking their prey.

"What do you think of Mindy?" Jeff asks, popping open a Natural Light. "Apparently she's into you. That's what Sharane said."

"When were you talking to Sharane?"

"I don't know, the other night. She's been calling me, I guess."

"Are you guys going out?"

"No," Jeff says. "I mean, nothing's happened yet."

He sips at his beer and avoids my stare. The scent of manure from some nearby farm makes me sneeze.

"Bless you," Jeff says, lowering his voice. "I didn't tell her anything about—you know. I wouldn't betray that."

He extends his arm around my neck, loosely then tightly, squeezing my skin. I'm watching the jocks without shirts upside down at the keg, all that wet and shiny flesh and my head begins to spin.

"You're a good friend, Cy. You know that, right?"

I get shy around Jeff and forget I'm supposed to speak.

"And no joke," he says. "I want two songs by Monday."

He pulls me close again, his warm body taking hold of me. I keep holding on.

THREE

JEFF MOVED INTO my neighborhood last summer from Red Lion, which feeds Dallastown High so he didn't have to switch, and I remembered him from freshman year, passing by my locker between 2nd and 3rd periods, close-cropped hair with preppy collared shirts, not the style at the time so maybe that's why I noticed him. That or the pinkish tint of his cheeks, even in winter, dimples wide with every smile and the brown hair turned blond under the hallway lights. I was out for a run before school started, training for cross-country, when I spotted him in front of his stepfather's house—back and forth along the lawn with a push mower, shirt removed. He waved at me—I'm not sure why because we never spoke at school, but I panicked and tripped over the bending curb in front of his house, falling face-first for the sidewalk. I reached out in time to keep my skull from cracking on impact, but it took weeks for the wounds to heal where the skin scraped the concrete.

When school started Jeff stopped by my locker, waited a beat and told me, "If there was a diving team here, you'd have to try out. Your form is impeccable." Then he smiled, his sideways smile beneath blue eyes. We've been friends ever since.

"Yo, Cyrus, mon, what you doing?"

This guy in a cowboy hat with a Jamaican accent stops me in Tyler Brower's uncle's kitchen.

"Um, what?"

White guy. Cowboy hat. Jamaican accent. I don't know him.

"I say, what you be doing?" he repeats.

Reggae is blaring over speakers down the hall but it sounds distant. I'm sober, or mostly sober, but I can't quite focus through the thick haze of smoke floating through the rooms. Cowboy is swaying next to me.

"I'm looking for someone," I say. "Do you know Jeff Connor?"

Jeff got wasted at the party—multiple shots with old friends from Red Lion—and I needed to piss, upstairs near the bedrooms because the bathroom downstairs was occupied, and now I can't find him, in and out of rooms filled with people making out, boys and girls who go to my school but I don't know them—I don't recognize anyone at the party, through crowded spaces full of strangers with no sign of Jeff. I'm freaking.

"Yah, he be downstairs," Cowboy says. "He be telling stories 'bout you mon."

"What?"

"Dude, you be tripping."

"I am?"

Cowboy laughs.

"You funny, Cyrus, you funny."

He waves me through the kitchen, down a set of stairs into the basement, where the walls are paneled with slate gray tiles, like floor coverings tacked along the sheetrock, peeling off from all the humidity or not enough glue or the drifting cloud of weed clogging the room. I spot Jeff through the mist.

"This is the guy, this is THE guy."

Jeff's shirt is off and he's perched on a circular table covered with cards and piles of poker chips for a game no one is playing. A bunch of guys are scattered on beat-up couches around a massive makeshift bong, the Marley loud out of speakers in the ceiling. No woman, no cry.

"We got a band," Jeff says. "Tell them we got a band."

He jumps off the table and wraps his arm around my neck. I feel his sweat on my skin.

"Cy, you gotta tell them, they don't believe me about our band."

He looks into my eyes like he's not quite there, more stoned than I've ever seen him. His hair is flat, matted down with sweat or water, and I'm having trouble concentrating with the music reverberating. The thick scent of musky skunk permeates the furniture.

"We don't have a name but we have some good names and I think Cy likes it. Did you guys meet Cyrus? He's the drummer."

"Yo, Cyrus," this red-haired guy shouts, near the bong, an oversized beaker with a pipe-shaped bowl molded into the side. "You want a hit?"

I shake my head and he dips his face over the opening, shaggy clown-wig hair spilling around the glass. The bubbles pop through my head.

"Can someone turn off this faggot music," this short squat guy says, nearer to Jeff and me.

"Excuse me?"

Cowboy steps forward but bumps against the table and stumbles sideways onto the couch. Everyone laughs at him.

"You're about as Jamaican as I am," the homophobe says. "And this shit is killing my buzz."

'Whatever, mon," Cowboy says, then loses the accent. "Marley is my jam."

"Why don't you fuckers play?" the red-headed guy calls out.

"Do you want to?" Jeff asks me, backing away.

The sight of his bare chest starts to clear my head. Or distracts me more.

"What?"

"We should play for them," Jeff says, pushing his face into my face. A wasted smile spreads across his lips.

"We don't have our instruments."

He watches me, more confused than anything, reaching out for my Cloud Nothings T-shirt to steady himself. It's fraying at the edges but I wear it all the time because it's the first shirt I ever owned with a band's logo on the front.

"Wait, what's happening?" Jeff says. His eyes won't focus.

"We have to go."

Angela was texting when I was searching for Jeff and I don't know if she's already left. She would definitely leave me.

"Nah, Cyrus mon, just stay. We all be chilling," Cowboy says, up off the couch and over to the bong. I hear footfalls above us, banging around the kitchen.

"We can stay a little longer, right?" Jeff asks, wrapping his arm around my neck again. I close my eyes for a second.

The banging upstairs turns to shouting and someone comes screaming down the steps.

"Cops!"

"Fuck!" the redhead shouts and then everyone is up, shoveling beer cans beneath the cushions and under the couch for some reason. The beaker bong sways on its axis but Cowboy reaches out to keep the glass from shattering.

"I can't get arrested, Cy," Jeff says, pulling me close to him, his pupils like pools I could sink beneath. "My stepfather will destroy me."

"Okay," I say. "I'll get you out."

We pick up his shirt and follow the crowd up the stairs to the landing, the flashing lights down the hall burning bright through the house. A bunch of girls push past us to the front, but Jeff yanks on my Tee, grabbing the Cloud Nothings until it rips all the way, the left side of my body from my armpit to my waist exposed to the skin. Like Jeff's naked skin. He points and indicates without words. We need to go out the back.

I follow—well I lead, but it's him directing—up a short staircase down a back corridor into an empty room with beer bottles strewn and spinning, abandoned mid-drink, the sound of the sirens louder now and the lights brighter from the front of the house. We push into the backyard.

Jeff slips from my grip, hurtling ahead on the slick wet grass but I catch up to him, latching around his waist. There's an open field to our left, past the street by the house, lit up by floodlights from the police cars, loudspeakers commanding kids to hit the ground.

I don't know if the Dallastown police are hardcore enough to shoot high school students attending a party but it's dark behind the house so we veer through the trees into the neighbor's yard. Jeff leans on me as we run, his breath heavy on my cheek, which would normally excite me but not now, in the neighbor's backyard chasing shadows toward trees I hope are fleeing students and not the fucking police.

We make our way to the road, away from the lights of the police cars where Angela parked, on the grass of an abandoned house down the street from Tyler Brower's uncle. We were late to arrive and that was the only spot we could find at the time, fortunate now, but Jeff can't run any farther—his body hangs on my shoulder, so I jerk him forward in one swift motion, digging deep into reserves built through years of cross-country to drag his body, limp beside me, across the road to my sister's car.

"Get in," she says, yanking Jeff up the step and into the Jeep's backseat with the strength of a thousand men. Or one pissed-off sister.

"He better not puke," she says after I climb into the front. "You're paying to get this detailed."

I nod as she rips the car into reverse, peeling away from the cops quicker than I would have in this situation. I lean back to see if Jeff's okay, his eyes half-open, the wind from the open roof spinning his hair in the air in feathery ribbons.

"Is he going to puke?" she says, hitting a hard turn to the right at top speed.

"If you keep driving like this."

"Fuck you, Cyrus." She hangs a left onto the entry ramp of the highway. I look back to Jeff again.

"Cyrus," he says, his eyes finding mine.

"You okay?" I say.

"I don't know, man, this is the weirdest feeling," he says. "Like everything is fractured, or distant, floating in front of me. And I can see so it's not my eyes, it's in my mind which is the most fucked up part about it. It's like I'm watching myself and I'm watching you and I wish you were here with me, Cy. High with me."

Angela switches lanes at full speed, shaking her head the whole time.

"He needs to come home with us," I tell her. "He's too wasted. His stepfather's sort of an—"

"—Asshole," Angela says.

He had a reputation in our neighborhood, even before Jeff.

"Yeah," I say. "We can't drop him off in this condition."

"No," she says. "I guess not."

"I appreciate it," I say, waiting for her to acknowledge, but she's too busy shouting at an SUV slowing down in the left lane. It's enough that she waited and is bringing Jeff home with us. With me.

I turn to tell him what's happening but he's asleep now, eyes closed and the tufted hair spreading in the breeze. He's never stayed over my house before, which isn't that surprising because we're not little kids and he only lives a couple blocks away, but sometimes when I'm falling asleep in my bed, I dream that he's with me in my bedroom, squeezed onto the mattress beside me.

Sometimes it's all I think about.

FOUR

JEFF IS PASSED OUT in my bed. I have many feelings.

It's difficult to rank them, difficult to process even, as I scramble to find my sleeping bag among the Christmas decorations and way too many blankets in the upstairs closet.

Angela got us home, which is more than I expected, but she didn't help with my search and Jeff is passed out half-naked on my mattress. I guess I could share the bed with him, and that shouldn't be too weird because he's my best friend and we're only friends, and he doesn't know that I think about him like that—the way I think about him.

"Is this what you're looking for?" Dad calls from the other end of the hall, stepping down the pull-down stairs to our attic. His poker friends were gone by the time we got home and I don't know if he knows I've been drinking.

"Thanks," I say as he hands me one of the rolled-up blue-and-white 'Penn State' sleeping bags he got for the whole family to celebrate Angela's acceptance into college last Christmas. "Good night."

"Cyrus." Dad waits until I turn back around. I wipe my nose to hide my alcohol breath. "Everything okay?"

"No. I mean, yes, I just—" I clutch the sleeping bag to my chest. "Heading to bed."

"How was the party?" he says, stepping too close.

I nod a bunch of times, afraid to speak. I need to get to my room and I need to check my hair and my face—maybe brush my teeth and throw half a bottle of Listerine down my throat—just in case I get close enough to Jeff. Close enough to kiss.

"Cyrus, this is probably not the time, and I don't want to make this more awkward than it needs to be, but—" He hesitates and now I don't think it's about the drinking but I don't know what's happening. "If Angela had a boy sleep over, I wouldn't let him sleep in her room."

He folds his arms beneath his Drexel Engineering T-shirt, the one he wears to impress his poker friends because they all wear sports jerseys and Dad's not into sports—I mean, he watches the games, way more than me because I follow no sports whatsoever even though I run cross-country but—what is he saying?

"You know I'm okay with your—" He pauses once more and this time I know why and I don't want him to say it because I'd rather sprint headfirst through the bathroom window than have him finish that sentence with a euphemism for gay sex. "So this is not a judgment. But you're fifteen for two more weeks and if you and Jeff are—"

"Oh god, Dad. We're friends," I say, shaking my head back and forth so hard it might break. "Jeff is straight. And he's passed out—err, sleeping. But straight. Fully."

"Okay." Dad nods. "Well, we will discuss the 'passed out' portion of the sleepover request tomorrow because you are also too young to be drinking."

Dad has a specific way of speaking, like an engineer speaks. Too exact or direct. The opposite of Mom.

"I love you," he says, turning and retreating down the hall to push the ladder back into the attic before I can respond. "Good night, Cyrus."

I don't have time for the bathroom so I open and close the bedroom door, as quiet as I can so I don't disturb Jeff but he's already awake, sitting up halfway in my bed, bare chest and disheveled hair, the hallway lights glaring through the opening.

"Hey."

"You're awake?"

"No," he says, slumping back to the mattress on his side. "But every time I close my eyes the room starts spinning, so—"

I feed him some water I brought into the room earlier, when I found a non-ripped shirt to pull over my chest. He coughs mid-swallow and spills it on my sheets.

"Sorry," he says.

"It's okay."

I unfurl the sleeping bag next to my bed.

"Cy, you missed some awesomeness in the basement. That bong was unreal."

"You disappeared," I say. "I couldn't find you."

"Did I?" His words are muffled, from the side of his mouth. "I'm sorry."

"It's okay. I found you."

I shift inside the sleeping bag, zippering it up around me because Angela keeps the air conditioning on full blast upstairs and doesn't let me change it. Jeff moves to the edge of the bed, facing me.

"So those guys in the basement were asking what we play and I told them hardcore, but hardcore means so many things to so many people, you know," Jeff says. "I think we need something more concrete. Like a song we can master, that could be our sound."

"What song were you thinking?" I say.

"I don't know," he says. "The room is still spinning."

My sleeping bag is centered beneath the ceiling fan, notably not spinning, between the twin bed on one wall and the desk on the other, the backyard behind me. I have a small dresser in the corner with an alarm clock I never set and deodorant I sometimes forget, plus hand lotion Mom told me to apply to my elbows and hands, to keep them from chafing in the winters of central P.A. The blue bottle with the lavender scent she used to apply every day.

"Where's your Cloud Nothings shirt?"

"It ripped," I say.

"It did?"

"Yeah. You ripped it. You don't remember?"

He laughs and shakes his head, his brownish-blond hair falling over his face. He leans over and whispers "I'm sorry" again.

It was hard on me when Mom died. How could it not be? And I know my depression was normal—even the therapist said it was normal, but I didn't want normal, nothing could be normal without her around. I retreated further, from Dad and Angela and the friends I used to have, the other kids in school who treated me like I had a disease—the "dead mother disease"—and the only thing I found that helped was to talk to her. Every night before I go to sleep. I tell her about my day, however shitty it was or how much better it's been since Jeff and I started hanging out. How happy I think she would be for me. I miss her all the time.

"Cy," Jeff says, leaning over again. "What are we going to do about Roland?"

"I don't know," I say. I texted the stepfuck from Jeff's phone and he responded with a series of escalating threats demanding he come home. Then his phone died and I haven't tried to recharge it.

"Can you set your alarm for seven? If I get home in time for church he might not lose his mind."

Jeff tries to avoid upsetting the stepfuck because his reactions are so extreme, like the thing with the garage or staying over a friend's house, apparently. I whip out my phone to set the alarm and notice a missed call from Cody.

"Who called you?" Jeff asks, squinting at my phone. "Did the stepfuck call you?"

"No," I say. "It's—no one."

I haven't told him about Cody. I'm not sure why.

"Is it a boy?" Jeff asks.

"No," I say, but I'm blushing, deep enough Jeff must have noticed. Even in the dark of the room.

"You're funny," he says, shifting his pillow over the edge of the mattress, closer to me. "I know you're gay, Cy. You can tell me if you met a boy."

It's so cold in the room I think my nipples are hard. "What?"

"Holy shit, you did."

Jeff reacts like this is the best gossip he's ever heard from me. Which it probably is.

"What's his name?"

"Cody."

"Does he go to Dallastown?"

"No." I shake my head. "I met him in California."

"Seriously?" Jeff says.

"Yeah, it's nothing. We've been talking, you know. Long distance."

"But you like him."

I close my eyes, shifting inside the sleeping bag. It isn't thick enough for any kind of comfort, but the bed is too small for the two of us and it's a ridiculous thought, to want to sleep with him. A ridiculous thought I can't get out of my head.

"Did you kiss him?" Jeff says.

I shake my head. I think the shade of red I've actually turned is not on the official color charts.

"Do you want to kiss him?"

"Maybe."

I open my eyes. Maybe it's better that we're only friends. I don't talk about this stuff with anyone.

"Cy, can I ask you something?"

"Sure."

The vents are still spewing frozen air but I can't see Jeff's face all bundled up in my sleeping bag so I sit up a bit and turn.

"Have you ever kissed a boy before?"

I shake my head.

"A girl?"

I'm still shaking.

"Have you?"

He nods.

"How many times?"

"Have I kissed a girl?"

"Yeah."

"Umm… I'm not sure. A few. But none this summer, it's been a bit of a dry spell." He laughs to himself, but not like he's upset about it. "Been spending too much time with you, I guess."

"Maybe I turned you gay."

I say it like a joke and I meant as a joke but he watches me. Considering.

"Maybe."

I catch the stars through the window because I forgot to close the blinds and they're shining outside. Or my brain exploded and this is the afterlife because then Jeff asks if I've ever thought about kissing him and I don't respond because I can't lie—not that I shouldn't lie, it's just I cannot at this moment formulate a thought let alone a lie and the room feels hot instead of Arctic cold and I want to rip off my T-shirt and touch his chest to my chest.

"So, you have thought about it," he says, his eyes clearer than they've been all night. He wipes his hair away from his forehead.

"Are you still high?" I say.

"Definitely. Why?"

"Because you'd never talk about this sober."

"No, probably not." He shifts closer. "Not this either."

It's still dark in the room so I kind of can't see when he leans forward and kisses me.

It's quick and it misses my lips and he pulls back even quicker. The whites of his eyes are lit up in the stars in the windows behind me.

He leans forward once more and we kiss for real this time.

My brain really did explode.

FIVE

JEFF'S PUNISHMENT is extreme. Strict quarantine until the start of school. He can't leave the house, not without one of his parents, unless it's something church-related, which he wouldn't do without one of his parents, and the stepfuck took away his phone for five days. He got it back last night, so we talked for a bit but he didn't talk about the kiss.

I wanted to—it's the only thing I've thought about all week—his lips on my lips, dry at first, or stiff, I guess. But when I tasted his spit on my tongue, every organ inside my chest pushed into my throat then burst through my mouth like a plant in bloom, fast-forward on the Discovery Channel, green flowered buds becoming white silken petals shot out from the stem.

After we separated, Jeff laughed—we both laughed—because we're best friends and we shouldn't be kissing, or maybe we should, and we did, and I wanted to—and we did—but I never had something I wanted that bad come true so I had no frame of reference. Then Jeff rolled over and fell asleep, or fake fell asleep, so I was sitting on the sleeping bag on the floor next to my mattress, thinking of moving to the bed, but the longer I sat there the more awkward it felt to try to make that move, not knowing how he'd react and knowing I'd have to wake him up to squeeze onto the mattress, so I decided a trip to the bathroom might provide some kind of cover but when I got back he was snoring and the next morning he was gone.

I didn't hear from him all week.

"Cyrus?"

Mindy Won is standing in the doorway of the guidance office in a rainbow-colored shirt, book bag slung over her shoulder.

"Hey, Cyrus!"

She's way more excited than anyone needs to be excited inside our high school in the summer.

"What are you doing here?"

"Great to see you, too." She scrunches her face and I feel bad but I didn't mean it to be mean, I'm just surprised. "I was supposed to meet up with Dr. Gallagher, but Ms. Stillwater said he wasn't in so I figured I'd come by and see you."

Jeff picked out a song for us last night so I stayed up late trying to learn "Younger Us" by Japandroids. It's super hard to master, the way the Japandroids' drummer rotates through the beats with unrelenting speed, but I have all weekend to practice. Jeff's on punishment so I have nothing else to do.

"Why did you want to see the principal?"

"I have all these forms to fill out to try to get students signed up as volunteers at the Food Bank, like as an after-school activity for service credits." She taps on her backpack and her eyes stray to the wall behind me, a collage of college brochures I spent way too long assembling. "I've been trying to make an appointment but no one seems to answer the phone."

"The secretaries here aren't the greatest," I say, although technically I'm supposed to answer when no one else answers, which is annoying. I hate picking up the phone.

"I'm not sure what the mix-up was but hey, I'm here now, so—" A wide smile forms across her lips. "What's up?"

"Nothing," I say, which is the truth.

"What are your plans for the weekend?"

I don't respond because "hoping Jeff calls" isn't an actual plan. But Sharane told Jeff she was into me so if I told her about Jeff and me, she would know that I'm gay and let me get back to pretending to work in peace. Which sounds meaner than I mean it, but I'm tired. And I miss Jeff.

"Earth to Cyrus," she says, waving her hand in front of my eyes. I don't know how long she's been waiting.

"I'm trying to learn a song," I say. "For the band."

"What song?"

"It's called 'Younger Us.' By Japandroids."

"Japan what?" she says.

"Droids. They're Canadian."

"The droids are Canadian? Were they manufactured in Japan?"

"No, I mean, um—they're from Canada. The band. They're white."

I turn thirty-eight shades of this-is-not-okay, because she's Asian-American and that had to be offensive, and now I realize I never asked which nation her parents emigrated from, which is even more offensive. I think.

"You're funny, Cyrus," she says. "Quiet. But funny."

Her hair is pulled back from her eyes, with a large blue clip at the center holding the stray strands in place, and her lips have a fresh coat of paint, this bright bluish purple, matching the tie-dye on her shirt. We've always been cool

in class but I haven't thought of her like that because I
don't ever think of girls like that. Not anymore. In sixth or
seventh grade I started to notice girls a bit, because all the
boys in my class were talking about the girls in class, but I
never wanted to kiss one—a girl—the way I wanted to kiss
the boys. And I know it's not the same for everyone—how
it's confusing for some—but Jeff's always been clear with
me about being straight. Then he kissed me in my bedroom.

"Well, first of all, I will indeed check out these droids
from Japan by way of our great neighbor to the north,
because if I am to play in this band, I will need a better
descriptor of your sound than 'hardcore,'" she says, waving
her hands as she speaks. "And I'm still not sure if you need
a bassist or a keyboardist, or a singer maybe? I do sing in
choir for the church."

"Jeff's the singer," I say.

"Okay, good. Because I'm a horrible singer. The church,
they take anyone." She laughs at her own joke and I force
a smile. "Anyway, other than practicing the song by the
hardcore band with the weird name, are you otherwise
free?"

I look toward the wall of windows separating the
guidance office from the hallway, pretending like I'm
figuring out whether or not I can rearrange my busy
schedule on such short notice. I do have FaceTime with
Cody planned, and I do feel bad for kissing Jeff without
telling Cody, because he's smart and funny and he wouldn't
have to be blackout drunk to kiss me, I don't think. Mindy
shakes her head.

"You know, Cyrus, I remember you being chattier in
English class. What was the word you used to describe Ms.
Patterson's breath?"

"Rungent."

"Of course. So pungent you need to run away."

She smiles and waits for me to speak but I don't know what to say. I wish Jeff hadn't said anything, or Sharane hadn't said anything to Jeff, because this shouldn't be awkward—Mindy and me—and if we were only friends, she could help me sort out what's going on with Jeff. I mean, I guess I couldn't tell her because then I'd be outing Jeff, but I'm dying to tell someone. To make it real.

"Well, if you are free, there's this documentary playing in Glen Rock I wanted to check out and I thought you might join me," she says. "It's about skaters and punk music and I don't know if you skate but if you're into hardcore, you must be into punk, right?"

"Uh huh."

"Okay, perfect. I'll pick you up tomorrow night?"

I squint and grit my teeth, like I'm confused about what's happening, because I don't know what's happening or what I just agreed to but she doesn't seem to notice.

"Text me your address. I'll send you the movie schedule."

"O—kay," I say, leaning back in my faux leather seat because Mindy is cool—she used to make Ms. Patterson's class bearable—but she's way more forward than I was ready for and I don't know how to get out of this.

"Don't be so frightened, Cyrus," she says, her wide smile spread beneath her purple lips. "It's just a movie. What's the worst that could happen?"

"It was a disaster."

Cody coughs on his coffee through the laptop, the liquid spilling up the straw over the sides of his cup.

"Let me get this straight," he says. "You didn't sit with your date. On your date."

"I mean, no. Not after the previews."

"But why? I need details." His wispy eyebrows furrow on my screen.

"Well, you know how the theaters have assigned seating—at least by me they do."

"We've had that in California for years."

He sets his cold brew out of view.

"Right," I say. "Of course."

His hair is curly and brown but the California sun turns most of it blond and he enhances the tips with a white-colored gel to keep it light and slick and straight.

"Well, Mindy texted which seat she got so I could get a seat next to her and I must have read the text wrong or fat fingered the request but we realized when we got there we'd bought different seats."

"Oh my god."

"Yeah, so at first it was fine and I sat next to her. But then some old couple came in and one of them had my seat and they wouldn't switch."

"So, you moved?"

I nod, reaching for my water on the nightstand next to my mattress but the bottle is empty.

"And you watched the entire movie in separate seats?"

"Pretty much."

"Oh my god, you're so gay." He laughs. Cody convinced his mother to convert the attic into a bedroom this summer, to give him more room and more freedom from his brother, a gift of sorts after she finalized the divorce from his father. The sunshine through the skylight bathes the surfing poster behind his bed in yellows and oranges and reds.

"She still doesn't know you're gay?"

I crinkle my nose. "No."

"You're crazy," he says, leaning away from his desk, tucked into an alcove next to a window, cater-cornered from the bed. "Is there going to be a second date?"

"I had no idea this was a date!" I say. "Not until she picked me up wearing a dress."

"And what were you wearing?" Cody says.

"This." I point to my METZ T-shirt—the one with the drums at the center on a stark black background—because that's what I was wearing when she arrived last night in her summer dress, low-cut with a pattern of bluish-green flowers over her breasts. "I haven't changed."

I haven't even gotten out of bed.

"Was there a mention of a second date?"

"No. We talked about the documentary after, which was really good. Side note, I did not realize documentaries could be good." Cody laughs. "But then we fell into silence for the rest of the ride home. There's no way she's doing that again."

"Don't underestimate yourself, Cyrus—wait, do I know your last name?"

"I'm not sure."

It looks like his FaceTime might have frozen for a moment.

"Is it going to remain a mystery?"

"Oh. Yes. Mystery. That's who Cyrus Dunn is. A man of mystery—hey wait—"

He laughs at my lame attempt at humor.

"Cyrus Dunn, huh?" Cody says, sucking at the bottom of his cup, the ice sticking to the plastic. "Is that Irish?"

"I think so. My mom was Polish and my dad is Irish and German," I say. "I don't know. I guess I'm just white?"

"Muy blanco."

I laugh. His brown eyes sparkle when he spins in his chair, the tips of his hair like icicles in the skylight.

"Um, es tu nombre?" I say, the accent all wrong. He laughs. Señora Diaz gave up on correcting my pronunciations two months into Spanish III.

"I appreciate the effort," he says. "Martin. Cody Martin. My dad is muy blanco."

Cody's parents were separated for years before the divorce and I guess they still get along. His mom and his brother live with him in Manhattan Beach and his father lives in a neighboring town a bike ride away.

"Well, Cody Martin, it's nice to formally meet you."

"Same here, Cyrus Dunn." He sticks out his hand to shake through the laptop and I follow suit, like we've just signed a contract for representation for our band. He laughs again.

"And maybe we could formally go to a movie next time I'm in California?" I say.

"I mean, sure," he says. "But I do prefer dates that sit next to me."

"Who said anything about a date?"

"Oh right, I forgot. Cyrus Dunn needs exact clarification as to what constitutes a date."

"This is true," I say. "Or at least some assistance on seat selection in a movie theater app."

He snorts through his laughter and drops the cup of ice. I like this, flirting like this—I think this is flirting—and taking the lead, because the distance makes it easier, easier than Jeff and me. And Cody's out, which is less confusing than Jeff, but also—he isn't Jeff. We still haven't talked—not for very long and not about the kiss. Last night before

Mindy picked me up, Jeff had Japandroids cranking on his laptop speakers while he spoke in short, low bursts so the stepfuck couldn't hear him.

I hear knocking at my door.

"Hey Cody, I gotta go," I say.

"No worries. Call me later."

"Absolutely."

He smiles, the sun in his eyes, bright and brown with the lashes dipping down, curly like his hair and shining in the light. I hold on for as long as I can before I stumble out of bed to let Dad in.

"You're not dressed?"

Cody called before his morning surfing session, which is early for us but he was eager for details when I texted about the "date."

"Did you forget your driving lesson?" Dad says, standing in the doorway. "Again."

"No."

I do have a vague recollection of driving practice, but Dad's been so smothering this week—more than his usual smothering—with Angela off to Penn State. It's like we don't have the balance of my sister's attitude to distract us from ourselves.

"I set aside this Sunday for you," he says. "You could at least be ready."

"I am," I say, adding. "I will be."

Dad's job involves managing massive schedules on projects he'll print out and tape to the dining room wall some nights, so he schedules everything in his life within an inch of a minute and doesn't quite get why I don't do that too. Like if I procrastinate on my homework or say I'll get to it later, he thinks it's a personal affront to him. Like his brain can't compute why I would let something fun get in the way of "my responsibilities" and then he'll ask formal questions like "were you not aware you had homework to complete?"

It's annoying.

"You're almost sixteen, Cyrus. You need to start being more responsible." He steps two steps inside the room. "I need you to follow through when I ask you to do things. I don't ask for much."

I don't know why he's saying that, because he asks me for a lot of things, I just don't have the energy for an argument this morning. Sometimes I think he makes up reasons to be upset because I never get in trouble in school and I never drank before Jeff and Jeff smokes way more than me. He gives me a curt "ten minutes," and leaves the door open behind him.

During our last session before the party at Tyler Brower's uncle's house, Jeff suggested we run away to Brooklyn, where all these punk bands play and they know each other and support one another and if we practiced long enough, we could become part of the scene, like Joyce Manor or Cloud Nothings, who both formed when their members were sixteen. I wonder if Jeff would come out if we ran away to Brooklyn, so we could be in the band and be lovers too.

I wonder if we'll still be friends if he doesn't want to kiss me again.

It's killing me.

SIX

I'M AFRAID TO DRIVE. The couple times Dad took me around the neighborhood I got so panicked when another car approached, I'd come to a complete stop instead of risking a crash. And I don't get it, the mechanics of it. I'll get behind the wheel and start thinking about what I'm supposed to do or where I'm supposed to look, so when another car comes I switch to the brakes immediately. Just in case. Dad tries to assure with calm, direct language but he's not at all reassuring. He can't explain things like a normal person explains things, like he's on step three of a thirty-eight-step instruction about a complex traffic situation and all I'm trying to do is not confuse the gas with the brake.

Angela says I'm afraid to drive because Mom died in a car accident. It's not something I like to think about, or talk about, the way her body got crushed beneath the tire of the tractor-trailer that lost control in the storm.

Her body. That's the way Dad described her before the funeral, that HER BODY was too damaged to keep the casket open.

It's not something I like to think about.

When I think about Mom, it's on Saturday mornings, when Dad played in a basketball league so Mom was alone in her bedroom, and I would wander down the hall, knock three times, and walk inside to her smile. My parents' window at the side faces the backyard with its overhanging trees, the flowering leaves extensions of her hair as I'd enter the room and climb up under the covers—even when I got older—letting her squeeze me super tight until I couldn't breathe.

Mom used to write out her lectures in long hand on Saturdays and I would tuck myself between her breasts and her stomach, eyes closed as she rehearsed the words she'd tell her students about racial disparities in economic outcomes or the inherent power of the word "feminist." I remember the scent of her skin, the powdery lavender of the lotion I still use as my own, but sometimes I forget what her hair smelled like, or the exact shade of her eyes. Sometimes I forget whether she showed her teeth when she smiled.

"Pull up there next to the cones," Dad says.

We're in the lot next to the high school, where Dad set up orange cones for me to practice parallel parking.

"The key is to pull up alongside the car ahead," he says, "and then as you're backing in, you reverse the wheel when your car is halfway past."

I stare at him. I'm not following.

"Go ahead, put the car in reverse."

He's a great dad, but it's like having a teacher for a parent and not the cool kind who lets you write creative essays in lieu of boring treatises about history. He's more like a math teacher who illustrates an equation in painstaking detail and if you fail to follow the formula exactly, like if you forget to carry the zero, the answer falls apart and he narrows his eyes thinking, "Is my son an idiot?"

At least that's what I'm afraid he's thinking.

"Okay," I say. I wind the wheel to the right to move the tail to the left and it's working at first, it always works at first, but then I start to panic.

"Keep going, keep going," he says, turning to check the cones behind as I ease off the gas, almost to a stop.

"Now you're at the halfway point, reverse direction."

It seems way too soon to spin the wheel without hitting the cones on my side but he nods, pushing his sunglasses into his eyes, and I cut the wheel in one swift motion as the car slides into place. I don't even touch a cone.

"Perfect! See how easy that is?"

I inch the Altima forward and release my grip on the wheel.

"It's all angles, Cyrus. You have to trust the geometry."

"Did you say 'trust the geometry'?"

"I did," Dad says and he laughs, a soft chuckle that gets stuck in his throat, like he's afraid to let it out. He hasn't laughed much since Mom died. I think he's afraid to.

"Cyrus, I wanted to talk to you about this week," he says.

Ugh. I feel like we've talked enough to last several months.

"My flight out of Philadelphia is at 7:42 A.M. on Tuesday so I'll be leaving the house by 5. I'll stop in and say goodbye even though you'll be asleep, but you're on your own for getting up for school—"

"We don't start school until Wednesday."

"I'm aware," he says, looking at me with a mixture of pity and disdain. "I meant you'd be on your own for waking up for school Wednesday and Thursday and Friday. I won't be back until Friday night."

His hair is thinning at the top so he grows it long on one side and sweeps the hair over to cover the looming bald-pocalypse. Sometimes it looks fine but when it's windy out like this morning, the hair spins sideways and gathers in a lopsided clump on one half of his head. I don't mention it.

"You know I've been traveling a lot with this project in Ontario and unfortunately, it's not going to let up—it's every other week until Thanksgiving. And without Angela home, you're going to have to handle things on your own. The cooking, cleaning up the dishes, your schoolwork. Everything, Cyrus." He pauses, gauging my reaction like an algorithm. "I know it's not fair to you and believe me, I'd rather not be traveling this much, but I'll be back for your birthday. It just won't be until you're home from school."

I came out to Angela on my thirteenth birthday, my first birthday without Mom. She was trying to cheer me up or at least keep me company and she said it flatly, not mean-spirited, "so you're into boys, right? Not girls?" And I nodded. I told her she could tell Dad because I didn't know how to tell him, the way I imagined him sitting and staring, studying my face, trying to gauge the statistical equation that turned his only son gay. But he sat me down after Angela spilled and he said that he loved me. Which is all I could ask for.

"I recommend you use your alarm clock and set it across the room so you need to physically get out of bed to shut it off."

"My phone is fine."

"Your phone is glued to your hip," he says. "And we all know you click it right off and return to sleep."

"Not always."

He frowns. He's had to drag me out of bed every day this summer to get me up for work. I'd stay up late with Jeff the night before, practicing with the band or playing video games in my basement. Dreaming.

"I won't be there to bang on your door," Dad says. "I need you to step up to the plate."

"Okay," I say, even though I don't know what plate he's referring to and my mind has already wandered to Jeff and me this week, his punishment over and Dad gone on a work trip. The house empty for just the two of us.

"Do you think you can handle all that?"

"Yeah."

"I'm serious, pal," he says. "I need to know you can handle it."

"I will," I say, coughing a bit because he keeps staring at me.

"Do you want me to have Aunt Donna check in on you?" he says. "Maybe cook a meal or two." He pauses. "I could ask her."

"Don't bother Donna."

I love his sister—she's an awesome aunt—and she helped us a lot when Mom died, because Mom was an only child and her parents live way the hell out in South Jersey, so it was just Dad and Donna and us, trying to survive. But she's a nurse at York Hospital and I'm pretty sure taking care of her teenaged nephew is not at the top of her To-Do List this week.

"Well, you have her number," Dad says. "I'll make sure she checks on you at least."

"Okay," I say.

"I love you, pal," he says and I don't know why he keeps calling me that. He reaches out and kind of rough-touches my shoulder because he could not be more awkward. I recoil as a reflex.

"I love you too, Dad," I say. Suppressing the grimace.

He smiles and reaches up to smooth his lopsided hair.

"Do you want to try parallel parking again?"

"Oh god no," I say and he laughs, not full-throated but closer this time.

It's nice to hear him laugh.

SEVEN

CHURCH FOR THE DEAD. It's a great name for a hardcore band and "Metronomy" is easier to learn than "Younger Us," which I couldn't quite master. It has less singing and more repeated drumming, the backing beat for an insane level of guitar playing, looping and twisting through a layered wall of sound, reverb then release, gathering speed as the singer screams, "there's no one I see" over and over then back again, like a towering crescendo brimming with rage. The first two minutes are more languorous, the drums a steady bass beat on repeat, and that part I have down, two hours into practice, the opening part before the song becomes insane.

"Do you want to break?" Jeff says.

We're down in my basement, on the carpeted portion near the stairs, my drum kit in the recessed space between the steps and the wall, Jeff to my right with the amp and a microphone in front of the water heater.

"Absolutely." I smile.

I've been trying to limit the awkward as much as possible even though it's close to impossible because the last time we were together, we kissed in my bedroom and we haven't mentioned it since.

"Wait—what do you mean?"

"Um, weed?" I say. We always smoke during a break.

"Right. Yes. But no." He shakes his head. "For all I know, Roland's going to drug test me when he comes home from work."

It's the last day of summer break and Dad's away so we have the house to ourselves, down in the basement where a single light bulb hangs down from the rafters on a rusted metal chain, brightening the whole space. Brightening Jeff's face.

"I'm sixteen. But crashing at my friend's house after the one fucking party I went to all summer is reason enough to send me away to school with Jesus freaks. It's such bullshit."

The stepfuck threatened to send him to some religious school near Harrisburg affiliated with his church, this super Christian place meant to indoctrinate, and now Jeff has to be on his best behavior just to remain in Dallastown. Which he hates.

"Okay, forget the break, we gotta get this down."

He strums the guitar through a loud, angry riff.

"But here's the hard part, right? It gets super fast after the bridge."

On the first day of summer break, we were down here in my basement playing Zelda or something, Jeff's iPhone connected to my portable speakers—Cloud Nothings maybe, or Joyce Manor—not Church for the Dead, because I didn't know them at the time, but that's when he told me we should start a band, a hardcore band, to make the scene in Dallastown. He was high and I thought he might not remember when he sobered up but that night after he left, I found my drum kit in the attic and dragged it to the basement one piece at a time.

"And I'm going to try singing on this one," he says, pulling the microphone on its stand and turning it on, testing one two one two.

To make room for the equipment we had to move the rusted bench where we sat playing video games all summer, the one that sat on our front lawn until too many storms rendered the paint too worn and Mom didn't have the heart to throw it away.

Jeff signals for me start, the way I'm supposed to start, clicking my sticks together with a quick riff on the snare. There's some reverberation on the microphone when Jeff starts out droning, low guttural vocals that match his guitar, just like Church for the Dead does. There isn't much drumming at the start, a few repeated steps—steady bass then the snare between kicks. And we've done this part all afternoon so it's almost rote memory now, thirty seconds, then sixty seconds, then ninety seconds of building before breaking with a wave of anticipation, then the song explodes—Jeff faster than me almost immediately—so I pick up my pace, elbows straight with alternating repeats, cymbals and bass, slipping to the snares, both hands focused on my quickening sticks as Jeff's voice emerges around me, filling the space with his sound.

"Now look what you've done.

Please look what you've done!"

The adrenaline sweeps through me as Jeff's vocals turn to screams, my foot on the bass trying to keep pace with his pace, but no one can drum at this clip. Not me. I almost miss and lose my sticks but Jeff keeps playing so I step up my steps, not on the beat of the song anymore but keeping my own tempo, kicking on the down beat, spinning through an awkward fill as Jeff turns to me, pointing.

"There's no one I see."

I scream the response: "No one I see!"

"There's no one I see."

"No one I see!"

"There's no one I see."

"No one I see!"

Jeff gives me the cut-it sign from the side of my eye but it doesn't register in the part of my brain still playing, this rush of energy sucking me in like the endorphin spin at the end of a cross-country race, my sticks on the snare then splashing at the cymbals as Jeff sets down his guitar and moves behind me, his hands on my shoulders. I keep playing.

He squeezes on my neck, his breath on my skin, and I'm slamming at the skins, faster and faster as he presses harder, his fingers ringing down my spine until I elbow him on instinct and he yanks me back, off the kit and into the wall, down to the floor next to the kit. And then we're wrestling, clutching and grabbing on the faded brown carpeting in the corner of the basement.

Jeff is stronger than me so he's holding me down but I'm not putting up much resistance or just enough to keep him guessing because he's peppering me with punches and I'm breathing him in, the ocean breeze or the summer sun, the sweat on his skin. It's everything.

We wrestled once before, earlier in the summer in my backyard after hammering each other with Dad's football— for fun—and it seemed normal enough that I didn't put too much into it—the touching and grabbing on the freshly mowed lawn. It's something all boys do, a quick release of energy, whether or not you're on the wrestling team, but this is more, so much more, this sweaty knotted mess of overheated flesh on the floor of my basement.

Jeff lets go long enough for me to scramble away but he's not only stronger he's quicker and he tackles me again, pulling me back to the carpeting, his warm body splayed over my body, punching at my stomach. I reach out for his arm to stop the thrusts, grabbing near his wrist and twisting.

He winces and I reverse positions, escaping to my knees. He rolls onto his stomach and his T-shirt drifts up his back, all bare and fucking beautiful.

"Wait," he says.

I climb up the bottom step, about to launch across the space like we're in a wrestling ring.

"Wait."

Jeff has a grip on his wrist, the one that I twisted, flexing his fingers. I'm breathing hard and I'm hard as a rock and I don't even try to hide my erection.

"Are you okay?"

He tests the fingers of his left hand then he's back to his wrist, squeezing with his other hand. His hair falls around his face.

"I think, uh."

He's focused on his hand, the one that holds the neck of his guitar and the future of our band. I step off the steps to move closer.

"Are you okay?"

He's shaking his head so I crouch down to my knees. The scent of his shampoo is intoxicating.

"I think it's, uh—"

He spins toward me and I see a smile slip across his lips before he attacks, an instant thrust into my gut that knocks me flat on my back. He screams—a primal scream—and lunges on top of me. The fucker faked his injury.

I try to fend off the barrage but he's punching too fast, straddling me and pounding on me, in the side and against my chest, but I can't block the jabs because my hands are trapped between his knees and my hips, and I can't resist— why would I resist—as his butt sinks into my groin and his hands keeps touching my chest. Something's happening, more than just us wrestling.

He leans forward, into me, the salty scents escaping his skin. I feel his heart against my chest, the rhythm not like mine at all—faster and more spastic, speeding up then slowing down. His face is close to my face, his blue eyes lingering, a few stray strands of his hair touching my check.

I lift my lips toward his lips. Just barely.

He pulls away, jumping off of me and up to his feet by the stairs.

"We should get back to practice," he says, breathing heavy.

I'm sprawled out on the carpeting with my erection showing through my shorts. He steps over to his guitar, his back turned to me.

"We need to get this down," he says, toying with the strings. "We were close."

I wait, the way I'm always waiting. And all of this waiting is nothing more than wanting because you can't wait without wanting the wait to be over.

"Come on, Cy, we don't have much time," he says, looking up from the guitar. "I need to be home before Roland gets back from work."

I pull my legs into my chest, adjusting myself, and he notices, he definitely notices, but he doesn't say anything. I need to know what he's thinking, if what happened in my bedroom is going to happen again.

"Now look what you've done," I say.

"What?"

I bite at my lip as he strums his guitar. I don't know why we aren't kissing. We were so close to kissing.

"Please look what you've done," I say.

"What the fuck, Cy?"

He watches me, picking at the frets with the tips of his fingers. I want to say something but I can't say something because what if he thinks the kiss was a mistake and he doesn't feel the same way and bringing it up would make it awkward between us. Too awkward to stay friends even.

"That's a great fucking line," I say.

"Seriously?" He looks at me for a few wasted seconds but then he laughs. "You're fucked up, you know that, Cy?"

I climb off the floor and straighten my shorts and wait for him to react but he doesn't react.

"Come on, let's play," he says.

You can't wait without wanting the wait to be over.

EIGHT

I DECIDED TO RUN home after practice today.

School was…or lunch was…Jeff was…

Even after practice, exhausted and sweaty, I didn't want to make the walk past Jeff's house, or be tempted to walk past his house, to stop by and say hi if the stepfuck wasn't home, ask him if we could talk about the kiss, actually discuss the kiss that seems more distant every second because I don't think he even remembers. I mean, I know he remembers but he's acting like he doesn't, with the way he was flirting with Sharane in front of me at lunch today. I had to run home.

Past the junior high through Inners Creek, which isn't a creek—it's a couple swampy ponds, back around the tennis courts and burnt grass fields where the football stadium used to be, cutting down the stretch of New School Lane that turns uphill at a 45-degree angle, straining with every stride along the span of massive homes that used to be farms, cresting the peak where I would typically sprint but I'm so out of shape I had to walk the rest of the way.

"I'm in here, Cyrus!"

"What the fuck?" I say, closing the door behind me. "What are you doing here?"

"That's a lovely way to greet your favorite aunt," Donna calls from the kitchen.

"I'm sorry, you just—you startled me."

"You didn't see my car in the driveway?"

I look at her confused because her car must have been in the driveway but I think I blacked out the last few blocks home.

"Well, either way, hi," Donna says, out of the kitchen to the living room to hug me tight. "Did you really think I was going to leave you alone for your Sixteenth Birthday Eve?"

"Birthday Eve?"

"That's what I said." She returns to the stove to maneuver a pot and two pans around the burners. "Birthday Eve is the last day before you turn too old to find a decent guy so you give up hope and decide to be celibate, but then you talk yourself into some cute creep on Tinder halfway through a box of wine and then you meet him in person and question your judgment on everything." She flips over several breasts of chicken in the pan. "Or maybe that's just my birthdays."

I laugh. Donna's always had a unique outlook on life.

"Anyway, how have you been?" she says. "You look sweaty."

I reach down for my calves because I should have stretched more and I also need to shower but I want to collapse in my bed and sleep until the morning.

"Cross-country practice."

"Right. What exactly do you practice? Running?"

"Pretty much."

She laughs as I pull a Pedialyte from the refrigerator.

"Ah, good ole Pedialyte. I've consumed way too many of those for—um, hydration." She's dressed in her scrubs so

I think she came right from the hospital. "Some real advice for you, Cyrus, now that you're almost an adult. It's always best to stop before you finish the entire box of wine."

Donna and Dad are not at all alike—almost like Angela and me. She babysat for us when we were little and she would let us stay up late to watch Adult Swim because I don't think she knew what it was or who it was intended for, but it was a cartoon and what cartoons are on at that hour so we watched a lot of Meatwad and Frylock on Aqua Teen Hunger Force, which was pretty hardcore for a nine-year-old, and my sister wouldn't last—she'd be appalled by some ridiculous scene like neighbor Carl getting gang-raped by genetically mutant dogs, and she'd storm off to her bedroom. But Donna was cool like that—she was always cool like that, and after Mom died, I would bike over to her apartment to get away from the house, from Angela and Dad's separate mourning routine. The way Mom hung over everything.

"How's school? What grade is this now?"

"Eleventh," I say. "It's okay."

It hasn't been okay. Sharane and Mindy decided to sit with Jeff and me at lunch and Sharane's been flirting with him. Nonstop. Jeff ignored at first but now he's touching her arm and laughing at her stupid jokes, and today they shared a candy bar from the vending machine. It's killing me.

"Jesus Christ, you're getting old. I'm getting old. Your father—every year he gets fucking older and drags me with him. Asshole."

Donna never talks to me like I'm a kid. That's why I like her so much.

"Dad's forty-five, right?"

"I don't fucking know." She sets down the spatula and steps to the refrigerator. "You have any wine in here?"

I laugh again. Donna was in a long-term relationship with this guy named Doug who proposed to her and broke up with her in the same week. I never saw her cry before—like I thought she was too cool to be upset by life, but I caught her crying in Dad's arms in the living room after Doug left. I knew I hated that asshole for a reason.

"So get this, Cyrus." She fishes a half-empty bottle from the back of the fridge and sets it on the counter. Her waves of blond hair are disheveled from her shift. "This kid—a fucking goddamn CNA—he asked how old I was today."

"Okay," I say.

"Do you not know how offensive that is?"

"Um, yes?"

Donna glares at me like she might kill me next. I glance over to the stove, smoke rising in billowing columns from each of the burners. She finds a glass and pours the wine, unconcerned.

"It's insanely offensive. And I gave him this psychotic look like I was going to yank out his tongue if he said anything else and then he started stuttering like an idiot."

I nod because I'm not sure if I should laugh. I wonder if the fire extinguisher is still under the sink.

"I don't know, I guess he's just a child. But apparently your fucking generation didn't learn the tenets of social relations."

"Donna—" I say, pointing to the stove.

"Shit."

She rushes over and pushes the pans off the burners then turns on the exhaust to suck up the smoke. The fire starts to dissipate.

"Dinner's ready," she says.

I help her set the table and dish out two plates of pan-burned chicken, yellow rice, and wilted broccoli, which is not exactly a birthday meal, but she's not exactly a chef, not that I mind. The burnt parts of the chicken are rather delicious and the meal I'd been planning tonight was microwave pizza from the freezer.

"But seriously, tell me how you're doing," Donna says from the side of the table where Angela sits.

Our kitchen is open with a half-height counter that blends into the dining room, a smallish space with an oval table tucked into a corner near the outside wall. The living room extends to the right, bigger and more utilized than the dining area, at least since Mom died. Dad's turned this table into his office in recent weeks, working down here almost every night.

"How's school, really?"

"Fine." I try to scoop up the rice with my fork but it keeps falling off the tines.

"Cyrus," she says, reaching back to form her hair into a ponytail, swinging it into a knot without looking. Like magic. "What's wrong?"

"It's nothing," I say. "I mean, it's fine. I'd rather not talk about it."

Lunch is the one class I share with Jeff this year so it's the only time I see him all day, squeezed in next to Sharane, across from me, and she wouldn't stop talking to him today, or throwing herself on top of him—it's so desperate it's almost pathetic because he's not into girls—unless he's bi, which he might be, but he won't even acknowledge the kiss. It's killing me.

"Are you sure?" Donna says, leaning forward.

"Yeah, it's nothing," I say, because Donna doesn't know I have feelings for Jeff—no one does—and that's kind of the point of the story, how Jeff seems to have forgotten our kiss because he was drunk, I guess, and he wasn't ever into me.

"Cyrus." She sets down her fork with a cling on the plate. "I worked a sixteen-hour shift at the hospital yesterday and another shift today and I haven't had a man to my apartment since you were in tenth grade so I don't care how pointless you think this story is." She picks up the chicken with her hands. "It's all I got."

"Well," I say, shifting to some gossip I can share. "I did go on a date last week."

"Wait, wait, wait—hold on a second." She rips off a piece of chicken with her teeth. "With a boy?"

"A girl."

"What girl? Do not tell me you're straight now."

"No." I laugh. "Still gay."

"Good. Good." She shakes her head. "Straight men are the worst. But why were you on a date—who's this girl?"

"Her name is Mindy," I say. "She's really cool and funny and I didn't know it was a date until I saw how she was dressed—in an actual dress, nothing too fancy but way more dressy than my dirty shorts and shirt."

"You wore dirty shorts?"

"Dad didn't do the laundry."

"Nice. You should learn how to do your own laundry you know," Donna says, wiping off her hands as she picks up the wine. There's a fake chandelier off-center over the table, casting indiscriminate shadows across her face. "But you should start dressing better if you want to start dating boys. All the gay guys I know are pretty into fashion."

I'm still in my running clothes, which aren't much different from my regular "beach-style" attire—board shorts and T-shirts and last season's worn-down running shoes. The gay fashion gene didn't make its way to me.

"I could use some help in that area," I say.

"I'll take you shopping," she says then she gasps. "No, really. I'll take you shopping. It will be awesome! Not here, though. This town sucks. But there's a couple places in Harrisburg we could go." She empties the rest of the bottle of wine into her glass. "Bring your father's credit card."

I finish off the last of the wilted broccoli and push the plate back from my seat, hoping she doesn't notice how little rice I ate.

"Okay, back to the date," she says. "She doesn't know you're gay?"

I shake my head.

"You should tell her. I dated this guy for six freaking months in college wondering why I wasn't getting some—or more," she says, oblivious to my embarrassment. "But then he spilled how he was into guys. I mean it was a different time and I wasn't mad at him but I was kind of pissed."

She spills some of the wine down her chin and suggests she might be crashing at our house tonight, which I'd be cool with. We connect way better than I do with my father, which is depressing when I think about it. I try not to think about it. And the last two nights were the first two nights I've been in the house by myself. At one point I was drumming in the basement and the water heater started making loud clanking noises like it might explode so I abandoned my sticks and sprinted up the stairs and I haven't been down there since.

"She wants to join our band," I say.

"You need to tell her. You need to not make it awkward when you hang out."

"I guess," I say. "She's in like three of my classes so we see each other all the time it's just—I don't know, the band was me and Jeff's thing and someone else might—" I can't finish the sentence without revealing what I don't want to reveal. "I like the band as it is now."

"Hmm, I think there's a lot more in that statement you're not telling me but I'll let it lie." She reaches behind her head to tuck a few stray strands into the ponytail. "You sure you don't want to tell me?"

"No," I say.

I'm never too sure what to reveal and to whom, this constant struggle to juggle my secrets.

"Okay," Donna says. "But you're turning sixteen tomorrow and you do need to start dating, or at least consider dating. Guys, I mean."

"I am," I say. "Sort of."

"Sort of?"

"There is a guy. I met him in California."

"Really?" Her eyes grow wide in the shadows of the light and I think she's more excited than when she talked about the shopping. "Does your father know?"

I shake my head.

"Wasn't he with you in California?"

"Yeah, but he doesn't know," I say. "He's oblivious to things that aren't math equations."

"This is true." She smiles. "So, what's his name? What's he like? When can I meet him? Are we going to California? Oh my god, when are we going to California?"

Donna talks fast when she drinks too much. She's already talking fast.

"His name is Cody," I say. "He's younger than me, but not too young, and he's about my height and has this perfect hair that's brown at the base but white at the tips and he has a smile that's sort of lopsided, like his teeth aren't perfect but it's almost perfect, you know. What were the other questions?"

I talk fast when I'm talking about boys. Apparently.

"You're in love," Donna says.

I shake my head. "He lives in California. It's very long distance."

"But still, I'm sure it's nice."

"Yeah," I say. It is. Cody started school like me and he's got soccer practice after school so by the time he called last night I was already asleep, exhausted from homework and cross-country and the near-death experience with the water heater in the basement.

And Jeff.

"Well, you know what you should do," Donna says. "You should have a date. Like get all dressed up—after we go shopping—and I don't know, watch a movie together on FaceTime but make it special, you know. Not a regular call."

"Oh," I say. "That sounds cool."

"It will be." She stands up to collect our plates. "Your Aunt Donna knows her shit."

I laugh. An official date would be nice and I think Cody would be into it. Plus, Jeff's all flirty with Sharane two days after we were wrestling in the basement, when he had the chance to kiss me again.

But he didn't.

He absolutely did not.

I guess he isn't gay.

"Listen, kid," Donna says, talking over the counter as she washes our plates in the sink. "Finding love for the first time is special. Super special. And yeah, the distance will make it complicated and it sounds like there might be other complications you're not willing to share but the point is, you're sixteen—or about to be—and all of this is special. You don't know it now but you'll look back and wish you had known and that's the point. You'll always remember these moments."

She wipes off her hands on the kitchen towel and pauses, considering.

"You might as well enjoy them," she says, returning to the table. "You deserve to enjoy it, Cyrus. You deserve happiness. Keep telling yourself that, okay?"

I nod. I think I nod.

"You deserve a boy who loves you back."

NINE

"HAPPY HAPPY HAPPY BIRTHDAY!"

"Ohmygod."

"Happy birthday, dear Cyrus, happy birthday to you."

Cody's excitement is infectious, his crooked smile contrasted with his darker skin. He extends the verse beyond what it necessary and I feel myself blushing, the way the heat stings my cheeks.

"Thank you," I say.

"Hey, I never asked you, what's with the name 'Cyrus'? It's not fully ordinary. Not that you are fully ordinary. Is it a family name?"

"My mom came up with it."

Mom had a friend in college named Cyrus who was sweet and shy and died an unfortunate death, which is not a good legacy to put onto a child, but the way she told it made it sound better, like he was her angel who protected her from the men she dated at the time—"I didn't have the best filter," she said—and this big bear of a friend called Cyrus rescued her "more than once," which again, now that I tell Cody is not something I should know about my mother, but I kind of like my name.

"You're glowing. There's a smile around your face."

I smile. Inside my face.

"Do you miss her?" he says.

"Yeah," I say, dipping my eyes, my cheeks still red. "Every day."

"I get that," Cody says. "I don't know how I would function without my mother."

He's lounging on a gray felt sofa near the entrance to his bedroom, a new addition to the attic because his mom's redecorating on the first floor. One time Cody took me on a FaceTime tour of his house, which is about the same size as my house but way nicer—there's an entire wall of glass at the entrance to the "parlor," not something we have in Pennsylvania. His living room is off to one side, the walls decorated with books, like Mom used to line up in massive piles in her closet, to fill a bookcase we never had. I haven't given Cody a tour of Casa de Dunn yet.

"Not that I'm even comparing it to your situation," Cody says. "But when I go to my dad's house for the weekend, I call her twenty times because I forgot something or I need something or—" He leans forward and whispers. "I just want to hear her voice."

"Awww," I say. "You're glowing."

"Screw you, Cyrus," Cody says, and he holds it for half a second before he breaks. He's thin—almost as thin as me—but his cheeks are fuller, or longer, and he has dimples even when he isn't smiling, the sun bright through the skylight above his head. Like always.

"What did you do para tu cumpleaños?" he asks.

"That's 'birthday,' right?"

He nods. Dallastown Spanish III coming on strong.

"Well, Mindy and Sharane, they found out it was my, 'cumpleaños,'" I say, screwing up the accent but Cody lets it slide. "So they snuck into the teachers' lounge for candles and placed them on a packaged cake from the vending machines. They sang 'happy birthday' in the middle of the cafeteria. Super loud and annoying."

"Ahh, that's sweet."

"It was mortifying."

I'm still dressed in my cross-country practice clothing—off-brand blue wicking T-shirt and short running shorts, not as short as some of the others on the team with their boxer briefs showing the whole time. Not sure why I'm thinking of underwear.

"And what's going on tonight, you having a party?"

Cody's wearing his white soccer shirt, stained with grass around the collar line—"slide-tackle," he said, and he's got a scruff of dirt above his cheek on the left side, visible when he shifts on the sofa and the sun catches him beneath the eye.

"Not exactly," I say.

Dad is on his way back from California and he's bringing Shake Shack with him—my favorite restaurant even though the closest one is all the way in Philly. I've been salivating ever since he called me from the airport.

"Why are you laughing?"

"There's a Shake Shack two miles from my house," Cody says. "I feel like you're so deprived out there in—what state is that—Kentucky?"

"Funny."

"I mean, do you have tractor pulls in corn fields? I hear that's something they do out in the 'heartland,'" he says, air-quoting with a wink.

I don't defend Dallastown because I will never defend Dallastown. I mean, it's not horrible but it's a carbon copy of all the other former farmlands between Philly and Pittsburgh, too far from both to be close to anything interesting. Dad's engineering firm is ten minutes from our house so that's how we ended up here, and Mom found a job at the nearest university—Penn State York. She took me there to show me her office and classroom and I didn't think so at the time but looking back at it now, I wonder if she regretted moving out here with him.

"I wouldn't mind visiting sometime, though," Cody says. "There's this guy that's super cool and he's already seen Manhattan Beach."

"We were only there for one night."

"That's true. You should come out for more nights."

He winks and I think to smile but I'm already smiling. We try to talk every night and I don't know what to do with it yet—the distance between us—but I do want to visit again, to see him again. Maybe then I'd stop obsessing over Jeff.

"So I have a proposal for you, Cody Martin."

"You want to propose?" Cody says. "I think I'm a little young to get engaged, but okay."

I laugh.

"My proposal is that we go on a date. A virtual date."

"That sounds awesome," he says, not waiting for the details.

"We could dress up, you know. Not formal wear, but like date attire, and then we could FaceTime while we queue up a movie on Netflix and watch it together."

"Awesome," Cody says. "We can even make popcorn."

"Kettle corn," I say. "I prefer the kettle corn."

"Right. Because you're from the country." I laugh again. "But yes, let's do it. Some type of popped corn product and our fanciest formal wear."

"You have fancy formal wear?"

"Of course," he says. "I mean, what I wear to church."

"You go to church?"

"Sometimes. Mostly at Christmas," Cody says. "Easter if my mom's feeling particularly penitent that year."

"Fancy word," I say.

"For our fancy date," he says. This is perfect.

I hear the whirring of his fan through my laptop, because the air conditioner doesn't reach the attic, he said, and when he leans back, the tips of his hair wave in the breeze like the wheat fields on the way to Lancaster.

"When shall we do it?" he says, shifting on the sofa. "Tomorrow?"

"Oh, um, I have band practice tomorrow and we're auditioning a new member. Does Sunday work?"

"It's not a major holiday, is it?"

"Not that I know of."

"Then church is not a conflict."

He licks his teeth and brushes at his cheek. The clump of dirt brushes free.

"Good, good. But I'm pretty sure the churches around here would not approve of two boys on a date, no matter how virtual."

"Eh, I don't think my church much cares," he says. "This is Southern California. Being gay is almost the point."

"Well, this is Central Pennsylvania, which not only does not have a Shake Shack but has more churches per square mile than anywhere else in the country. Even Kentucky."

"Is that true?" he says.

I'm not sure if it's true but I heard that it is, from several sources aware of the repressive nature of a town filled with churches.

"There's an intersection on the way to Red Lion with a church on all four corners."

He laughs. That part is true. I've ridden past many times.

"Seriously, they love their Jesus around here."

"Well then, we'll have to figure out a way to do some sinning on Sunday," Cody says.

"I can't wait," I say. Glowing.

I must have fallen asleep after talking to Cody because I can smell the Shake Shack from my bedroom so Dad must be home. I throw on a hoodie and run to the bathroom to splash some water in my eyes because my contacts get super dry when I sleep without removing them and—

"Jeff?"

"Happy birthday, man," he says from the bottom of the stairs.

"What the?" I say, stepping down into the living room.

Dad emerges from the kitchen with a pair of burgers on a tray, "1" and "6" candles sticking out from one of the buns. "Happy birthday to—"

"Please don't sing."

"Youuuuuuu," he continues and Jeff chimes in and then they sing the entire song with insane sincerity. It's super awkward the way I'm standing in front of them and I wish I'd checked my hair before I bounded down the stairs.

"What are you doing here?" I ask Jeff when they finish.

"Your dad invited me."

He follows me to the dining area and I clear off space on the table. I didn't know my dad had his number.

"I didn't get a cake but I figured a shake would suffice," Dad says. "Except they melted on the drive so I put them the freezer."

"Thank you," I say. "How was your trip?"

Dad hands us each our burgers, some napkins, and ketchup. I've already removed the candles and taken a bite before he can answer.

"Good. Got a lot accomplished. I'm hoping from now on, I can take an earlier flight and be home when you're home from school on Friday."

"Still Friday?" I say.

"Yeah," Dad says, dipping his head. "It'll be all week for the foreseeable future, I'm afraid."

"You go away every week?" Jeff asks, eyeing his burger like it's a foreign substance and not the greatest meal in the history of humanity.

"Every other week. Through Thanksgiving at least."

"That sucks," Jeff says. "I mean, I would freaking love if my stepfather went away every other week but it might suck for you guys."

I laugh but Dad shows no expression. Even though I tell him all the time how much the stepfuck sucks, I guess as a parent you always have to take another parent's side.

"On the bright side," Jeff says, "they're attending some church event in Hallam this weekend."

"Really?" I say.

"Yeah. We can use the garage," he says, eyeing the grease dripping from the burger along my palm. "What time can you come over? We need to move the equipment back."

"I have my permitting exam at the butt crack of early but—after that?"

Jeff laughs but Dad glares before retreating upstairs to get changed out of his work clothes. He has no sense of humor. We take seats at the table.

"This is good shit," Jeff says, taking his first bite.

"I told you."

It's difficult to describe the taste of a Shake Shack burger because it's the same beef as any other burger but the way they make it, I don't know if it's fried in butter or lard or maybe bacon grease, but every single inch is filled with this amazing flavor unlike a regular burger—Mickey D's or whatever homemade patty Dad grills up, where the middle is dry and overcooked or under-seasoned. Every bit of a Shake Shack burger—mine loaded with cheese and bacon and lettuce and tomato—is pure perfection. Jeff licks at his lips.

"I can't believe I've never had this before," he says, bits of bacon stuck to his chin, wet from the grease in the living room lights.

"I told you."

He's got on his baseball cap, the black-and-white Brixton he bought at the York Galleria at the start of the summer, before we started the band.

"I got you a present."

"Really?"

I didn't get him anything for his birthday but I did accompany him to the guitar store in York where he spent most of his summer earnings on our band. He hands me his phone.

"You're giving me your phone?"

Jeff shakes his head. "Look."

He points but the screen is blank so he uses his fingerprint to correct.

"What the hell? You got them!"

"Yes," he says. "Two tickets. Two weeks from tomorrow. Joyce Manor, baby!"

"Holy shit," I say.

"Yeah. It's going to be insane."

Two tickets to see Joyce Manor at Union Transfer in Philly and the sound of those words is the greatest present I could ever get—better than all the Shake Shack burgers in all the world. Joyce Manor is my favorite band or at least top three and I've never been to a concert before. With Jeff.

"You're excited?"

I'm glowing.

"There's one catch."

I unfurl my lower lip.

"We need someone to drive us to Philly and back. I know there's a train but I don't think Union Transfer is close to the train station and it's a pain in the ass either way. Do you think your dad would take us?"

"Maybe," I say.

"I mean, he's welcome to get a ticket for the show," Jeff says. "But ideally, he'd go do something in Philly while we're inside because I love your dad, he's cool for a dad it's just he'll stick out at a Joyce Manor concert, you know. With like—" Jeff glances up the stairs to make sure Dad's not there. "He's old."

"I don't think he'd want to. His favorite band is called Superchunk. Like who calls themselves that?"

"I don't know," Jeff says. We still haven't come up with a name for our band.

"Oh, I forgot to tell you," he says. "Sharane is coming over with Mindy tomorrow, but just to watch. She has no musical talent whatsoever. Her words."

"When did you talk to Sharane?"

"I don't know. Before coming over here, I guess."

"Oh," I say, crumpling the wrapper from my burger. The grease is stuck in my throat.

"What's wrong?"

"Nothing."

I shouldn't hate Sharane. It's not her fault for liking Jeff and if he likes her back, that's his choice. He's over the fucking kiss. And he's still my best friend, which is all I said I wanted and I have a date with Cody on Sunday night, so that should be my focus. But I can't get it out of my head.

"Are you dating Sharane?" I say, squeezing the wrapper in my palm.

"No," Jeff says. "She wants to, I think."

"And you don't want to?"

He pauses, like he's considering, and there's something in the way he dips his head that makes me think he's already considered it.

"Did you kiss her?"

"No," he says but he doesn't meet my eyes. He looks up the stairs again to make sure my father isn't coming.

"Listen, Cy, I shouldn't have sent you mixed signals with—" He hesitates again, afraid to look at me. "With what happened after the party. I don't know why I did it. I was pretty wasted."

I start to blink, my contacts dry enough they're pinching at the sides.

"I'm not gay," he says. "It's great that you are, it is. But I didn't mean for it to happen."

"You didn't kiss her?" I say.

"What?"

He looks up.

"Did you kiss Sharane?"

"No. I told you I didn't."

"Do you want to?" I need to know.

"I don't know," he says. "Maybe."

I blink a bunch of times because I can't actually see.

"Are you okay, Cy?" Jeff says, reaching across the table for my hand. The refrigerator clicks off with a clang. I pull away.

"I'm sorry," he says. "I just—we're not going to kiss again. I need you to be okay with that."

Dad comes clomping down the stairs to barge into the conversation because I still can't get privacy, even on my birthday. The contacts are slicing into my retinas.

"I got you another present," he says, handing me the gift box he bought on his trip but I don't even look at it, I just set it beside me.

"You want your shakes now?" Dad says. "They should be frozen."

"Sure," I say. Just go away.

I look into Jeff's eyes until he meets mine.

"Cy?" he says.

"It's okay, Jeff. Sharane can come tomorrow. It'll be good to see her."

I stand up and follow Dad into the kitchen, rooting through the drawers for spoons for Jeff and me.

"You okay, Cyrus?" Dad says, setting down the shakes and reaching for my arm. I shake free and shake off the moisture in my eyes. I can't breathe.

"My contacts are just dry," I say and return to the dining room with a forced, crooked smile, avoiding his face. If I can't get past this, I'll lose him.

"Their shakes are amazing too," I say, spreading wide my fake smile.

I can't lose my best friend.

TEN

"WHAT UP, BOYS?" Mindy says from the driveway, bass in a case in her hand. "I'm sorry I'm late."

"No worries. We just started."

Jeff invites her in through the garage door opening and plugs her bass into the amp near the wall.

"The Food Bank had too many callouts so I had to fill in," she says, setting her bass against the shelves of half-finished woodworking projects. I'm at my spot at the kit, the sticks in my hands like gloves.

"You were at the Food Bank today? Handing out meals and stuff?"

"Yeah. Well, not handing out 'meals and stuff.'" She laughs as she air-quotes my words. "I volunteer at the warehouse that supplies the distribution points. You guys should come with me one time. It's a lot of fun."

"That doesn't sound like fun," Jeff says.

"No, it is," she says. "And if I'm gracing your band with my presence, I think it's only fair you join me at the Food Bank."

"Okay," Jeff says and I give a quick riff on the toms.

"Plus, it looks great on a college application," Mindy says. "And let's be honest, that's what we're all after."

Mindy's at the top of our class and she probably knows what college she wants to attend, because she's conscientious like that and I'm the opposite. I spent all summer staring at stacks of brochures in the guidance office, bucolic landscapes brimming with smiling faces but none of it interested me. The secretaries implored me to start exploring, to figure out what I wanted to do in life, career-wise, but it's hard to think like that, so abstract. I just turned sixteen and I'm six feet from the first boy I ever kissed. And all he wants to do is forget.

"Sharane couldn't make it," Mindy says as she takes out the bass and moves next to my kit at the garage door opening, the sun at her back. "Her parents invited her relatives over for a family barbecue with the weather so nice."

Jeff steps to the near wall with his guitar, taking up position by the Rockville RPG speakers that came with the amp, a joint purchase on Amazon that arrived the week I returned from California. Jeff has his pick between his lips, flicking it with his tongue as he tests the amp with Mindy's bass.

"What are we playing?" Mindy says.

"Whatever you're comfortable with," Jeff says. "Cyrus said you know about Japandroids?"

"Well, I've heard of them now, yes. And I've tried playing along on YouTube a bit." She adjusts the strap around her neck, letting the bass hang to her side. "They're loud."

"We like to play loud," Jeff says.

"Not to worry, I brought my ear protection." She whips out a little baggie from her shorts pocket with earplugs. "It's lame, I know. But my mom bought them for me as soon as I floated the idea of 'rock band'. She's old-school Korean and goes right to the sex, drugs, and rock-'n-roll connection between bands with tattoos and long hair and whatever Ozzy Osborne did to a rat onstage." She squeezes one of the foam plugs and pulls back her left ear, sliding it into the canal. "She's ridiculous sometimes."

"She was okay with you coming?" I say.

"She'd prefer I practiced classical piano, but she no longer tries to completely control my life. She settled on a happy medium of indiscriminate nagging and sad-face guilt trips."

"Sounds like my dad," I say.

"Your dad?" Jeff says. "Don't get me started on Roland."

"Roland?" Mindy says.

"His stepfather," I whisper, as if saying his name too loud in this space will conjure the specter of his being.

"My real dad's in Florida," Jeff says. "I tried to go visit him this summer but…" He trails off, tuning his guitar. He hasn't seen his father since he left P.A., when Jeff was ten.

"Are we going to play?"

"Sure," Mindy says. "What are we playing?"

"Just try to follow."

She nods and we start out with "Metronomy," the one song we know. Jeff has the lyrics down and his singing is better, a little less screaming and more intonation but I spend the beginning focused on him, his skin in the sun's splintered rays, the way his eyes begin to squint as he strings the words together, his fingers at the frets faster and less spastic, and my drums lag behind, still a beat behind. He signals for me to stop.

"No good?" Mindy says.

"No it's good, real good," Jeff says, glancing at me. "Um, you okay, Cy?"

"Yeah, I'm sorry. I messed up there in the middle."

I wish I were better at this. Getting over him.

"It's cool," Jeff says.

It's not cool. He got a haircut this morning while I was taking my driver's test—I passed, I have my permit—and the sides are shaved tighter now and the top's not as long, the wispy strands on his forehead gelled to the right. He looks better. I don't know how, but he looks better.

"Cyrus?" Mindy says.

"Huh?"

Jeff laughs.

"Wow, you're out of it today."

I wanted clarity and he gave me clarity but now it's final. I won't ever kiss him again.

"So am I in?" Mindy says. The sweat lines are forming beneath her shoulders on the floral-printed blouse, billowing a bit despite no breeze from outside. "I don't know if that was the audition but I was pretty good and you guys are excellent. How long have you been playing?"

"A few weeks," Jeff says, looking at me.

"You're better than expected," Mindy says. "No offense. I mean, I didn't know." She blinks at me and I forgot that she has feelings for me, or she used to.

"You're good too," I say. Like an idiot.

"Oh, Cyrus. Don't make a girl blush."

I slam the sticks into the skins.

"And what is the name of this band I will be joining?" Mindy says.

"We're still deciding," Jeff says. "'Dallastown Sucks My Balls' was in the running for a while—"

"Classy," she says, setting down the bass on the concrete.

"You have any suggestions?" Jeff says.

"Hmm, let me think about it." She steps between Jeff and me. "Have you written any songs yet? That might give me a clue."

"I wrote one the other night," Jeff says, pulling out a crumpled piece of paper from his pocket. "But it has no name."

"You're not big on names," Mindy says. "Maybe that should be the band's name—'No Name'."

"Or nonamé," I say, envisioning the words strung together and adding a phonetic pronunciation. "It's like French or whatever."

"You have some strange thoughts, Cyrus," Mindy says. "Maybe that's why I like you."

I dip my head behind the kit. The sweat slips into my eyes.

"As a friend," Mindy adds. "I realized halfway through our date watching the same movie from separate seats that we were not meant to be as a couple."

She laughs like she's laughing it off but we never talked about it, why we didn't have a second date.

"I'm sorry," I say, because I never said it.

"I'm good, Cyrus, really."

"Should we jam some more?" Jeff says. Trying to save me.

"Sure," Mindy says, turning her back to me and picking up the bass. I look to Jeff but he's down at the amp, adjusting the levels. No one can save me.

We play some more Church of the Dead then give Mindy a chance to solo and she's good—you can spot the natural talent—not that I should be judging her bass playing ability, or anyone's ability, but I think I can tell, the way I can tell about Jeff. And I didn't want her to join the band because I'd rather it be Jeff and me, but maybe it's okay, maybe it's better this way. I could focus on drumming and less on Jeff's face in the sunlight filtering through the maple tree on the front lawn.

"This was great, guys," Mindy says, rolling up her cords and packing them into the case with her bass. "I haven't played this much in a while, so I do apologize for my mistakes but I'd like to play with you guys again. Even on the regular. If you'll have me."

I mop up the sweat on my forehead with the bottom of my T-shirt. My forehead's been breaking out since we started the band, the heat and the perspiration and a distinct lack of showering, maybe.

"We'll need to discuss the logistics of it," Jeff says. "But we'll let you know."

"Hmm." Mindy edges toward the door. "I hope that's not your way of letting me down easy."

"No, no," Jeff says. "We're only allowed to use the garage because my stepfather's at some stupid church outing this weekend and Cy's basement is already cramped for two people."

"I see," Mindy says.

"But we can figure something out," Jeff says. "Right, Cyrus?"

I nod. I'm okay if Jeff wants her in the band but I don't know what he's thinking.

"Okay," she says. "Well please let me know. I'd rather a definite 'no' than a slow dribble of unresponsive texts." She looks at me and I feel my face flush at once, the way it always does. "Sorry, Cyrus. I couldn't resist."

"No, I—" I don't have anything resembling a valid excuse. "I'm sorry."

"It's fine."

"I'm sorry," I repeat, even though it's way too late.

"Cyrus, I'm good. I was kidding. Mostly."

Jeff looks between Mindy and me like he wants to help but there's no way to help me. She's a good person who helps other people and I should have told her the truth.

I should tell her the truth.

"I'm gay," I say. Blurting it out like an idiot.

"What?"

She's standing to the right of me, by the open door to outside, and if she wants to run and hide now would be the time because I don't think I could have come up with a worse way to come out to her.

"I'm gay," I repeat. "Jeff knows. I should have told you before I agreed to the date but I didn't know it was a date and then I didn't say anything. I'm sorry."

"I see." She nods a bunch of times in a row, but slow nods like she's contemplating. The birds in the branches of the maple start trilling all at once, like they're making fun of me. "No, that makes a whole lot more sense now."

"I'm really sorry," I say.

"Dude, do not be sorry." She steps inside from the edge, approaching my kit. "I'm glad you told me. That means a lot."

"I didn't know how to tell you," I say.

"It's not easy, I'm sure." She looks back to Jeff, watching us. "My cousin came out to the family—her parents and grandparents, who are my grandparents, back in Korea, like a week before she was heading to America for school. She was so afraid they would kick her out of the house if she told them earlier."

"Did they?"

"No." She pauses. "But it's been a few years now and they don't exactly march in the gay pride parades, which I'm not sure they even have in Korea. I need to research." She smiles. "But she's happy here. Got a place in Queens with her girlfriend. Now that I have a car, I'm definitely going to visit."

"Awesome," Jeff says.

"It is," Mindy says. "And Cyrus, I'm cool with it. If you want to come to Queens with me, we'll find all the gay clubs that let minors in and we'll find you a guy, okay?"

"He has a guy," Jeff says.

"Oh?" Mindy says, spinning between Jeff and me. "Really?"

"No, not really," I say. "We're friends."

"Their first date is tomorrow," Jeff says. "Although I'm still unclear how you can have a date on a computer."

"Huh?" Mindy says.

"He lives in California," I say.

"Oh." She steps back two steps, in the shadow of the garage door. "That's not one of those 'I have a girlfriend in Canada' things, is it?"

"No, he's real," I say. She laughs.

"I'm kidding. But I do have to go. Thanks again, and Cyrus—if the position of gay guy's female best friend is not yet filled, I'm happy to apply."

She gives a wave and picks up the bass as she slips from the garage across the lawn to the street.

"You want to break?" Jeff says.

He takes a seat on the overturned crate next to my kit and pulls out the Altoids tin from the pocket of his shorts, the beige ones with the grass stain on the side. He packs the pinkie-sized bowl imprinted with a gray-and-purple skull we found at the flea market near Woody's Body Shop last month.

"I thought you were afraid of a drug test?"

"Fuck Roland," Jeff says and I laugh. It's nice to laugh. After everything.

I carry my stool around the front of the drums and we sit and smoke for a bit and I figure he's going to ask me why I came out to Mindy in front of him, but he doesn't. He just sits next to me and smokes. It's nice.

"You wrote a song?" I say.

"Yeah." He pulls out the yellow sheet of paper again, dotted with scribbled lyrics. "I don't know if it's any good."

"We could play it," I say, touching his fingers as I hand the sheet back to him. The wispy strands slip down his forehead again, returning to their natural state despite the haircut and gel.

"I'd like that," he says, that sideways smile in the fading sunlight through the opening. The birds flap their wings all at once, disappearing into the sky. He hands me the bowl.

We haven't smoked since the day of the kiss. We haven't kissed since the day of the kiss. I know I need to, it's for the best that I do, but I don't want to forget.

ELEVEN

DAD AND DONNA TOOK ME out for my birthday last night—third straight night of celebrations, I guess since sixteen is a big milestone or because Dad felt bad for being away all week. We went to the Texas Roadhouse in York and I had baby back ribs and fries. Dad and Donna split a bottle of wine. He let me drive home, insisting I needed to practice, and he even suggested I merge onto a highway ramp as a shortcut but I ignored, sticking to the local roads doing a solid twenty-five. I don't want to die.

"I want to try to record this time," Jeff says, over to the entrance from the house to the garage, two steps down on hard concrete.

"Okay."

He's been patient with me, encouraging, but we need to get it right, to learn his song—because it's got an amazing beat and Jeff's an amazing talent and I don't know how much longer we've got until his stepfather comes home.

"What do you think of the lyrics? Do they match the sound?"

"Yeah," I say, even though I only took a glance. I tried to come up with a song like Jeff asked me back at Tyler Brower's party but all the words I put down had everything to do with him, maybe not overtly, but not hidden enough, and hardcore shouldn't be about sappy stuff like love, and lust, or whatever fills my brain when I think about Jeff.

"I memorized them last night," Jeff says. "After you left."

I wait behind my kit as he sets up the 8-track he bought from a guy at the Parks Department so we can record our music. He laid down a guitar track before I came over this morning, adding another row of tempo to expand our sound—more hardcore than it was, with the layers of rhythm that'll turn two guys in a garage with a drum kit and guitar into a real band, he says. He fiddles with the machine.

"Mindy texted," I tell him.

"Did she ask if she was in the band?" he says.

"No, no," I say. "About—the other conversation."

I don't know how to say it, not because I'm afraid to say it. It's more like there isn't a normal way to say: "When I blurted out in the middle of your garage yesterday that I'm gay."

"Got it," Jeff says. "What did she say?"

"Just that she's glad I told her and if I ever want to talk or whatever, you know. She's here for me."

"She's good people," Jeff says.

I came out to Jeff in my basement, the first time we ever got high. He asked if I wanted to tell him anything about "anything," because we were talking about girls, or he was talking about a girl he used to date and how she broke up with him, I forget why now, or whether he even told me but he said I never talked about girls the way guys talk about girls and he asked if I was gay.

"Okay, I think I got it," he says, moving away from the table to set up the microphone stand in front of me, closer to my kit than where he usually stands. We have the garage door closed, the rain coming down after I arrived and not letting up, the shower tip-tapping on the rooftop above our heads.

"You ready to record?" he says.

I nod and he presses the remote, signaling with his guitar to start, and I click my sticks together as I count in my head—one, two, three then crashing down with the four, into the toms with a double stroke at my wrists, Jeff right behind with a strum that speeds up all at once, this pulsing flourish at the start, our first song as a band.

"*They broke me.*
They tried to break me.
I said I hate them.
And I know they hate me.
They pretend to like me.
They pretend to love me.
But I hate them
And I know they hate me."

He's standing in front of me, low murmured singing like a guttural growl that sinks through my skin, through my kicks at the bass, this heavy staccato rhythm blending back on his guitar, spilling from the speakers along the wall. Jeff's voice kicks up an octave or two and the next verse explodes through the microphone.

"*They scream at you with their lies*
And the shit they spew in your eyes
They say the devil is fate for everyone that they hate
But how do you know you're not the one they despise?"

He's screaming now, spinning sideways from me, thrashing up and down on his guitar strings then pointing at me like I should solo, which we haven't rehearsed but

I slam my foot through the fill, into the bass, the sticks against the snare into the cymbals, snapping them off then snatching back into double strokes on the toms until my fingers take over, circling the rims with practiced precision, reverberation from the speakers echoing off the walls like our fans are screaming at us, from the mosh pit beneath us, Jeff turning back to my kit, microphone at his lips—

"Hail you and hail me,
Hail everything we thought we could be.
Hail you and hail me,
Hail Satan.
And God died."

My arms are spread, one stick in each hand on the snare and the cymbals, in rhythm with his screaming, full volume over the sound of everything.

"Hail you and hail me!
We're better than they'll ever believe!
Hail you and hail me,
Hail Satan.
And God died."

The guitar stops and my drums stop, right on cue, resonating so loud I didn't hear the car approaching, the garage door opening. Jeff's stepfather's SUV pulls halfway into his parking space, the rain pouring down in torrents on the concrete.

"What did I tell you about playing in this garage!" he shouts, climbing out in an ill-fitting suit, the jacket crumpled. His eyes are spinning back and forth like he's not sure what he's seeing or what he should be saying but he wants to be yelling and he can't quite start.

"You are not allowed to have visitors in this house while you are on punishment," he says, stepping past the woodworking shelves into our makeshift space. Jeff moves over to the 8-track, preserving our song. "And you are not allowed to have your goddamned equipment in this garage. Ever. And you absolutely cannot play this revolting trash at such volume inside my house. This is my house. Do you understand me?"

I stumble out from behind my kit, the rain splashing through the opening onto my sneakers. Jeff's back is facing us.

"I said do you understand me, Jeffrey?"

I spot his mother emerging from the passenger's seat of the off-gray SUV, wearing a flowered blue dress, clutching an umbrella. The stepfuck turns to her.

"Carol, go inside," he says. "I can handle this."

She waits, watching the confrontation inside the garage for a moment, Jeff stepping away from the table with the 8-track, so she can see him. Then she retreats past the car out into the rain, up the sidewalk the long way inside. I don't know what the fuck is happening.

"I know you heard my question, Jeffrey," the stepfuck says, moving closer to him. "And I will not repeat myself."

"It's my fault, Mr. Danforth," I say, hoping to diffuse the situation. "We needed to practice and my dad was doing some work in the basement so I asked if we could use your garage this weekend. I apologize."

My voice is pitched and desperate, like I'm talking to an adult who demands respect, even though he doesn't, and he doesn't listen.

"I will ask you one last time before I take these instruments and smash them on the concrete," he says, waving his arms around the space. "Do you understand what I am telling you about what can happen in my house?"

"You touch Cyrus's drums and I'll kill you," Jeff speaks.

"Oh, you did not just say that to me."

Mr. Danforth takes two deliberate strides up to Jeff, his thick gut the only thing separating them.

"Cyrus, go home," he says, the rain splashing at my feet at the edge of the garage. His suit is thick and wool, too warm for the season, and his red speckled tie is off-center from his shirt. He turns back to Jeff, noticing the table behind him.

"What is this?"

He steps around Jeff, reaching out, and I think for a second, he's found our Altoids tin, but it's worse. Way worse.

"That's mine."

Jeff reaches for his sheet of scribbled lyrics but his stepfather shakes him off, shoving him back with a swift rough push.

"This was what you were playing so loud in my house?"

He shakes the page in his hand like a fist.

"I could hear it down the street."

Jeff lunges back to grab the lyrics but the stepfuck's too quick, ripping the sheet away and taking hold of Jeff's arm, twisting hard before releasing.

"'Hail Satan'? 'And God died?' You take the Lord's name in vain in my house. For all the neighbors to hear?"

I step forward, out of the rain, waiting for Jeff to speak but he's silent, clutching at his wrist. I can't see his face.

"You stupid, unrepentant child. What do you know about Satan?"

"I've lived with you for two years now."

The stepfuck moves forward into Jeff again, bumping into him with his thick-waisted stomach, towering over him and raising his arm like he might strike all at once but Jeff backs away, into the microphone stand, his fists clenched. The stepfuck coughs, breathing out, and adjusts his wrinkled jacket. Turning to me.

"Cyrus, I've asked you to leave," he says, calm and deliberate. "I'm not going to ask you again."

I look out into the rain cascading through the opening now, but I'm not leaving Jeff, not alone with this raging fuck, and I think to call my dad or run inside to Jeff's mom to keep from happening what I'm afraid will happen when Jeff charges into him, lowering his shoulder and ramming full speed into the massive man's gut.

The stepfuck loses his balance and stumbles back into the woodworking shelves, knocking the structure over. Half-finished birdhouses and metal tools crash around us.

"You little shit!" the stepfuck shouts, righting himself and storming forward. I hear his fist hitting flesh before Jeff can react. I scream out.

Jeff staggers after the strike but plants his feet to the floor in front of my kit and launches himself into the stepfuck's legs, lifting up just enough to take them both to the ground, onto the splintered wood and tools littering the space.

Jeff climbs up his body, cocking his fist about to hit, but the stepfuck grabs hold of his neck with his thick meaty hand—choking him—and Jeff coughs, his arm going limp. I step forward, about to jump in to save him, but the door to the house opens and the stepfuck stops choking. Everything stops.

"What is going on out here?"

Jeff's mother is in the entryway while her son is crouched over her husband on the concrete. Jeff dismounts and grabs at his throat.

"Your delinquent child attacked me," the stepfuck says, pushing up to his feet, knees first then off the concrete, tucking his collared shirt into his stretch-waisted slacks.

"Is that true, Jeffrey?"

Jeff coughs. "Is what true?"

Jeff's mother looks from Jeff to me, the rain at my back still beckoning. We've never spoken in all my times at the house so I've always assumed she hates me because most mothers talk to their children's friends.

"It's that attitude right there," the stepfuck says, between halting breaths. "He's not even supposed to have anyone over and yet here they are in my garage. Playing the devil's music for all the neighbors to hear. You should see what he wrote on this sheet, forsaking the word of our Lord." He looks for the lyrics among the scattered debris on the concrete. "Then I confront him and he curses at me and attacks me physically. You saw him attacking me."

Jeff's mother is standing with the door propped against her hip. Silent.

"I've said it before and I'll repeat it until you accept it. He's going to end up in prison if we don't curb his delinquency."

I look to Jeff, stationed between his mother and the stepfuck near the microphone stand, and I want to say something, about his stepfather provoking the fight and punching Jeff in the face. I can already see the welt on his cheek where his fist connected.

"Cyrus, you should go home now," his mother says.

"No," I say.

"Excuse me?" the stepfuck says.

"Mr. Danforth started it. Jeff didn't do anything wrong. We were practicing for our band and—"

"Cy, forget it," Jeff says. "Just let it go."

I'm not sure what he means or why he's saying it but the look he gives back begs me to stop—that my presence isn't helping.

"You can come back for your drums," Jeff says.

"Take it now," the stepfuck says. "Take it all. Because whatever is left in this garage tomorrow, I'm donating to the church."

I don't listen to him, I'm focused on Jeff, and I don't know why his mother's not taking his side.

"Are you okay?" I say. I thought someone should ask.

"Yeah," he says, rubbing at his neck, red marks forming on one side, like the welt beneath his eye. "I'll be okay, Cy."

Jeff never complains about his mother, the way he saves his anger for the stepfuck. But I hear her tell Jeff to clean up the mess as I exit through the opening out into the rain.

I sprint all the way home.

TWELVE

VOLUNTEERING AT THE FOOD BANK was my idea—well it was Mindy's idea, but I never planned to agree. It's just I couldn't think of a way to spring Jeff from his punishment other than a charity, sponsored by a church, and I get to see Jeff for the first time all week.

We follow Mindy past a series of offices—"Hi, Mr. Evanston" and "That's Gladys, she's always smiling"—back through a double set of doors into the warehouse, this huge space with hip hop blaring and all the employees and volunteers running around at top speed. They station us in the "Special Packaging" area off to the side by the dock doors, and our task is to load food into brown canvas bags for less fortunate families who need the assistance "our government refuses to provide," according to Wanda, the white-haired woman who explains our duties in between wheezes and seems relieved Mindy arrived to take over her job.

"No fucking way," Jeff says, straining to be heard over the music. "There's more?"

One of the workers on a forklift drops off another pallet of bags at our station. I thought we were almost done because the bags were almost gone. Mindy advertised this would be more fun.

"Jeff, you're putting one can of tuna in each container?" she says.

"Yeah."

"You're supposed to put two in, one of each kind," Mindy says.

"Right." He stops. "Wait, what?"

Mindy moves around me to teach Jeff how to count to two and she squeezes my arm as she returns to her spot. We spent all week at the lunch table sans Jeff—Mindy and Sharane and me—and it was the two of them talking and me eating real quick before escaping to assist Ms. Patterson on a research project in the library—cataloging which fiction gets borrowed the most, assigned readings or more contemporary stuff like Harry Potter, and it wasn't interesting at all but at least I didn't have to listen to Sharane ask every other second whether or not I'd heard from Jeff.

"Cyrus, have you ever done anything like this before?" Mindy says.

"Help people?".

"No." She laughs. "Work in a warehouse like this."

She points at the rows and rows of pallet racking and the workers racing past on massive forklifts. The concrete floors are pressing at my shins and there's a faint scent of sawdust mixed with exhaust fumes permeating the space.

"No, but this is what my dad does for a living," I say. "I mean, he doesn't work in a warehouse. He builds them. Not physically, but he works on the drawings of the design—the insides I think, not the building itself."

"You have no idea what your father does, do you?" Jeff asks.

"He tries to tell me all the time but I zone out as soon as he mentions 'gaining efficiencies.'"

I smile at Jeff but he just lifts another stack of fruit snacks from the crate behind us. I got my first text from him last night, after a full week of radio silence. I actually Googled "child abuse" to see if there was something I could do since I witnessed Roland punching Jeff. And I didn't know if the cops would believe me or if I could talk to someone other than the police, but that was a wormhole I shouldn't have entered and I had to close my browser before I started weeping.

"Where's Sharane today?" Jeff asks Mindy.

"SAT prep," Mindy says. "Her first week."

"Oh," Jeff says.

"I'll tell her you asked," Mindy says.

I guess Sharane didn't get a text when he got back his laptop.

"So when's the next practice?" Mindy says.

"I'm not sure," Jeff says.

"I thought you were feeling better?" Mindy says.

He coughs a bit, for the "bronchitis" he told Mindy he had all week. The stepfuck found the Altoids tin while cleaning up the garage and now they're talking about "rehab"—or "worse," he messaged without context, and that's when I suggested the Food Bank.

"I'm allowed to do this and church this weekend." He hesitates. "That's it."

I straighten out my spine, tense from all the pressure of the hard concrete. I don't know how people work here all day. Or help people. Mindy is a saint. I glance across to the docks where a large man in a trucker hat is arguing with white-haired Wanda.

"What about next weekend?" Mindy asks.

"We have a concert," I say.

"Right," Jeff says. "I almost forgot."

"What concert?"

"Joyce Manor in Philly," I say.

I lean onto the table because my legs have started to vibrate, like a shaky quiver sending signals from my calves through my quads to my spine. I ran forty-seven miles at cross-country this week and today is supposed to be my day off from physical activity.

"Did you talk to your dad about driving us?" he asks.

"Not yet," I say because I haven't thought about anything all week except the fight in Jeff's garage with his stepfather. I postponed my date with Cody because I was too upset. "Can you go?"

"I'm going," Jeff says. "Fuck him."

Mindy looks confused.

"My stepfather's an asshole," he says.

"You've mentioned that."

He hasn't told me why he missed school all week but I assume it has something to do with the mark beneath his eye, because teachers ask questions, the way that teachers ask questions. And Jeff wouldn't want anyone to know.

"You know, I could drive," Mindy says.

Another worker has waded into the argument at the docks and now they're pointing in our direction.

"You want to go?" Jeff says.

"Sure, why not?"

"You know Joyce Manor?" I say.

"Nope," she says. "But how bad could they be?"

Mindy has done her best to forge the straight-gay alliance between us ever since my "coming out," which feels like a lifetime ago but I think it's only been a week. We haven't talked at school, because we're in class with other students or in lunch in front of Sharane, but she's good with a secret and she's been sending a barrage of one-line texts awash in sexual innuendo. She wants to FaceTime Cody with me.

"Well, we only have two tickets," Jeff says. "But if it hasn't sold out, that would be awesome, Mindy. Thank you."

"Absolutely," she says, her long black hair tied up with a blue-dotted bow behind her head. "I mean, we're in a band together now. Right?"

Jeff leans back as Mindy leans forward and laughs. The overhead fans blow hot air into my eyes.

"You guys are a tough crowd," Mindy says.

White-haired Wanda and the guy from the docks walk up to our station.

"Mindy, we have a problem," she says. "Mr. McLaren says these orders went out already."

"We shipped them yesterday," McLaren says. He's got a thick mustache and a thicker accent, like he's from New York or New Jersey. "Who told you to pack these?"

"Mrs. Phillips left the packing lists at her desk," Mindy says, fumbling through the sheets of paper spread around the table. She hands one of the slips to Wanda. Jeff keeps packing.

"Oh, I didn't see that earlier." Wanda speaks at a deliberate pace, inserting pauses between her words. "These have Friday's date on them. Mrs. Phillips must have had a volunteer crew here yesterday."

"That's what I told you," McLaren says. "You're supposed to be in charge of the volunteers."

"I am, but usually Mindy—"

"I'm sorry, Wanda, I didn't look at the date," Mindy says, leafing through the packing slips.

"It's okay." Wanda turns to apologize but McLaren isn't paying attention. Jeff reaches across me to grab more cans.

"Hey kid, what are you, stupid?" McLaren barks.

"Excuse me?" Jeff says.

"Stop packing this shit."

Jeff pauses mid-motion, in the frozen glare of the larger man.

"Mr. McLaren, you can't talk to the volunteers that way," Wanda says.

"Listen, you've got my people pulling pallets for these goddamn kids and now they have to put them back into storage and you know we're getting charged overtime as it is."

His voice is loud and his hands spin through the air with every word. Jeff drops a can of pasta sauce on the table beside me.

"You got a problem, kid?" McLaren says.

"Yeah, you need to chill the fuck out," Jeff says.

"Who the fuck do you think you're talking to?" McLaren spits, stepping closer to our table.

"I didn't come here to be yelled at for volunteering on a Saturday morning."

"Well your 'volunteering',"—McLaren adds the air quotes—"just gave my men an extra hour's work. Paid work. For your stupidity."

Jeff steps out from behind the table, moving past me so fast the pile of bags tumble to the concrete. Wanda shouts through the radio.

"Kid, I will beat that smirk off your face, so help me God."

Jeff steps forward and McLaren meets him, next to an empty pallet Jeff would need to stand on to even reach the chest of this massive asshole.

"Mr. McLaren!" Wanda screams.

"You ain't worth my time, boy," McLaren says, stepping back and spinning sideways, next to Wanda.

Jeff gives a two-handed shove at his back. McLaren turns, about to send Jeff sprawling across the concrete floors but some guy on a pallet jack speeds up to our station to save him. Wanda keeps screaming.

"What the hell just happened?" I say, hoping a lighter tone might help us figure out what the hell just happened. We're outside on the curb by Mindy's car. Waiting.

"Fucking asshole," Jeff says. "He's lucky they broke it up."

"You realize he was twice your size, right?" I say.

He squints at me, the sun bright in his eyes. Steam rises from the pavement.

"He would have folded if I hit him, one smack and guys like that, they crumple. You can't take shit from them, you know."

A hot breeze blows through his hair and I reach out to touch his knee, the faded jeans against his hamstrings. I pull back before contact.

"They'll walk all over you if you let them," he says.

"We should apologize to Mindy. I hope she doesn't lose her job over this."

"It's a volunteer job," he says. "Who cares?"

"It means a lot to her." He notices my hand in the space between us.

"Yeah," he says. "Of course."

Employees are starting to leave the building for lunch and Jeff's eyes follow them. Waiting.

"That's great if she can take us to Joyce Manor," I say. "Do you think you can go?"

"I'm going, Cyrus," Jeff says. "Why the fuck wouldn't I go?"

"I thought—with your stepfather."

He shakes his head and slams his fist into the curb. Sweat has formed in little puddles between his ear and his cheeks.

"I don't care," Jeff says. "He can't rule my life."

"No," I say. I don't know what else to say.

"I talked my father yesterday," Jeff says. "I asked if I could live with him."

"What did he say?"

I try not to panic but Florida is way too far from Dallastown not to be upset immediately.

"He said 'no'."

A group of warehouse workers climb into the car next to Mindy's and Jeff waits until they pull away. My calves are cramping now that we're sitting.

"He made up some crap about being between jobs and staying with my grandmother—temporarily—in a back bedroom of a tiny house, so there's no room." He turns to face me. "He sounded drunk."

"Oh man," I say.

"I just wanted to see if it was an option, you know. But I knew what he'd say."

"Yeah."

"They're talking about sending me away, Cy."

The curb is getting hotter the longer we're sitting and I feel the burn through my shorts to my skin.

"Send you where?"

"New Bredford. That Christian school up near Harrisburg," Jeff says. "It's over an hour from here."

"Are you serious?"

He nods, the moisture tumbling down his cheeks. The heat is so oppressive I can barely breathe.

"That's ridiculous."

"I know," Jeff says, the sun reflecting off the blues in his retinas. "And this place is hardcore. From what I could find online—not on their official site, because from the outside it looks all normal and nice, but the kids who went there—those who survived—they posted all this shit on Reddit because it's one of those 'Kidnapped for Christ' places that indoctrinates you in Jesus and has you speaking in tongues by the time you graduate. And they have all these rules and 'obediences'—that's the actual word they use—so you can't do anything other than schoolwork and chores and church. Plus, there's prayer circles and Bible study and drug counseling, I'm not even sure they have time to teach English and History."

I'm not following with how fast he's speaking but I don't want to interrupt.

"Can you believe that shit?"

I shake my head.

"Cy, it's like a teen prison run by Jesus freaks or a Brainwash Institute for all these smiling kids who get taught to obey if they don't do a billion chores or whatever." The bruise beneath his eye is more noticeable outside. "I can't fucking go there."

"No. That's insane. All because he found the weed?"

"Yeah. Roland hates me. You know he hates me. And he's trying to convince my mother to send me away."

"What are you going to do?"

"I don't know," he says, dipping his head. The sweat drips along his cheek. "But she doesn't hate me yet, I don't think."

He laughs, to himself, because none of this is funny and I hear the shuffling of shoes on the sidewalk as Mindy approaches.

"I'm sorry to keep you waiting," she says. "I had to talk with HR and call Mrs. Phillips at home, it's—" She looks over to Jeff and then to me. "It's a mess."

"Are we going?" Jeff says.

Mindy coughs and her eyes grow wide in the sunlight. I elbow him.

"Oh," he says. "I'm sorry, Mindy. I didn't mean to get you in trouble."

"It's fine, Jeff. It'll be fine." She sighs. "They're not in the business of turning away volunteers. That jerk McLaren's in a lot more trouble than me."

"Good," Jeff says. Mindy steps back from the curb.

"I'm sorry too," I say.

"What did you do?" Jeff says.

"I brought you along."

He laughs. It's good to hear him laugh.

I don't want to think about it, the way I know I'll think about it, but I can't survive high school without him. My life would end if he leaves.

THIRTEEN

HAVING THE FIRST MEET at home is an advantage in cross-country. We know the route, starting at the far corner of the football stadium between the stands and the woods, up the grassy slope toward New School Lane then downhill on pavement in an abrupt change of pace across the parking lot, a wide-open sprint so you have to watch your momentum to conserve your energy—that's what we know that the other teams don't. We practice it all the time.

I start at the back of the pack of forty runners, pacing behind a Biglerville idiot in a banana costume, waving his yellow arms with his green top flopping up and down against his face until I pass him, near the woods by the baseball fields, gliding through all the runners who went out too fast, picking them off one by one. We loop around the tennis courts, crossing New School Lane at the mile marker, and I check my watch—six minutes—which is fast for me, but the pace feels relaxed, an afternoon jog through Lions Park. But the second mile is a slog along the road toward Myers Farms and I lose my momentum, caught from behind by my teammate Jarrett then trailing behind him, hoping to stay attached because I only count four or five ahead of us and if we finish this way, we would win the meet. I can't stay attached.

We cross back across the street and go the long way around the softball fields, where the Dallastown girls give a cheer that helps—a brief rush of energy that speeds me up a bit, powering through the strain in my calves, and I spot Jarrett ahead of me, his long tan legs gliding through the grass. But my lungs start to press into my chest with every breath, threatening to burst through my ribs like that alien from that movie about aliens. Aliens, I think. It's hard to think when you're as exhausted as this. Jarrett pulls away.

I'm laboring as I reach the parking lot, students and cars and bodies a blur when I pass, the finish line close enough to taste in the thick, wet air clinging to my throat and I don't look back—I can't look back—but I hear the runners catching up from behind, their clomping shoes on the hard black pavement. I do my best to ignore, throwing my focus on the gold shirt in front of me, down the grassy slope for the football stadium.

They haven't cut the grass because they're waiting for game day, the way everything at Dallastown High revolves around the football team. But the thick, wet lawn is weighing the gold shirt down and I think I can catch him without straining it's just I am straining, my legs and my lungs and my guts and my brain, pushing past the pain consuming my body, my torso ahead of my legs, my arms now flailing as we pass the stadium, and Gold Shirt hears me—he kicks into another gear but I have some hidden reserves built up in all my training and I lunge to the finish just ahead of the other runner with a miraculous time of 18:29.

I can't feel my calves and I can't think to breathe but I crushed my personal best. 18:29. I lift my hands above my head to get some air into my lungs, counting down the runners finishing behind me. Blue, gold, green, another green, then the white-and-blue striped singlets of Taylor and Tiger, sophomore twins on our team finishing at the same time, and if I counted correct our first five finished faster than the other three teams so I pump a fist with a half-hearted declaration of victory.

And collapse on the grass next to the stadium.

I can't breathe.

"Oh my god, Cyrus, you won!"

I lift my head to find Mindy, the haze from the sun obscuring my vision. She hand-waves in the direction of the rest of my team celebrating by the scorer's table.

"And I saw you finish—you were in fifth place. Is that?" She hesitates. "Is that good?"

"By far my PR." I sit up between breaths, or one long breath to help me sit up. "Personal record."

"Oh wow, that's awesome!" Mindy shouts, way more enthusiastic than my brain can handle. "Did you hear that, Sharane?"

Sharane steps forward with a thick red backpack on her shoulders.

"Hi, Cyrus," she says. "Congratulations."

"Thank you." I don't often have a rooting section. Once or twice my father got out of work early so he came to watch and Jeff showed at our last meet last year. "What are you guys doing here?"

"We came to see you, stupid," Mindy says. "We are now best friends, Cyrus. That should not be too difficult for you to grasp. Well, Sharane is my best friend always and forever but you're tied for second-best now, along with Regina and Devin, and we're here to support you." She bends down in the grass because I haven't managed to stand. "Okay?"

"Yeah," I say. "That's really nice of you guys. Thank you."

"Jeff's not here, is he?" Sharane says.

I shake my head as I catch a banana tossed by the assistant coach, passing them out to everyone on the team.

"Is he home, do you think?" Sharane says. "Would his mother mind if I stopped by and dropped something off?"

"What are you dropping off?" Mindy says.

"A pot of soup."

"A pot?" Mindy says.

"A bowl."

"Hold on, hold on, hold on," Mindy says, bending her legs in a cross as she takes a seat beside me. "Is this soup you are making from scratch or are you just opening a can?"

"Can," Sharane says and Mindy laughs. "But he liked it yesterday and I thought maybe I could bring him more."

Sharane brought in soup for him at lunch—to help with his 'bronchitis' recovery—and I caught them holding hands under the table.

"Well, I have many thoughts," Mindy says, shifting to her knees on her pleated jeans. "Including why is there a banana running toward the finish line."

"Oh. Yeah," I say. "That happens at some high school meets. It's kind of a thing."

"That's weird. Or awesome. I'm not sure which but I'm intrigued," she says, rubbing her chin like she's a Disney villain. "What team is he on?"

"Biglerville," I say. "They suck."

"Well, your team did awesome, Cyrus," Sharane says, shifting the heavy backpack from one shoulder to the other. "Congratulations."

"Thank you."

"I'm going to go find Court, okay?" she says to Mindy.

"Okay," Mindy says.

Sharane waves and disappears and Mindy steals my banana, taking a big bite.

"Her cousin runs for Dover. She wasn't here just to see you. But it's still nice, right?"

She's talking with her mouth open and I can see the desiccated remains of banana in her teeth. She stretches out her legs on the grass.

"I bought tickets for the concert Saturday," Mindy says.

Runners are still finishing with the requisite fake applause thirty yards away.

"Really?" I'm not sure we're still going. "I'm not sure we're still going."

"Why the hell not?"

"Jeff. He hasn't gotten permission from his parents yet."

"I see." She brushes her hair behind her ears. "I thought my mom was the strictest parent in Dallastown but she allowed it. Sort of. She's not aware we're going to Philly, or to a concert, or leaving Dallastown at any point because Sharane's house is prominently involved in my fake plans, but can't he lie—I mean, just say he's doing something else? Maybe we can all go to Sharane's?"

"Huh?"

"Like, maybe you can be part of my fake plans." She slips her arm around my shoulders before releasing because I'm a sweaty mess. "We can double date. Fake double date."

"Maybe," I say but even the idea of a fake date between Sharane and Jeff is unsettling.

"You know, I never told my mom that our date didn't work out and she's always asking if you and I are like— more than friends, so that makes it an even better excuse."

The crowd around the finish line begins to disperse for the parking lot so I guess the last runner has finished. Cross-country meets tend to break up pretty fast.

"And it might get her off my ass about a boyfriend, although it would be infinitely better if you were Korean. You're not Korean, are you?"

I look at her strange. She laughs.

"Don't worry, Cyrus." She wraps her arm my head and holds it there this time. "I'm not asking you out again—this would be a fake date. And my mom doesn't need to know you're gay."

"Okay," I say. I trust her with my secret.

"Oh my god, that reminds me. You never told me how your date went."

Cody and I had our virtual date last night after much delay. It did not go well.

"It did not go well."

"Hmm." She reaches for my arm, the banana peel in my hand. "I'm sorry. You okay?"

"No, it's fine. We're good."

"What happened?" she says, a stiff hot wind blowing her hair into her face. "Was it as bad as your date with me?"

"Actually, yes," I say and she gives me her "eek" face as I relay an abbreviated version of our date, when we tried to watch a movie together but the connection wasn't great so there was this lag where I'd be laughing or making a sarcastic comment but Cody hadn't seen the movie before and he kept missing the dialogue or my failed attempts at humor so at some point I stopped speaking and we spent the last hour in silence.

"What movie did you watch?" Mindy says.

"Scott Pilgrim."

"Oh, I love that," Mindy says.

"So do I," I say. It was a go-to flick for Jeff and I this summer in my basement. I probably shouldn't have tried to recreate it with Cody.

"Was he upset? Are you upset? Is this going to interfere with our trip to California to meet him?"

Mindy's obsessed with Cody. She stalked him on Instagram and sent me cute pictures of him with his brother. She's dying to meet him.

"No, he wasn't upset. We even made tentative plans for a second date."

"That's good," she says. "Maybe you're better at second dates?"

"I hope so," I say. "God, I hope so."

She laughs and I look past her to see Sharane with the Dover runner and his parents. He looks cute from a distance.

"Well, we need to figure out the plans for Saturday but I'm pretty sure they will involve you and me on a second date," she says. "And hopefully my mom won't call your dad to interrogate him on his knowledge of Korean-American history."

"She would do that?"

Mindy nods a bunch of times. "Absolutely." She stands up and pulls me off the grass at great effort on her part. My calves are broken. "But don't worry. Tell Jeff we'll find a way to break him out this weekend because I already bought tickets and I'm attending my first hardcore concert and my mom is definitely calling your father, so give him a heads-up for me please."

I laugh. She looks down at her arm and wipes my sweat off her sleeve.

"Now, please go shower because you're disgusting."

FOURTEEN

THE PERSPIRATION PUDDLES on my shirt, down my chest and along my sides, and not just mine. I've been banging into bodies bouncing around the mosh pit, flailing arms and legs and smashing chests, surging into me then over me, surfing the waves of hands above me. We got here early enough to stake out a place close to the stage but once Joyce Manor came on, the mosh pit formed around us and Mindy pulled us back, out from the stage and away from mortal danger. But when the opening chords of "Derailed" spilled from the speakers, Jeff smiled at me and I followed him into the crush of bodies, sucking us in and making us whole.

I've been trying to respect everyone else's space, pogoing up and down in one place, but every few seconds I get blindsided by a cannonball attack by some lunatic who knocks me sideways into another person and sends that person sprawling into another stranger. And I can barely see the band, not with all the bouncing bodies up and down around me, the constant fear of random assaults from oversized drunken dudes slamming into my body. It's amazing.

I find a little daylight to catch the band up on the stage, the lead singer of Joyce Manor leaning out into the crowd with the microphone stand and a full sleeve tattoo covering his left arm. So cool. His raspy voice echoes from the speakers, along with the guitars and drums, an implausible level of amp explosion besieging my ears at once. He's kind of cute—or really cute—and I'm bouncing up and down next to Jeff, so it's a wonderful feeling, a full perfect feeling, and I can't believe I never attended a concert before.

Union Transfer is in a shady part of Philly, so Dad said under no circumstances were we allowed to drive down here without him, but then Mindy had me put him on the phone, and she used some kind of friend/parent jujitsu because he ended up giving us permission and I didn't even have to beg. Jeff's stepfather was harder to convince.

We enlisted Aunt Donna, who happened to be moving this weekend, so Jeff and I volunteered to be part of her moving crew—just as an alibi—but the stepfuck didn't believe us, the way he hates everything fun and doesn't trust Jeff, but also who moves to a new apartment on a Saturday night. Donna called him, though, and explained how she works the day shift on weekends at the hospital and she somehow convinced him because Jeff is here and Joyce Manor is on the stage and I owe Donna more favors than I can ever repay. She said I have to let her move in with me when she's too old to take care of herself. Seems like a small price to pay.

Joyce Manor's singer climbs down from the stage and pushes out into the audience, wading into the center of the pit, almost on top of me, and we all spread out to give him room but I'm bursting, holding onto Jeff and all these fellow fans, catching our collective breaths like a wave about to break. The drummer slams the skins behind the two guitarists up front, freaking out on the stage like all of us in the pit. I can't breathe.

The singer jumps back to the platform so I focus on the drummer—short brown hair and forearms flexing up and down behind the kit, head turned to the left, clasping the cymbals and crashing down again, elbows straight with no wrist, hands above the snare then back to the toms like he's not even concentrating. I don't know how he does it, drumming with such speed while looking out at the crowd long enough for me to see, but then "Five Beer Plan" erupts from the speakers and the crowd collapses around me. I can't see.

"Holy fuck, this is incredible!" Jeff shouts during a break between tracks. My ears are numb so it takes a second or two for his words to register. I don't know what happened to Mindy.

"I can't breathe," I say and he pulls me closer, away from the thunder of the pit, his sweaty grip around me.

"I know, man. It's awesome."

The drummer lays down the beat for the next track, one two three before the guitars kick into gear and the audience reacts to "Christmas Card" in one extended spasm, a tsunami more than a wave this time. We try to stay at the edge but the mosh pit expands around us, these flailing bodies whirling past me, the speakers above the stage blasting the music so loud they shake. I feel Jeff's hand on my side, clutching my waistband to help me stabilize, to keep me from sprawling across the concrete. Keeping me safe.

Joyce Manor was the first band Jeff introduced me to last year and I almost forget what I was into before I met him—indie rock I guess, like my dad listens to. Death

Cab for Cutie or Arcade Fire, maybe, but Jeff says you're not listening to anything meaningful if it ends up in a commercial for a minivan. And there's beauty in hardcore, the way it fills you with a sense of something bigger than yourself, or better, this swelling emotion swept up with the rage until you release all your thoughts and disengage. Revel in the beauty of the sound.

I focus on the drummer again, to see if I can learn how he keeps up with the beat, all controlled but rapid motion, no respite from his motion, a double bass attack over to the cymbals to the snare, hi-hat and then back again, speeding up and spreading thin and I need to begin practicing again. Impress the shit out of Jeff by playing that well, or close to that well. The audience roars as Joyce Manor finishes their set and Jeff moves over to me.

"I think I've sweat off ten pounds tonight," he says.

I nod and find my breath but I still can't hear, my ears ringing with every sound. I almost forgot Mindy was here until she steps up beside us.

"That was great," she says.

Jeff touches my back, ignoring.

"Can you breathe?" he says.

"A little."

He laughs and his lips stay parted for a smile.

"Nobody's leaving," Mindy says. "Why is nobody leaving?"

"It's not over," Jeff says. "They'll be back for an encore."

The crowd is clapping and some in the audience are stomping their feet and I don't want to leave. I don't ever want to leave.

I catch Mindy checking her phone so maybe she wasn't as into the show as Jeff and me but I don't care, I just want to be here. To live in this moment, Joyce Manor on the stage and Jeff and me in the mosh pit, slamming into strangers and bouncing into each other. His sweat on my skin.

"They'll play at least three more songs," Jeff says. "They haven't played 'Leather Jacket' so that's a definite and probably 'Catalina Fight Song'—that's a short one. Maybe 'Beach Community'?"

Mindy laughs. "You really know their music."

"The best band in history," I say. Breathing out loud.

Mindy laughs, longer this time.

"You guys are hilarious," she says and that's the last thing I hear because the band returns and the crowd explodes and Jeff pulls me back into the pit.

"You know, I didn't agree to be your chauffeur this evening," Mindy says, pulling her Civic out into the streets of Philadelphia. "This is way beyond the expectation of our friend compact."

"I'm sorry," I say. Jeff sat shotgun on the way down, taking over Mindy's radio with Joyce Manor on his Bluetooth, but he slid into the backseat next to me before we left the parking lot and I didn't move. "If you want to pull over, I could—"

"It's fine," she says through the rearview. "What did you think of the concert?"

Jeff's head is planted in my lap, face up with his eyes closed, and I can't tell if he's awake but his chest is moving in and out with his breathing.

"They were incredible," I say.

"Yeah," Mindy says. "I knew none of their songs before tonight and while I admire and respect the talent it takes to play in the multiple symphonies I've seen in person, this was another level of exciting."

Mindy merges onto the highway, west toward central P.A. and I think we're late—I know we're late, but I'm afraid to look at my phone to see how late we are. I know Dad's been texting. The windows are down and I can hear Mindy's hair flapping against the seat, beneath Joyce Manor through the sound system.

"How come you didn't come into the mosh pit with us?" I ask her.

"That didn't seem safe," Mindy says. "Didn't you fall?"

"I did?"

"Dude, you totally fell," Jeff says from my lap, his eyes still closed. "I picked you up."

I don't remember. I think I was in a daze from the moment they started playing.

"Don't worry, I saved you."

"You're awake?"

"No," he says. "Just dreaming."

I adjust my jeans with his head between my legs. It's so loud in the car with the wind and the music I don't think Mindy can hear us.

"Dreaming of what?"

"Our band. Being up there on the stage. With you."

I try to swallow but my mouth is too parched so I scratch at my throat instead.

"I'm sorry," he says, opening his eyes.

"For what?"

"I just—" He bends his neck toward the front seat to see if Mindy is listening but she's focused on the road. "Sorry about what happened after our—you know."

He lifts his hand to his lips to make a kiss.

"Okay," I say. I'm not sure what to say. He apologized already.

"I didn't mean to hurt you," he says. "I think—I think I might have hurt you."

When Joyce Manor finished their set, Jeff and I were still in the mosh pit and he leaned on top of me—his hands on my shoulders as I cheered and clapped at the final flourish of "Beach Community." He didn't let go.

"I've missed you, man. These last two weeks. I've missed the band and my guitar and us."

He shoves his legs against the door to push himself up, closer to my chest. He's no longer whispering.

"You're the one person I can count on of all the people in my life. Not my mom, not my dad—my real dad, I mean."

I catch Mindy's eyes in the rearview, watching us. I don't know if she can hear us but as long as Jeff keeps speaking the way he's speaking, the world could end right now.

"But you're always there for me, Cy," Jeff says. "And it wasn't fair to dismiss it, you know. What we did."

The wind pummels my face through the open windows, Jeff's head on my chest. I let my fingers reach out for his hair and he lets me caress and I don't want to say anything because I don't want to say the wrong thing so I just pat the curly waves of brown like a pet. He keeps speaking.

"I don't think of Sharane like that," he says. "I try to—but—it's not the same."

I'm not sure what he means but I want him to mean it. He looks up at me. Smiling.

"It's not the same as when I think about you."

He reaches behind my head and pulls me down, my face to his lips. Upside down and strange but we're kissing.

And it's better this time, with the rush of the wind and the heat of his body pressed into my body. I keep my eyes open—watching him kiss me. His face and his skin. On my skin.

I feel like I'm bouncing about in the mosh pit, the adrenaline rush or the endorphin spin, Joyce Manor in my ears on the stereo system, louder than the wind. I don't know how long we kissed before but this is longer. Better.

Mindy slams on the brakes too late and I hear a scream, an awful scream, then a punishing crunch under the tires and a high-pitched howl. My face smashes into the seat in front of me, Jeff on my lap crashing through me.

The car stops. Everything stops. I reach up to catch the blood streaming down my cheek. A long, low wail echoes in my ears.

"Shit!" Jeff says. "What the fuck was that?"

FIFTEEN

MINDY PULLED ONTO the shoulder behind the body of the animal, headlights bright on its mangled limbs, spread out at unnatural angles, matted fur mixed with blood. One glance and I nearly puked but I kept it down, close to me.

Jeff's bent beneath the tire at the side of the road, screaming by with passing cars that won't stop, might not even notice us in the dark, the fallen dog clinging to life on the highway's shoulder.

"Where did it come from?" I say. Out loud I think. "Did you see it?"

Mindy is pacing back and forth in front of the Civic, wincing like she might have injured herself but she doesn't answer me. I can hear the dog whimpering—a plaintive wail that bores into my skull. The blood seeps down my cheek onto my tongue. Like silver.

"You have a spare?" Jeff says, climbing out from underneath. The right rim is dented into the tire and the whole corner by the bumper is crumpled back onto itself. Mindy doesn't speak.

"Are you okay?" I say. She looks at me like she's looking through me.

"I'll check the trunk," Jeff says.

The cars keep screaming by. We're stopped by a thicket of trees, and the shoulder is wide enough we might be fully out of view from the road, if it weren't for the Civic's headlights, throwing a harsh glare on the four-legged victim. It launched into the air upon impact and Mindy slammed her car to a stop. I almost wish she'd kept driving.

"Cy, give me a hand," Jeff calls out. He drops the spare and a jack onto the shoulder next to the wheel. The dog's howls keep getting louder.

"The dog is alive," I say, but I don't think anyone can hear me with the cars passing by so fast and the lug wrench clanging off the rim. The blood stings as it coagulates on my skin.

"We need to get it to a hospital," I say.

It's some kind of husky breed with white speckled fur, lying on its side with the front legs curled under and the back legs so crooked they almost look detached. The white is marred by red in the fading headlights.

"That dog is done for, Cy," Jeff says. "We should put it out of its misery."

The rim is bent back too far for Jeff to loosen the lugs so he stands up, close to me. The entire front corner has buckled under, tilting the car sideways, and the tire keeps losing air, filling the gaps between the dog's wheezing.

"No, it's alive. We need to get to a hospital."

"What hospital?" Jeff says. "Where the hell are we?"

"I don't know, an animal hospital or something." I remember my iPhone and its GPS capabilities. "Maybe there's one near here."

The signal isn't great and the mapping feature is slow and my hands are wet with sweat or the blood dripping from my cheek but a few results for 'animal hospital' come filtering in.

"Fuck," Jeff says. "What time is it?"

"Late," I say. We were already late when we hit the dog but I don't want him to panic. More than he already is.

"We gotta get back, Cy," Jeff says. "Fuck."

Google lists a bunch of places in York or wherever the hell faraway, then the ASPCA, which is that place where some singer warbles about "angels" at 3 a.m., but I manage to click near one of the choices. The dog keeps howling, louder still.

"Cy, can you give me a hand?" Jeff says, back under the wheel to jack the car off the shoulder but the tire is flat and the rim is a mangled mash of rubber and steel.

"I found a vet hospital a few miles away," I say. "An emergency center for dogs and other animals."

"We don't have time for that," Jeff says. "If we can't fix this tire and get the fuck home right now, I'm so fucking fucked."

He stands up and starts to pace at the edge of the asphalt, slapping at his hip for several frightening seconds. We left too late—I knew we left too late but I didn't check the time when we still at the concert and I should have said something but I didn't want to leave. A dog is dying at the side of the road and Mindy's car has a tire we can't possibly fix.

"I have to call AAA," she says, wincing a bit as she steps around to the other side of the Civic, away from the dog. The right headlight flickers from the accident, on and off like a spotlight.

"Should I call the hospital?" I say. "Maybe they have an ambulance?"

"Are you kidding me, Cyrus?" Jeff says. "If I don't get home right now, I'm going to that Christian school up in Harrisburg. Can you call your aunt—maybe she can pick us up?"

"We're half an hour from home, Jeff," Mindy says. "AAA would be quicker. And maybe they could help with the dog."

"Jesus fucking Christ," Jeff says. "What the hell was a dog doing in the middle of the fucking highway?"

"I don't know," Mindy says. She recoils again, holding her side as she steps forward, away from the highway. "But we can't just leave it here."

I notice its fur sticking from the bumper, clinging tight to the sheared-off metal in the headlights.

"It's dead," Jeff says. "It's as good as dead. Do you see its hind legs?"

The dog's moans start to wane, like it's tried hard enough and it's ready to give up.

"But maybe the AAA guy can fix the tire and we can hurry to the hospital to drop it off," I say. "It's not too far."

"What part of we have no fucking time do you not understand, Cy?" Jeff steps over to me at the front bumper, exasperated. I think we kissed. Before the accident. I can't quite remember.

"I never should have come tonight. Why the fuck did you make me come?" Jeff says, his mouth square and eyes ablaze. The jack collapses from the weight and the car slams to the pavement.

"Fuck!" Jeff shouts. "Fuck." The cars keep screaming by for no fucking reason.

"I'm calling AAA," Mindy says, stepping around to the front with us. "I'm sorry Jeff, I need them to fix the tire.

And if he sees the dog, I'm sure he'll have to report it. He won't just leave it here."

I watch the dog's face in the flickering headlights— the jaw jutting out almost sideways, the white fur turned crimson but its eyes oddly clear, looking back at me. Mindy walks to the back of the car as she gets AAA on the phone.

"Call an Uber," I say, handing my phone to Jeff. "It's my dad's account. I'll wait here with Mindy and we can deal with the dog. Just get home."

"Forget it," Jeff says. "Uber will take even longer. We're in the middle of nowhere."

He lifts the lug wrench off the ground and steps forward, toward the animal. Its howls grow louder all of a sudden and the air feels colder, like we've been out here forever.

"Jeff, what are you doing?" I say.

He moves past me, clutching the shiny metal in the shape of a cross.

"We have to get rid of the body," he says, moving away from me. "Mindy's right. The driver won't leave it here at the side of the road."

"Yeah, but Jeff." I jump in front of him, blocking his path to the dog. "What are you doing?"

"Move aside, Cy," Jeff says, teeth clenched, his blue eyes dulled like he's looking through me, not at me. I grab hold of the lug wrench in his hands.

"Let the fuck go," he says, jerking the wrench from my grip and pushing me back in one motion.

I trip on the asphalt, reaching out to break my fall, and Jeff slips past, quick and deliberate. Mindy shouts "No!" when Jeff lifts his arms above the animal's body and I scream, a desperate scream, hiding my eyes from the scene.

But the metal clangs off the pavement without impact. The dog keeps howling.

"Jesus, Jeff—what were you going to do?" Mindy says.

Jeff falls to his knees beside the dog at the side of the road. Whimpering.

The cars keep speeding past for no fucking reason.

The dog died on its own, before the AAA guy arrived, but the driver took extra time to call the police and make a report so we had to wait longer, like Jeff said we would. He stopped speaking—none of us were speaking, the entire drive home in silence once the driver jacked up the Civic, got the tire fixed, and sent us home.

"Maybe he's asleep," I say as we turn into our neighborhood but before I can finish, I spot Jeff's stepfather in the driveway, his hulking figure perched against the closed garage door. Mindy drops us off and speeds away without saying goodbye.

"You realize what time it is?" the stepfuck says.

His shirt is tucked into stretchy khakis, belt fastened and straining under the pressure. We stop at the edge of the driveway, the cracked concrete at my feet.

"We were in an accident," Jeff says. "We hit a dog."

"You realize what time it is," he repeats with a matter-of-fact tone more frightening than a shout.

"I didn't happen to catch the time as we watched the dog die at the side of the road," Jeff says. "We're okay, thanks for asking."

Mr. Danforth moves out from the garage, focused on the street as Mindy's taillights fade in the distance. She said she might have broken a rib, the way her side is sore to the touch. I told her I'd go to the hospital with her but she just wanted to go home.

"Your aunt looks awfully young, Cyrus," Mr. Danforth says, that same disinterested tone. "And if I'm not mistaken, Asian."

"That was my friend Mindy," I say. "She was—uh—helping with the move too." I'm not a good liar but I need to pull it together. "She was driving us home and the dog, it came out of nowhere. We didn't want to just leave it, and we had to wait for AAA."

"Funny," Mr. Danforth says. "Jeffrey didn't mention her in his texts about coming home late. And your aunt didn't answer when I called."

Jeff and I stay at the edge of the driveway, one foot in the street.

"You have any explanation that resembles the truth?" Mr. Danforth says.

I'm not sure if he's talking to me or to Jeff but I'm afraid I'll make it worse if I speak again. Jeff glares at him.

"We're done here." The stepfuck says and heads up the walkway toward the house with long, unnatural strides. I wait until he's inside.

"What just happened?"

"It doesn't matter," Jeff says.

"What did you text him?"

Jeff shakes his head, stepping forward on the concrete, scratching at his neck. I think the bleeding stopped from the gash on my cheek but I haven't looked. It hurts.

"I didn't mention Mindy. Just that we were driving home from your aunt's and we had an accident. I said I'd be home soon."

"When was that?"

"While we were waiting for AAA," Jeff says. "And you and Mindy weren't speaking to me."

Jeff lifted the lug wrench above the dog's head like an executioner and I get that it would have died anyway because it did die anyway and we couldn't do anything to save it but I can't get past the look on its face. The way Jeff shoved me away. The porch lights fade.

"Go home, Cy," Jeff says.

"What are you going to do about Roland?"

I step onto the lawn, beneath the overgrown maple tree. The branches spread from the garage to the front door of the rancher.

"I can handle it," Jeff says, moving for the house. "Just go home."

"But the last time this happened you had a black eye for a week."

I reach up to my own cut, which isn't bleeding anymore.

"Leave it alone, Cy," Jeff says.

I step across the soft wet grass, bridging the gap between us.

"Come home with me, don't go inside," I say.

"I can handle it," Jeff says, his voice sharp and deep but I can't see his eyes, the dark of the night enveloping the house. "He tries to hit me again and I'll fucking kill him."

He steps onto the porch and disappears into the house as I wait under the maple tree, the pain in my cheek spiking through my head, a surge of vomit shooting up from my stomach onto the stepfuck's well-manicured lawn.

I sprint all the way home.

SIXTEEN

THE NIGHT MOM DIED, I was in Angela's room watching the rain through the windows, because we hadn't heard from her—she was supposed to be home from class hours earlier and Dad kept calling and getting no answer, so Angela and I were trying to keep distracted playing Monopoly or some old game like that, when the flashing lights of two police cars pulled up to the house, the officers climbing out wearing caps protected by plastic coverings, the water rolling off the surface into the puddles that formed between the driveway and the front lawn. Angela and I went to the top of the stairs as Dad met them at the front door, dropping to his knees on the hard-tiled floor before the officer even made it inside.

Angela sprinted down the stairs ahead of me, her screams met by his cries. I stopped at the bottom step, across the faded blue carpeting of the living room, an ocean of medium pile texture between us. Dad stood up and held Angela, waving me over, but I didn't move—I wouldn't move—I thought if I stayed long enough on that bottom step, I could avoid the news they'd already heard, the news I never heard because I refused to move from the stairs the night the officers pulled up to our front door to tell us our mother was dead.

Dad said time would make it easier. Not better, just easier. But I didn't want easy. I didn't care how hard it would be or how long it might take. I wanted better. It never got better.

Not completely.

Dad didn't either.

He drove me to the hospital Sunday morning to get stitches for my cut, after it bled overnight and reopened on my pillowcase, crimson stains on the cotton. Mindy's been admitted with more severe injuries and I haven't heard from Jeff—his phone going straight to voice mail the couple times I tried. I don't know what happened after I left but it can't be good.

Nothing is good.

"Well I didn't think it was possible, Cyrus," Mindy says. "But the second date was worse than the first."

She's sitting up in the hospital bed, her back in an almost upright position, and she's got her legs spread to the limits of the gown, the sheets askew at her feet.

"Date?"

"You know, the Joyce Manor concert. Our second date." She laughs to herself. "Maybe we're not meant to hang out outside of school."

Her laughter turns into coughing then a few violent wheezes, forward in her bed. She had trouble breathing when she got home and her mother rushed her to the hospital. I went upstairs to visit after the doctor stitched up my wound.

"Are you okay?"

"I'll survive," she says. "Gnarly bandage, by the way." She points to my cheek. "How many stitches?"

"Six."

"Will it scar?"

"They say probably not, but it's the 'probably' that's concerning."

The doctor who applied the stitches said I might have a concussion—I've had a headache all night—so we took X-rays to check. The results were negative, which is actually a positive. Hospitals are confusing.

"I think there's a cream or something you can put on that helps with scarring. I'll ask my mom."

"Thank you," I say. "I appreciate it."

It's awkward seeing her like this—in the hospital with her gown spread wide, twelve hours after we watched the husky die at the side of the road. I think she saw Jeff and I kiss. Before the accident.

"How are you feeling?" I say.

"Not horrible." She closes her legs and lifts up a bit. "Cracked ribs. Punctured lung. But they've already fixed that. The lung part. So, I'm breathing okay. They took me off the oxygen and I'm on painkillers so—"

"Did you say 'punctured lung'?" I step closer to the bed, approaching from the side. "You neglected to mention that in your texts this morning."

"Yeah. Sorry. Apparently, I could have died if we didn't go to the hospital last night."

"Are you serious?" She lifts her hands to her head, shaping her hair to part it in the middle, away from her eyes. "Why didn't you tell us that last night?"

"I didn't know I had a punctured lung, Cyrus."

"I know but—" I set my hands on the metal railing, gripping tight. "Wow."

"Yeah." She scrunches her nose like what happened was a mild inconvenience, not a potential death sentence.

She plays with the sheets as she speaks. "I mean, my chest was tight and my ribs were sore but it wasn't until I got home that I realized I couldn't actually breathe. Must have been the adrenaline or something. All better now, though."

"Wow." The sunlight through the windows shines on her smile. I don't know how she's smiling. "Do you know what caused it—a punctured lung?"

"The steering wheel, I guess," she says. "My mom always told me I put the seat up too close and I guess this is why."

She shifts forward to pull up the sheets and winces this time.

"Are you sure you're okay?"

"I'm fine. It'll take the ribs a little longer to heal, they said."

"Are you going to school tomorrow?"

"Funny, Cyrus." She can't help but roll her eyes. "I'll be in here at least a couple days."

She's hooked up via multiple tubes or wires to various monitors, her gown hanging low off her neck, the sun and the room's fluorescents casting a split-layered light through the open blinds. We're at Wellspan York, the nearest hospital to Dallastown, a fifteen-minute drive Dad and I made in silence after I woke up with blood on my pillowcase.

"I'm sorry," I say.

"It's not your fault. Even though I was distracted by you kissing Jeff in my backseat." My heart drops into my feet like an elevator on speed. "But I don't think I ever would have spotted that dog racing out from the woods. Might have been better that I didn't have time to react, you know."

"Yeah," I say. "Maybe."

"I mean, not better for the dog, of course." She dips her head.

I haven't had time to process what happened with Jeff and the husky at the side of the road. What we did in Mindy's backseat before the accident. What the stepfuck did to him when he went inside last night. My face was a throbbing ball of ache once the adrenaline faded. I'm trying not to think.

"Where's your mom?" I say.

"Getting us lunch. I am not beat for this hospital food." She points to a tray on the table beside her, a mound of untouched mash potatoes and half-eaten meat. "Speaking of which, I have to offer my resignation from your band. The band with no name and the distinctive singing of the dear departed Jeff, which yes, I know Jeff is not dead but he is departed from my life and that's why I can't be in the band. I'm sorry."

"Wait—what?"

"Yeah, you see my mom forbid me from driving without her again or driving at night, or you know, leaving her sight, since I was supposed to be at Sharane's last night and not in a concert in Philly, which I did not admit to but I had to give her some reason I was out on the highway so late and I blamed it on the band. I'm not supposed to speak to either of you again, actually."

She reaches out to me, touching my hand on the railing.

"But I'm ignoring that part. The 'you' portion of it, at least. Because listen, Cyrus, you're a great guy and I know you and Jeff have something special—more than something, apparently." Her skin feels clammy on my skin. "And we don't need to talk about that. Honestly, I'm not ready to talk about that. But the thing is, I can't get past what he was about to do to that dog. I can't."

I can't either. I keep seeing its eyes.

"And I know the dog was in horrible shape, which was my fault." She shakes her head and releases my hand. "I'm not excusing my fault in all of this, believe me. It's haunting me. And thank god, he didn't follow through because this would be a whole different conversation. But what he did was insane, Cyrus, to even consider striking down that poor helpless creature. I just don't know how someone could do that."

She blinks a few times in the fractured light and I think I should tell her what will happen to him if he gets sent to that religious school, how his stepfather treats him, how desperate he must have been. And he didn't go through with it—that has to mean something.

"I don't think I can be friends with him anymore, Cyrus. I don't know how you can, honestly, but I'm not forcing you to choose or anything."

Mindy looks past me at her mother, coming into the room with a tray full of food.

"But thank you for stopping in to visit me, Cyrus, this was sweet," Mindy says.

"Who is this?" her mother asks in a heavy Korean accent. Mindy emigrated to the United States when she was five and her father didn't come with them so she lives alone with her mother in Red Lion. She never talks about her dad.

"This is Cyrus," Mindy says. "He's in my grade."

"Cyrus?" her mother says. "Is he one of the boys from last night?"

"No," Mindy says. "This is the boy from the movies."

"Oh, I see." Her mother's mouth forms a half-smile, one side rising up from her chin. "Well, it was nice of him to come. Would you like some lunch?"

"Oh no, I'm okay," I say. She must think Cyrus is a much more common name than it is. "I was just, I have to go. My father's waiting in the lobby."

"How nice of him," her mother says, exchanging places with me by Mindy's bed, so quick I don't realize I'm leaving until I'm out of the room.

SEVENTEEN

Dad's client in California had a "conveyor emergency," a statement so ridiculous I never would have let it slide under normal circumstances, but I was too upset to respond with anything but goodbye as he headed to the airport while I got ready for school. It's been a slog this week without Jeff and without Mindy and now Dad is gone all weekend. I'm trying not to think.

I walked home from school today, backpack loaded down, hoping studying might take my mind off things. Jeff. I could have taken the bus but the route goes round past half the town before they get to my development even though we live across New School Road. I missed a whole week of cross-country practice—the doctor recommended I rest after the concussion, or possible concussion—and the wind on the walk spikes against my stitches. I don't mind. I want to feel something.

"Is your dad home?"

Jeff climbs off the curb by our garage door, shrouded in the cover of the overgrown bushes lining our driveway.

"Jesus, Jeff. You scared me." I didn't even see him.

"Is your dad home?"

"No, he's in California," I say. "Conveyor—stuff."

"I need to use your phone." He's wearing a heavy flannel shirt hanging loosely off his back.

"Okay," I say, pushing the backpack off my shoulders and dropping it onto the concrete.

"Roland's sending me to that school."

"Are you serious?" I say.

"They already transferred my records from Dallastown."

He shields his eyes from the sun with the sleeve of his flannel.

"Fuck."

"Mom told me it will just be until Christmas and I'll come back more mature and have a relationship with God or some bullshit like that, as if she could possibly convince me."

A car drives past and Jeff looks over my shoulder to watch, ducking for cover in the shade of the garage. His hair is a mess—tangled and spread across his forehead, stray strands straight up, tufting in the wind. His blue eyes look dark, red veins webbing through the white.

"She said I might be able to come home on weekends but I don't know if that's true." He finds my face. "I need to use your phone."

"Wait—what do you mean, home for weekends?"

"It's a boarding school. Like, you board there and live there and they don't let you leave."

I blink to make it make sense, but he isn't making any sense. He can't leave me.

"And they don't even let you have phones or Internet. No access to the outside world at all." He hasn't had his phone all week—I know because I've called and texted every single day and the messages don't even deliver. I haven't spoken to him since the night of the accident.

"That's insane," I say, stepping closer, but he ducks under the garage again and the wind against my back blows several leaves from the gutter above his head.

"It's basically a prison—they're sending me to fucking prison, Cy. A goddamn Jesus prison because I went to one fucking concert in Philly."

His lips are charred or a little chapped in the light behind me, breaking through. We kissed. I know we kissed because Mindy saw it and told me. It seems distant.

"Can't you talk to your mother?" I say. "Can't she do something?"

"It's too late." He scratches through his flannel at the side of his chest. "Roland found my stash."

"The weed?"

"Yeah. He convinced my mom I was on drugs so she let him search my room. It didn't take long. He already had the Altoids tin."

"Shit."

"My mom was resisting about the school until then but now it's over. She's on board. It might even be her idea at this point."

"I'm so sorry, Jeff."

I should have been the one stashing the weed. He taps his foot against the door and his hair sweeps down his face. He doesn't brush it away.

"How's your cheek?" he says.

"It's okay," I say, touching on instinct. "Six stitches."

"Does it hurt?"

"No." Not as much.

"Have you heard from Mindy?"

"Yeah. She's doing better. She got out of the hospital yesterday."

I wait for him to ask why she was in there, or ask about our kiss. His bloodshot eyes are spinning around my face.

"She broke some ribs in the accident," I say.

"Oh," he says. "That stinks."

I keep waiting.

"I need to use your phone," he says. "Please."

I bend down to dig it out from the front pocket of my backpack, sitting on the concrete. He takes it from me.

"I need to call my father, try again to get him to let me live with him."

Jeff walks to the front of the house, underneath the pair of oaks at the side of our driveway, the leaves turning brown in the early autumn breeze. The front lawn was bare when my parents bought the house and Mom planted the trees for Angela and me, when each of us was born. Mom would sit on her bench in between them every spring, reading her books or grading papers for school, watching the leaves return from a winter of waiting.

"What happened?" I ask when he returns. He looks past me into the street, scratching at his side through his shirt again.

"He said no. I knew he would, I just—" He's shaking his head back and forth so hard I think he might break. "You got to do me a favor, Cy."

My cheek starts to itch from the wind picking up, this sharp pressing ache.

"They're driving me up there Sunday. After church."

"This Sunday?"

"Yeah." He nods and keeps his eyes down. This is happening way too fast. "But they do their Bible study after church so I need you to do me a favor."

"Okay," I say.

"I thought I could catch a train to Florida but that's out now—" He grinds his hands against the flannel, the hair in his eyes spinning around his face. "So I need cash—whatever you can spare—for bus fare or a train ticket, because I don't have a car and I don't have my phone and I can't get far with what I have in my savings. I spent a lot this summer on the guitar and the amps and everything."

The rush of words spread through my brain. I don't know what to do with them.

"Can you help me, Cy? I'm leaving."

"Wait—where would you go?" I can't let him leave. "What if I came over, explained what happened again. Better this time. That it was all my fault—the concert, the accident, the weed. I'll say you were stashing it for me."

"It's too late, Cy, let it go."

"It can't be too late," I say.

He steps forward out of the shadows, into the faded sunlight behind me.

"When Roland found my stash, he closed the door to my bedroom and told me he wasn't going to let me hurt my mother like my father did. That I needed to accept what was happening and get the proper treatment." He pauses, gnawing on his chapped lips. "I told him to go fuck himself and then he hit me."

"Oh my god."

"And I fought back, Cy, I told you I would. But he's so fucking huge—he's a big fucking ape—and I hit him as hard as I could but he was punching too."

He lifts up his flannel and the T-shirt underneath. Sharp black bruises cover the skin around his ribs.

"Jeff." I reach out to touch. He pulls back.

"It looks worse than it hurts."

"Jesus, Jeff. This is ridiculous."

He yanks on the flannel, stepping back against the door again. A few fallen leaves have gathered between the driveway and the garage, the start of a pile that Dad's going to force me to rake in the coming weeks. They spin in a circle next to Jeff.

"It doesn't matter now, I'm leaving."

"Where are you going?" I say. Desperate.

"I don't know. Maybe Brooklyn, like we talked about. That's why I need money—for like a motel room and the train ticket or bus—I don't know, do they even have trains to New York from here?" I start to nod but he doesn't wait for my response. "I'll pay you back. I'll definitely pay you back."

"But Jeff, wait—"This is insane. "You're running away?"

"Yeah," he says. "They've been doing Bible study after church at the house so they'll have all these people around and won't notice when I leave. Will you help me?"

I don't think I'd survive if he got sent away to religious school but if he ran away, I might never see him again because he couldn't come back to Dallastown and I don't have a car or a license so I couldn't go visit him. I can't function without seeing him, the way I haven't functioned all week. He hasn't even mentioned the kiss.

"Cy?" He leans forward, into the light. "Please."

I nod. I don't know what else to do.

"Thank you."

He cracks a sideways smile and for a second I think it's a joke, the end of a wild dream that started with the kiss. I wait for him to laugh, tell me his punishment is over and he's staying in Dallastown for good and giving all his money to the ASPCA. But he's not laughing.

"I need to go, Cy," he says, handing me back my phone and stepping from the shelter of the garage. "Please be home Sunday, I'll be over right after church. I need you, man."

He taps me on the shoulder and rushes down the driveway, picking up into a sprint as he dashes into the street. I squint as he speeds away.

EIGHTEEN

"DID I WAKE YOU?"

"No, no," Donna says, her voice trailing off as I follow her into the kitchen. She's wearing her navy blue hospital scrubs and slippers, scratching against the hardwood floors. "Maybe."

"I'm sorry."

She pulls out a stool at the counter for me to sit.

"It's okay, Cyrus," she says. "Do you want the grand tour?"

"We were here last week."

Dad and I stopped by on our way home from the hospital.

"Right, right," Donna says, back around the counter into the kitchen, reaching for the fridge. "Your aunt's coming off on an overnight so I'm kind of out of it right now."

"I could go—"

"Don't be ridiculous," she says, setting water in front of each of us. Her hair is uneven, the left side matted like she was sleeping on that side. "How's your cheek? When are the stitches out?"

She steps around the counter to examine my face.

"They said Monday."

"Good, good." Her breath is ripe with stale coffee and a hint of sweet, like donuts. "Looks like they're healing well."

I biked the eleven miles from our house to her new apartment and in spite of the autumn, it's still super hot. I open up the bottle and swallow half in a single gulp.

"What's going on, kid? You haven't biked to see me since—" Her voice trails off again as she takes a seat at the counter beside me, on tall black stools with stiff backings. "It's been a while."

I used to bike to her apartment all the time, to get out of the house after Mom died. She'd let me play video games on this old PlayStation one of her ex-boyfriends left behind, and she never pressed with questions on how I was doing—not well, obviously—and she didn't offer vague generalities about how things would get better with time, like Dad tried. I stopped coming so much after I met Jeff.

"I need your advice," I say. "And you can't tell my dad."

"Okay, okay. Is this 'I should get some wine' advice or—" She stands up from the stool. I laugh. "I'm getting the wine."

The kitchen table behind me is stacked with boxes from her move and the adjacent living room has half-opened packages and folded cardboard strewn about the space. We offered to assist when Dad and I stopped by but the pain in my cheek increased the longer we stayed, so we didn't do much.

"What you got, kid?" Donna says, returning from the kitchen with a Drink Wine or Die tumbler. "Lay it on me."

"Jeff's leaving."

"Where to?"

"Some religious school up near Harrisburg," I say. "And he's rooming on campus so he can't leave or access the Internet or phone. It's like a prison almost."

"Sounds lovely," she says. "The Catholics?"

"No. It's his stepfather's medieval evangelical church."

"I see. That's a tough one."

Donna doesn't mess with church, which is pretty rare for an adult in Dallastown, and maybe it's her influence that turned me away from God and his very existence, at least since Mom died. Dad said he used to believe when he was a teen but the Catholic Church was riddled with so much hypocrisy over its treatment of gays and women, of science and reason, he couldn't support its teachings any longer. Mom wasn't religious either so they never imposed any of that on me but she used to talk to me about her vision of an afterlife, something that would happen when you died, to your soul or your energy, but I never knew what she meant. Sometimes I forget the way she sounded, the exact accent, sophisticated but with a touch of South Jersey. Or the way she paused before she spoke, like she was formulating her response with particular care. I talked to her last night about Jeff leaving. I don't know what to do.

"And why is he being sent away?" Donna says.

"His stepfather lost his mind when we got back late from the concert."

"Right, right." Donna takes a lengthy sip of the wine. "You know he called that night but I think I was asleep. I'm so sorry, Cyrus."

She crosses her legs on the stool, set low for the countertop, my neck just over the surface.

"Is there anything I can do?" she says.

"Well, you can't tell anyone this," I say.

"You know we have an ironclad agreement."

"I was under that impression but then Angela found out about Cody."

"Oh—" She uncrosses her legs and laughs. "I mean, that's just because I was excited for you. I had to tell someone. I didn't tell your dad, so I did not officially violate the terms of our agreement."

"I guess."

When I was thirteen, Donna printed out and signed a sheet that guaranteed any secrets I told her would not be revealed to my father. It's hidden in my room inside the box of cards I made Mom for her birthdays.

"Jeff's running away." I feel the sweat dripping off my forehead onto my legs. "He said he's not going to that school and he wants me to help him. He asked for money to get him a motel room and said he'd pay me back—" I think that's what he said. "And I have the money—my savings from the summer. I just don't want him to leave."

"All right, all right, I need to step back a second," she says, climbing off the stool and stepping back. The slippers clack on the flooring. "First of all, as an adult-type person who is an official of the state since all registered nurses have to be registered with the state, I can unequivocally say it's a bad idea for him to run away. Like horrible. You have any idea how many kids end up in the hospital after running away and living on the streets?"

I shake my head.

"It's a lot," she says. "I would wholeheartedly recommend he not do that. And you should not give him any money to help him do that."

"But if he has money for a motel won't that make him safer?"

"I don't think so, Cyrus. Do not give him money." She reaches out for my hand and lifts my chin to make sure I'm listening. "I know religious school sounds horrific, and believe me, if I were Jeff at that age and my parents wanted to send me to some kind of Jesus camp—which they did, by the way—your grandparents thought your father and I were going to Hell or whatever bullshit they made up in their heads to justify their rage, but either way it's not as bad as running away. He'll survive school. Tear up some shit if he needs to. And maybe he won't have to go for too long before his parents come to their senses."

"But what if they brainwash him and he comes back different?" I say, swiveling the stool left then right, the blasting central air cooling me off a bit. "If he runs away, at least he can call me, right? And maybe I can go visit."

"How?" Donna says, spreading her hands and lifting them sideways. "You're six months from your license. If he runs away, you'll never see him again. I can guarantee you that. Even if he survives."

"Jesus," I say. "Morbid enough?"

"I'm sorry, Cyrus." Her lips form a lopsided frown that matches her hair. "I don't mean to be so rough but you need to talk some sense into him. You need to convince him not to run away. I'm telling you, some of the cases we get—kids younger than you, strung out on drugs and malnourished, or beaten and bruised—and that's not even mentioning the ones who get kidnapped and sold into sex slavery."

"Donna—"

"It happens," she says. "It happens all the time. You need to convince him."

"I don't know if I can," I say.

"Well, don't give him any money. That might convince him."

I've saved almost $2500 from the summer at the guidance office, which is supposed to form the bulk of a down payment for a car next spring but I would give him all of it, if it would help him. I'd do anything.

"Maybe you could talk to his mother?" I say.

"I don't know her," Donna says. "I barely know Jeff. I'm not sure I can intervene."

"But they beat him."

"They beat him?"

"His stepfather does," I say. "They got into a huge fight the other day and he beat him up. He's got bruises all over his body."

"Shit." Donna steps back around her stool to get to the wine bottle. "That's serious, Cyrus. More serious."

She picks up her glass, pouring more in.

I didn't plan to tell her about the beating—or the fight, as I'm sure the stepfuck would describe it—because I know Jeff wouldn't want anyone else to know, but Donna wants him to go to that Jesus school which makes no sense at all.

"Well the protocol at the hospital is if any child comes in with bruises we need to tell the nurse manager or the hospital administrator and they'll do the questioning," she says, back around the counter again, setting down the drink. "And if they deem it appropriate, they'll notify the police, who take it from there. It's a pretty formal process and if you think he's being abused, I can call someone and have them start the process."

I shake my head. No way Jeff would want that. She pulls out a folder from the drawer beneath the counter and starts to leaf through it. Her hospital's name is on the front.

"When does he leave?"

"Tomorrow."

"We'd have to act fast," Donna says, pulling out a sheet of paper. "It doesn't always happen fast."

I don't think Jeff would want it but what if the cops did come to the house and take the stepfuck away— they'd have to see the bruises all over his stomach, they'd have to believe him. And that way he wouldn't have to leave and we could be in the band again in his garage every day.

"Can I ask you a question, Cyrus?"

Donna sets down the sheet and leans forward, setting her elbows on the counter. Her eyes are bloodshot but focused on me.

"Are you and Jeff more than friends?"

I look away. Yes. Of course we are. But I don't know what that is.

"I don't know."

"How do you not know?"

"It's complicated."

"Kid, I have been in more complicated relationships than years you have been on this earth so lay it on me," she says. "Maybe I can help you figure it out."

"We kissed," I say. I needed to say it. To make it real. "Twice. But after the first time, he said it was a mistake. And then the second time we were in the backseat of Mindy's car and we hit the dog. We haven't talked about it since."

"Oh, Cyrus."

She moves from the kitchen around the counter to me, outstretched arms enveloping.

"Do you, um." She backs off so she can see me. "Do you have feelings for him?"

I nod. Up and down so many times it hurts. My head still hurts.

"That's good, Cyrus. That's nice." She backs up and leans on the stool next to me. "And Jeff's a good guy. I mean, I've only met him a couple times but he's always been polite. And maybe he's not ready to admit that he's gay. Honestly—" She looks into the living room, the pile of boxes on the carpeting. "Maybe that's why his parents are sending him to that Jesus school—to 'pray away the gay' or some bullshit."

"I don't think so," I say. Jeff didn't mention that. But maybe his stepfather found something in his bedroom other than drugs and he didn't want to tell me about it. I don't know why he wouldn't tell me about it.

"Well, either way, religious school is a shitty sentence, especially for gay kids, but he'll be back, you know, sooner than you think." She stands up and heads for the living room but keeps speaking. "And maybe being around all those Jesus freaks will convince him to come out to himself."

"Or the opposite," I say.

"Sure." She reaches into one of the half-opened boxes on the living room sectional. "There is that. He could go the other way. Like get super into the Bible and start speaking in tongues." She returns to the counter at the edge of the kitchen, a book in her hand. "But that doesn't sound like Jeff."

"No. That's not him."

"And that's the point," she says, handing me the book. "You have to convince him not to run away. Because I bet you that school won't be as horrible as he thinks and in a couple months, he'll be home for Thanksgiving break or Christmas break—I'm sure they go all out for Christmas there—so you'll see each other again and you know what? He'll miss you more than you'll ever miss him because at least you'll have your other friends at Dallastown High. And he'll kiss you. He'll run right up to you and kiss you again." She sips at her second glass. "Believe me, your Aunt Donna has a sense about these things."

Aunt Donna is already on her second massive tumbler of wine but I do trust her. I just don't want to lose him.

"Listen, how about we make some popcorn, order Chinese food, and watch a movie to take your mind off of your stress for a bit. We'll have a Donna and Cyrus night, okay?"

I nod. That does sound nice.

"And look—" She points to the book, a faded paperback called It Gets Better, with a rainbow flag spread across the front. "Your mother gave me this, years ago. One of her students in one of her classes, he'd read it when he was a teen and they were discussing gay marriage or homophobia in class—you know your mom was always trying to preach progressive values to whomever would listen in central P.A. But I guess this student gave it to her, in case she knew anyone who needed it and she gave it to me, afraid you might see it. Afraid you would think she was forcing it on you before you were ready to come out. I guess she knew. I guess she always knew."

I leaf through the pages, still crisp despite the wear, sharp across my fingers.

"I forgot about it, honestly, because it was hidden among the stacks of nursing books on my shelves and I didn't find it until I was packing last weekend." She hesitates, watching me read. "I thought you might want it."

The book appears to be a series of coming out stories and narratives. I could share it with Jeff. I close the cover and take a sniff. No trace of Mom's scent.

"Thank you, Donna," I say.

"Aww, Cyrus," she says, wrapping her arms around me, this time from behind. I swallow up my tears. "It'll get better, kid."

"That's not—" Her tangled hair drops around her face and touches my cheeks. She squeezes tighter.

"Thank you," I say.

She spins around the counter into the kitchen and I set the book in my lap, keeping it close to me.

I don't want to let go.

NINETEEN

I BIKED DOWNTOWN from Donna's this morning, to the Wells Fargo on Main Street, where I attempted to take out all the money I've made this summer. But the ATM was capped at six hundred dollars, which is not enough for Jeff, nowhere near enough. That's when I decided to join him.

Donna was right—it isn't safe to run away, but it won't be running if we go together, and once we get to Brooklyn, I'll find a Wells Fargo to take out the rest of my cash and we'll get a motel room—someplace cheap—and we'll find him a job so he's not living on the streets. And I'll come back. I'll definitely come back. But we were going to go to New York after he got his license anyway, to catch some hardcore shows in DIY places emerging from empty warehouse spaces. And we can figure out what's going on with us, so it's not so abrupt.

But Jeff never showed.

I packed my backpack to near bursting with my laptop, speakers, headphones and chargers, four pairs of shorts, three pairs of jeans, as many T-shirts as I could squeeze, and enough socks and underwear to last a week. I even packed the credit card Dad keeps in the lockbox under his dresser—only for emergencies, which I only planned to use in an emergency. I looked up Amtrak schedules from Lancaster to Manhattan and I figured we could ask somebody what subways would take us to Brooklyn from Penn Station. And if his mom doesn't change her mind and let him come home without going to religious school, I could visit on the train every other weekend and we could start up the band again so we could get good again, with the way I've been practicing and the way he'll have more time to write more songs. We could maybe even book some shows in those DIY spaces in warehouse places, like Joyce Manor and Cloud Nothings did when they were our age.

But Jeff never showed.

I waited all morning on the steps of my house with my backpack beside me, venturing as far as the front lawn, the two oaks providing a bit of shade against the heat of the pressing day. Dad isn't back yet, still dealing with the conveyor emergency in California, so I sat all morning at the front of our house. Waiting.

When I couldn't wait any longer, I ran over to Jeff's house, hoping he might be home and unable to escape, but there weren't any cars in the driveway for the Bible study group he said was taking place, and no one answered the doorbell or came when I knocked so I kept running, all the way down to the high school. I jump up on the concrete as soon as my phone rings.

"Where are you?"

"By my high school," I say. "I'm out running."

"Oh," Cody says, up close on my screen, the tips of his hair dripping water down his face. "You look hot."

"It's ridiculously hot out," I say.

"That's not what I meant," he says.

He's trying to joke but I wasn't ready for the joke and I don't react. I thought it was Jeff.

"Where have you been?" he says. "It's been days since we talked."

He pulls the phone back from his face and the sun is blinding over his naked shoulders. He takes a seat on his surfboard on the sand, squatting cross-legged with his wetsuit around his waist.

"I'm sorry," I say. I start to walk away from the high school, the hot asphalt of the empty parking lot at my feet. "It's been a rough week."

"What happened?" Cody says, moving closer to the frame, flecks of beach stuck to his cheek. "Are you mad at me?"

"No-no-no-no," I say, in rhythm with my neck, swiveling left then right in exaggerated fashion. "It's not you at all."

"What is it, then?"

I reach the edge of the lot and head up the grassy hill away from the stadium.

"Just some stuff at school," I say. I've kept him in the dark about Jeff—him leaving or me wanting to leave with him, which is why I haven't talked to him because I'm afraid to tell him, how much I love him. Jeff. Not Cody.

I should have told him before we ever started something, however remote and long distance, even though at the time I didn't know Jeff might be gay and might like me like that. But I should have said something. The sun obscures Cody's face, an odd orange hue around a frozen sideways smile. The connection from the beach isn't great.

"What happened? Did somebody—do I need to fly to Pennsylvania and kick someone's ass?"

"No, no." He pulls the phone back as he climbs off his surfboard. The wetsuit is hugging his legs, tight against his body. "Nothing like that."

"What's wrong, Cyrus?"

I catch the ocean in the background as he spins the phone around him, other surfers or maybe swimmers in the distance. It's tough to tell.

"I'm just tired," I say.

I want to say more. I should tell him, the way I need to tell him, how I'm breaking because Jeff is leaving. I sprint across the street past the honking horn of a pickup truck I didn't see.

"Fucker!" the driver curses at me through his open window but I keep running, down the road toward Lions Park, the phone in my hand and Cody calling my name for several spastic seconds as I sprint full speed before gliding to a stop and collapsing, at the edge of the baseball fields where I used to play as a kid. They built better fields at a newer park on the other side of town so these are always empty now. Cody hears me crying.

"Cyrus?" he says. "Ohmygodwhat'swrong?"

I have my phone down so he can't see me crying. The mosquitos buzz around my head and I hear the ocean behind him. Cold, inviting waves. I wipe my eyes with the back of my hand, the sweat mixing with the tears on my cheek.

"I'm sorry," I say. Letting him see me. "It's Jeff."

"What happened?" He returns to his seat on the surfboard, twice as long as him.

"I should have told you. I shouldn't have led you on."

"Led me on?" He's blinking through the phone, holding it close to his face.

"Jeff's leaving," I say, half into the phone, half into the fence separating the grass from the abandoned field. "We kissed and then he didn't talk to me and then he got punished and then we went to Joyce Manor and it was amazing—I sent you the pics and it was amazing, you were right—they were amazing." I let him see me, the tears flowing. "And then we kissed again in the backseat of Mindy's car and hit a dog, and the dog died and now Jeff's getting sent away to a religious school in Harrisburg so he's running away and I told him I'd go with him, run away with him, or—I guess I didn't tell him because he never showed and I guess he's gone now and I shouldn't have led you on because I'm in love with him, Cody." His face looks frozen. "I've always been in love with him. I should have told you."

"Okay," Cody says. His eyes pull close together and the sun on his skin softens a bit, the natural tan on his cheeks through the screen. "I—that's a lot."

I swat the bugs away, watching his fallen face.

"I'm sorry," I say. "But I have to see if he's home."

"Oh."

I stand up. I should have kept waiting. Maybe church ran late or something.

"Cyrus?"

"I'll call you back," I say and return the phone to my pocket, kicking into a sprint along the street, left past the big purple house with the faded clapboards where this old man lives that used to scream at us when we were little, whenever a foul ball entered his driveway. I don't know if he lives there anymore.

Jeff's house is three blocks down on the left, the overhanging maple blocking the view of the driveway but when I get close enough, I spot his mom's blue Hyundai parked where it wasn't parked earlier and I start to panic at once. I never should have left.

I rush up the walkway to the front door, two steps to the doorbell, and I wait before knocking but no one answers. The stitches are stinging at my cheek and the sweat is pouring down my skin.

I sprint the rest of the way home.

My backpack is still sitting where I left it, in the shadow of the front door, up the steps onto the patio, and as I reach for my backpack, I spot a note—a yellow folded sheet tucked into the aluminum edges of the screen. I struggle to unfold with the sweat on my fingers, my calves pressing at my shins.

Scrawled in thick black letters are four words.

THANKS FOR NOTHING ASSHOLE

Jeff showed.

THREE
MONTHS
LATER

TWENTY

COQUITO [KOH-KEE-TOH]: A Puerto Rican beverage typically made with rum, sweetened condensed milk, coconut milk, and additional spices that is traditionally consumed during the Christmas season.

Sharane's mother is Puerto Rican and her uncles do not mess around with the rum. They added a "floater" to my glass, which is an extra shot, served by a pair of short squat guys with goatees who refilled my cup as soon as I finished the first. The room is spinning.

"You need to try this Mindy," I say, super fast, the way I'm talking super fast because I haven't drank this much liquor before and it doesn't even taste like liquor, it's this sweet perfect concoction, cold in my palm and warm in my stomach, just in time for Christmas.

"I'm good," Mindy says. She digs her fork into her plate filled with pernil—slow-roasted pork—and a second serving of yellow rice, hardened a bit but soft in the middle. I ate my first plate so fast I broke my fork on my teeth.

"What?" I think Mindy was speaking. She shakes her head.

Coquito [koh-kee-toh]: A Puerto Rican beverage sort of like egg nog that fucks white boys up.

"Come on," Mindy says, leading me from the side of the kitchen around the counter where the drinks are set, across the dining area past the chafing dishes arranged on folding tables, a few latecomers in festive dresses serving themselves from the wide selection of pork and beef and chicken and rice.

Mindy's mom doesn't celebrate Christmas so she always goes to Sharane's for Christmas Eve and this year I got an invite. My dad didn't mind because we don't do church at all and Angela wanted to hang out with her friends in Dallastown now that's she home on winter break.

Sharane is down the hall in an enclosed porch, chatting with her grandmother on a ripped vinyl couch. Mindy introduces me but I don't respond because her grandmother speaks Spanish to me and I don't have much contact with Cody anymore so I don't have the opportunity to practice anymore, outside of Spanish III.

"She says are you enjoying the party?" Sharane translates.

I nod, taking a sip from the coquito to avoid spilling it again. A gaggle of children are playing video games on the carpeting.

"He's usually chattier," Mindy says. "Actually, he's usually quiet but tonight he's been chatty."

"That makes no sense," I say.

"Exactly."

Sharane's grandmother pushes herself off the couch and Mindy rushes over to give the gray-haired woman a hug.

"Feliz Navidad, Nana," Mindy says as they separate then everyone turns to me.

I'm not sure what to do, looking for a spot to set down my glass before stepping toward Nana, but she frowns, looking me up and down, and shambles out of the room.

"I love her so much," Mindy says.

"She's the best," Sharane says.

Mindy and I fill the empty seats on the couch, hard green vinyl with duct tape layered on several ripped spaces but built-in tables on each side for drinks. I set down the coquito. The children on the carpeting scream something about Fortnite, then they tackle each other in a wild frenzy. They're ten.

"You want some?" Mindy says, offering some pernil to Sharane.

"Cyrus?"

She slides the plate my way but I decline. More pork will not help with the spinning.

"Rude," she says, punching me on the side.

"Bitch," I say.

"Dick," she says.

"There are children in here," Sharane says. Laughing.

I return to the coquito, lifting it carefully, the floating rum at the center surrounded by golden yellow foam. It's not helping with the spinning.

"So Cyrus, have you heard from Jeff?" Sharane says. "Is he home for Christmas?"

"Sharane, we discussed this!" Mindy says, slapping her on the side. "Cyrus is happy for the first time in months and you have to bring him up—he who shall remain nameless."

"It's Jeff," I say. "His name is Jeff."

I take a massive sip on the coquito, the floater sliding down my throat all at once. I grit my teeth as the poison coats my tongue and pick at the fuzzy threads on my sweater, red-and-white-striped with a green glittered tree above my chest.

"See!" Mindy says. "He's already upset. Now we'll have another week of sad, depressed Cyrus. Right through New Year's."

"It's fine," I say. "I'm fine. I haven't heard from him."

"Hey, that reminds me—" Mindy says, deftly changing the subject. "What are we doing for New Year's?"

Sharane starts to speak but the ten-year-olds screaming at the game drown out the sound so I can't hear what she's saying.

Jeff has his phone back because the "Happy Christmas!" message I sent this afternoon got "Delivered" for the first time in three months, but he didn't respond. He may have also seen the string of lost messages I'd sent him, which could have freaked him out, or did freak him out. I've been kind of crazy since he left.

"That sounds awesome," Mindy says to Sharane. "Does Devin have access to a car? You know I'm not driving."

"I think so," Sharane says.

Mindy's Mom drove us here and she's still under the impression we're dating, or sort of dating. Mindy's been unclear about how much she tells her mom which makes it awkward every time she drives us anywhere but it's better than having a conversation with an adult about my sexuality.

"Courtney!" Sharane jumps up off the couch and greets this boy coming into the room with a kiss on the cheek. "You came."

"Of course I came," he says in a deep-timbered voice, his hair cut short, tight curls on all sides. "It's tradition." He spots me on the couch and smiles, a wide white smile contrasted with his skin. He looks familiar but I can't place him. He might go to our school.

"Coquito?" I say, offering my glass. He laughs.

"Don't mind Cyrus," Mindy says. "He's drunk."

"Nah, it's cool, man," Courtney says. "Those are delicious. If Sharane doesn't mind, I'd love one."

Sharane laughs, says "of course," and heads for kitchen, leaving Mindy and me alone with Courtney. And the ten-year-olds slaughtering strangers on the Fortnite screen.

"Do I know you?" I say, as he takes a seat on the other side of Mindy.

"That's rude, Cyrus."

Mindy slaps me again. She hits her friends a lot. It's kind of her thing.

"No, I meant—I think I've seen you?"

"You have, idiot," Mindy says. "This is Sharane's cousin. He runs for Dover."

"Oh, okay," I say. "We raced you guys."

"That's right, that's right," Courtney says, leaning forward around Mindy. "Sharane pointed you out at the meet. You guys smoked us."

He laughs and I smile. We had Dallastown High's best cross-country season in over a decade. In the last meet, I finished in the top three.

"We were surprisingly good this year," I say. "But it was a long season. I'm still walking lopsided, I think."

"Are you sure that's not the coquitos?" Mindy says. Courtney laughs again.

I pick up the drink even though I don't drink, or I haven't since Jeff left. I haven't even gotten high. I've run and I've studied and I've spent lunch with Mindy and Sharane and we've gone out a few times—movies and the mall and walking Mindy's mini-schnauzer in the park near her house. Her name is Elie and she barks with excitement every time she sees me.

"Everybody up!" Sharane announces as she returns to the porch, drinks in her hand. She's dressed in a V-neck sweater with red-and-white vertical stripes over green jeans, casual and festive at the same time. "We're playing white elephant in the living room."

"White elephant?" I say.

Sharane hands Courtney a coquito and offers another to Mindy, who passes, so I end up with a third somehow.

"Just come on," Mindy says, pulling me up by my elbow. "I'll explain it as we go."

We reconvene in the living room off the entrance to the house, a baby grand piano in the corner as you enter. They have a formal dining room to the right, with a wall of bay windows centered between the two spaces. Most of the family is seated on chairs around the large dining room table but the others are spread out on sofas on the carpeting. Mindy and I squeeze in next to Sharane on the piano bench. Courtney takes a seat at my feet, cross-legged. He's taller than me.

"Don't," Sharane says as I attempt to set a glass on the piano's surface so I just hold both of them. Mindy takes a number from a hat and sets a slip of paper on my lap. I don't know what's happening.

"What's happening?" I ask her.

"What number are you?" Mindy says.

I consider unfolding the slip while juggling the two drinks but instead I down the first and set it on the carpeting. Courtney laughs, backing up against my knee.

"Eighteen," I say.

THE BEST HARDCORE BAND IN PA   171

"Okay," Mindy says. "Just watch."

One of Sharane's cousins, a short woman with straight black hair and blue-rimmed glasses, announces the rules for the game but she's speaking so fast I don't follow. But after a few gifts are opened, I get the gist. You open random wrapped presents when your number is called and if you don't like what you get, you can exchange it with a gift that someone already opened. There's a limit on the number of exchanges per gift, which gets invoked after a set of wine glasses are claimed three times. It's a lot of fun.

"Okay, okay, this better be good," Mindy says as she selects the extra-large box at the bottom of the gift pile, the one that everyone was avoiding because of the effort to uncover it from its surroundings. Courtney moves next to me on the piano bench, its leather padding against my butt. His jeans touch mine.

Mindy takes a seat on the thick gray carpeting, pulling off wrapping paper by the sheet and opening the box to unveil a massive fake wreath.

"What the?" she says.

The cousin who announced the rules starts to apologize as Mindy struggles to lift the oversized decoration with both hands, the fake needles jabbing at her skin. Everyone in the room is laughing.

"I ordered it online, not realizing the size," the cousin explains over the continued laughter as Mindy lays the wreath on the floor. "It doesn't fit on my front door, or I imagine, anyone else's. I don't know what it's for—a barn?"

One of the uncles that were mixing coquitos gets up to inspect the glued-on decorations. Mindy's already eyeing available exchanges.

"I do appreciate it," Mindy grits her teeth. "But the thing is, my mom doesn't actually celebrate Christmas so…" She stands up and heads to the table. "I'm just going to be taking these candles, Gina, because my mom loves to cook kimchi and while it is the most delicious condiment on this planet—outside of maybe the beans Mrs. Williams made tonight—" Sharane's mom smiles, tucked behind the table with her sisters. "Kimchi does not smell very good when cooked all day on a low simmer so—candles!"

"Good choice," Courtney says as Mindy returns to us, sniffing the candle and eyeing her abandoned seat on the bench. Courtney slides closer to let her sit down but she kneels on the floor, spreading out on the carpeting.

A young girl is up next—maybe the same age as the boys playing video games. She grabs a small box Mindy dislodged from the pile.

I haven't gone yet, which is an advantage, since you pretty much get your pick of all the previous gifts. Courtney got a playing card deck and a set of poker chips, which he's got hidden behind us on the piano surface, hoping no one steals it. Worst case, I'm stealing it.

"Wow!" the girl exclaims, opening a Bose stereo speaker that surpasses the wine glasses as the night's best gift. Her relatives start clapping as she's beaming and if I were good at math, I'd start calculating how many people were left before I made my selection. Dad would know immediately. But he also wouldn't be this drunk.

"Don't even think about ruining my daughter's night," this tall guy announces, standing up to threaten Uncle Coquito, who's up next. The girl has the speaker open and is already linking it to her Bluetooth to play her Justin Bieber or Taylor Swift or whatever is popular with little girls in Dallastown. I've been on a deep dive with Iceage this month, this awesome hardcore band from Norway. I even included their song lyrics in my last letter to Jeff but he didn't respond. He didn't respond to any of my letters.

"Cyrus, what number are you?" Courtney says. I blink and reach into my pocket to unwrap the slip of paper again, trying to read, but the numbers are fuzzy and the room hasn't stopped spinning. Courtney reaches for my hand, wrapping his fingers around my fingers. "You're next," he says. His breath is warm on my neck.

"Who's eighteen?" one of Sharane's mother's sisters asks.

Uncle Coquito takes a seat, upset with his set of perfumes but he doesn't try to exchange it. Courtney helps me up and I need to steady myself, walking the long way around the wreath taking up all of the space on the living room floor.

There's a small box at the edge of the table and I open it as fast as I can, which I'm pretty sure is pretty slow— a coffee mug with a Christmas and/or snow theme that's about the fifth coffee mug gifted tonight. I thank everyone sitting nearby because somebody bought this gift and it wasn't me—I didn't bring anything—and I steady myself as I step back around the wreath to the sound of "Speaker!" being chanted, first by Uncle Coquito then a bunch of the others in the room. Courtney is smiling at me from the piano bench, waving me back to the little girl on the sofa next to Sharane, clutching the speaker with both hands. I want to ignore—I would always ignore—but the way Courtney is looking at me, encouraging, the rum swimming in my head as I veer to the left and rip the speaker out of the girl's screaming fingers. I leave the mug behind.

"Holy shit," Courtney says as I sit next to him, head low, the entire room erupting in laughter except the girl's father, out from behind the table and across the carpeting, getting held back by several sets of hands, but he's playing—I think he's playing, or he might be serious and he might actually kill me so I keep my head down, sliding the speaker into the box and hiding it beneath the bench. Courtney wraps his arm around my shoulder.

"Dude, you have a death wish," Mindy says as the crowd settles down.

The voices are a mixture of Spanish and English so I can't tell what anyone is saying. Several people have to guide the father back to his seat. Maybe he wasn't playing.

"That was bad ass," Courtney says, his arm still around my neck. I pick up my coquito but the glass is empty. I don't remember how it got empty.

"It's getting stolen next turn," Mindy says, which is an eventuality I didn't consider.

"Nah, nobody's that crazy," Courtney says, lifting off the bench. "You want another?" He holds out his glass.

I shake my head but he ignores, emerging from the kitchen with another glass of Puerto Rican Death Wish, which distracts from the speaker getting stolen next turn. Mindy takes on a seat on the sofa with Sharane.

Courtney and me are alone. "You play?" he asks, lifting the guard from the piano keys. The White Elephant game is over but I'm not sure what gift I wound up with. I turn sideways to look into his eyes, dark and clouded.

"No," I say.

"I don't know much, just from visiting Sharane."

He plays a couple chords and laughs, then plays them again. I can't tell if it's a song.

"Sharane told me you were in a band," Courtney says. "She did?"

She never talked about him to me. I came out to her last week, by accident, when Mindy was asking about Cody. I wonder if she told Courtney. He's watching me.

"I mean, I am. Or I was," I say. "It's kind of on hold."

"Oh," he says.

I kept practicing every night like I said I would, so I could get good enough when Jeff got back that we could run away together, for real this time. To some cheap apartment in Brooklyn where we would start up the band again, better this time. I haven't drummed in a while. Jeff was gone for three months.

"What's your name?"

"Cyrus?" I say.

"I know that." He laughs, spinning from the keys to face me. "Your band name."

"Oh." That's a long story. "It's still under discussion."

"I see," he says, moving his fingers to my knee. I bend my neck to peek around the room but the crowd has thinned completely, except for Sharane and Mindy and Uncle Coquito now at the dining room table sampling his fragrances.

"You, um, mind that I'm doing this?" Courtney says, his dark eyes penetrating.

Because his hair is so short, his face has more face, which is ridiculous I know but Jeff is all hair and Cody is all hair and Courtney's eyes are beautiful, watching me. He leans forward and kisses my cheek.

I lose my balance and my elbow falls onto the piano keys with a clang. Courtney smiles and I blink. I can't see. Or think.

"Was that okay?" he says and before he can finish his thought, I lurch forward, into his lips and his chin, a bit of stubble on my tongue.

"Yes," I say when we separate. Salsa music penetrates my brain.

I lean forward once more but Courtney backs off, and I follow his eyes toward Sharane and Mindy and Uncle Coquito watching us. Courtney takes hold of my hand.

I think about Jeff. Because he was the last person I kissed, in the backseat of Mindy's car, and that was the last time we hung out because we hit the dog and then he got sent away and now he's back and he hasn't called me and I shouldn't be thinking of him right now, with Courtney's fingers caressing my skin and his taste on my lips. But I am.

I'll never stop thinking of him.

TWENTY-ONE

"PRESENT PATROL coming through," Donna announces, the packages spilling out of her arms.

I jump up from the couch to assist but my head shakes from the movement. Hangovers are a bitch, as far as I can tell. I never want to drink that much again.

"Merry Christmas, Donna," Dad says, over to greet his sister with a hug. She sets down her purse on the dining room table, still dressed in her scrubs. "I can't believe you had to work today."

"I always have to work."

She enters the kitchen and fills up a plate with meatballs and pasta salad that Dad prepared as part of our annual Christmas tradition—Angela, me, and him opening presents in the living room then watching Christmas movies all day. We started the tradition the year Mom died, because Dad hoped to get our minds off Mom dying, and it worked, as best as it could. We're up to Christmas Vacation this afternoon, Clark Griswold trapped in the hole in the attic floor, lamenting his choices in life.

"Frozen?" Donna says as she takes a seat at the dining room table, plastic fork inserted into the center of her meatball.

"No, I woke up Christmas morning and made them fresh," Dad says, several layers of sarcasm spilling from the sides of his mouth.

"Ass," Donna says. He only talks that way with her, like he saves up any attempt at humor for his sister. Not us. "Where's Angela?"

"On the phone with her boyfriend," I say. "They've been separated for an entire day now so she's been on the phone with him all morning."

I'm pissed because she woke me up at the butt-crack of early to join Dad downstairs with the presents, despite my hangover. I took a long nap that did little to stem the pressure on my temples. Thank god Donna came.

"Good for her," Donna says, mouth half-full with meatball. Dad's "cooking" is fine but it doesn't compare to the pernil or the rice or the sausages and peppers and cake—I think there was cake. After Courtney kissed me. "Is he visiting for the holidays?"

"They are supposed to be going to Philly for New Year's," Dad says, pulling out a seat at the table across from Donna.

"And you're okay with that?"

Donna digs into the store-bought pasta salad. Mom would always make homemade meatballs that stewed on the stove all Christmas morning, filling the house with the unmistakable scent of garlic and onions and Italian seasonings, and by the time we got to dinner I'd devour several plates of pasta with oversized meatballs that were never frozen and perfectly sauced. Even Sharane's mom's cooking doesn't compare.

"He's supposed to stop here to pick her up so at least I can meet him."

"Oh, that's perfect," Donna says. "I'll come over and meet him too. My New Year's plans right now are day shift at the hospital followed by a fresh box of wine. Unless this guy I met last week calls me back which I don't even know if I want him to because men are disgusting pigs who don't call back if you don't put out on the first date—"

"Donna," Dad says, jerking his head toward me.

"Relax," she says, wiping her mouth with a napkin. "Cyrus has heard everything I've got to say."

"I guess," Dad says. He's given up trying to control Donna at this point. Or Angela even. All he has left is me. It's annoying.

"Anyway, get ready for me on New Year's Eve," Donna says. "Are your poker buddies coming?"

"Not sure," Dad says. "But most of them have wives so if we do have something, it'll just be the single guys."

"Oh," Donna says, pausing before the last meatball on the plate. "No, never mind. Your friends are gross."

"Gross how?"

"Just, you know." She reaches back to pull her hair into a ponytail, wrapping it up into a knot faster than I thought possible. "They're men."

"Well, you know, if you want a boyfriend you might have to make an adjustment in your assessment of men."

"She could go lesbian," I chime in.

Courtney and I exchanged numbers before we left and he texted "Happy Christmas" this morning but I was sleeping. I haven't responded yet.

"Ehh, I tried that in college," Donna says. "It didn't take."

I laugh and Dad frowns at the thought, or maybe the discussion, even though it's a discussion he should be comfortable with. He has a gay son. We just never talk about it.

"How's the boyfriend front with you, Cyrus?" Donna says. "Are you and Cody still—"

"Not—no," I say.

We never got into a fight—it's just, it hasn't been the same. Since Jeff left, nothing's been the same. And it's too hard to think with the leftover rum spinning through my brain. I wish I'd puked and gotten it over with.

"What happened?" Donna says, setting down her fork and turning her chair to face me on the sofa.

"Nothing," I say. "But he doesn't call as much."

"Do you call him?"

"Sometimes," I say.

I keep hoping he'll call me first, like we used to. Every day, like we used to. But I blew it when I told him about Jeff and me, and then after Jeff left, I got so depressed I didn't answer when he called or when I did, I wasn't brimming with conversation. I know it's my fault. I've tried calling a few times lately, but he hasn't gotten back to me. It's been a couple weeks.

"Have you heard from Jeff?" she says. She just goes and says it. Dad lifts his coffee cup, which I'm pretty sure is empty, and coughs.

"I saw him this morning," Angela says, bounding into the room from the bottom of the stairs, in the same shirt and sweats she wore to bed last night.

"What?" I say.

"I saw him at Sheetz getting coffee."

"Did you talk to him?"

"No." Angela shakes her head. "I was already at the checkout line with our breakfast sandwiches so I just waved."

"He saw you?"

"Yeah." She nods. "Why?"

The vomit begins to gurgle in my stomach, all of a sudden with the scent of the meatballs.

"Haven't you talked to him?" Donna says.

I shake my head.

"Really?" Angela says.

I look to Dad because I don't know where else to look. I've been waiting three months for him to come back, for some kind of contact, because he didn't respond to any of my letters and now it's Christmas Day and he saw Angela at Sheetz and he hasn't even messaged me. I pull out my cell to check whether I've inadvertently turned it off because I'm too hungover to think but it's there and it's on, two messages from Mindy and three from Sharane. Courtney messaged again.

Not Jeff.

"You should go over there," Donna says. "You should talk to him."

I want to. I do. But he hasn't even attempted to contact me.

"At least find out how long he's home for," Donna says. "Maybe you guys can hang out?"

The first letter I wrote explained how I waited for him, how I had the money from the bank and that I was going to go to Brooklyn with him. Then when he didn't respond, I thought maybe that scared him so I sent another letter, asking how he was and that I was thinking of him, the way I can't stop thinking of him, and maybe that scared him too, or maybe he never got my letters so I called the admins at the school to make sure the students could receive mail and they said they could. But I never heard back from him.

"I will," I say, looking at Dad because if I look at Donna, I know I'll cry and I've been trained by society not to cry in front of my father. But Dad's got that look like he's sad for me, like he wants to help but he can't. No one can.

"How about we open your presents?" Donna says.

"Okay," I say, focused on the television. The Griswolds are about to light up the house with the decorations. I fish out my phone as Donna distributes the presents, dropping a box next to me.

Hey, I type. I'm sorry for everything. But I waited for you. I hope you know that. Can I please stop by and say hi?

I stare at the screen until the iPhone's designation turns from Delivered to Read. Angela opens up her present and runs over to hug Donna, and the Griswolds' neighbors are stumbling all over themselves, blinded by the lights. I'm staring at the screen.

The little dots that show he's responding light up for a second—a split second—then disappear.

I'm sick of waiting.

TWENTY-TWO

Mrs. Danforth's hair is pulled into a tight bun behind her head, straining lines down to her eyes, thick wooly nightgown hanging off her body.

"Cyrus, it's awfully late," she says. "Jeff cannot have visitors this late."

"I know, Mrs. Danforth. I won't be long, I promise."

"Hmm."

She looks down on me from the doorway, one step up from the porch, the screen door shut between us. I've been by a few times since Jeff left—asking about the letters I sent, whether he might be home for Thanksgiving. I'd wait until Mr. Danforth's SUV was gone from the garage—which you could tell by peeking through the windows—but his mom always had some variation on the same answer: "I'm not sure, Cyrus," or "We haven't made that determination yet," or "You need to stop coming by."

She looks behind her, down the hallway, no lights in the shadow of the entrance. I hate her.

"Is Mr. Danforth home?" I say. I need to see Jeff. I'm desperate.

"No." She shakes her head. "He's at the church helping to clean up after the day's festivities."

"Festivities?" I say, hoping vague interest in whatever the hell she's talking about might get me an invite inside. It wasn't too cold out today so I didn't grab my coat but I didn't realize how much the wind picked up, cutting through my sweatshirt.

"It's Christmas, Cyrus," she says. "I know you're not active in your religion, but surely you are aware of the birth of Jesus Christ?"

"Kind of," I say. I can't help but be a smart-ass because she's fucking ridiculous, and she's not letting me inside.

"You'll have to come back tomorrow," she says, backing up so she can close the door behind her but I pull open the screen and step into the frame, throwing my knee against the wood until it connects, smacking hard enough to make a sound.

"Oh Cyrus," she says and I grab my knee, rubbing against the jeans. "I'm sorry."

I wince and step back, full of exaggeration, keeping the screen door open against my hip. A fresh blast of wind blows through my clothes.

"It's…okay," I say, gritting my teeth like I just tore a ligament. "Cross-country season is over."

The door is open now and Mrs. Danforth leans forward, her resting frown softer in the green bulb lighting the porch. The Christmas decorations are sparse, a lone wreath on the picture window to my left, an angel lit up in white. The rest of the house is dark.

"I—I guess you could see him for a minute," she says, clutching her nightgown and looking around like she's uncertain.

I hurry past before she changes her mind and I'm already up the stairs when she calls out "Five minutes!"

His door is closed so I knock three times.

"Come in."

"Cyrus?"

He's seated on the spare recliner we found abandoned at the end of our street last spring, this multi-colored patchwork of stuffing and stitching with holes ripped into the sides. When we brought it home his stepfather freaked, the clutter of the chair disturbing the order of his house. But Jeff's mother let him keep it. That was before she lost her mind.

"You can't be here," he says. "Roland said I can't have guests over Christmas break."

"I know. Your mom told me."

The bedroom walls are painted puke green, the same color scheme as the hallway, no posters or pictures or any trace of his personal space. He told me he hoped it was temporary, them moving into Roland's house, so he didn't bother to decorate. It's been over a year.

"How come you haven't texted?" I say. "When did you get home?"

"Yesterday," he says. "I got back yesterday."

"Oh."

I step to the side to try to meet his eyes but they're buried in a book, something called The Rise and Fall of Third Leg. The cover has a strange cartoon of a purplish humanoid with a protruding eyeball over its nose and a head coming out of its ass.

"How long are you home for?" I ask.

"Just the week."

He's wearing the red bandana he used to wear to work sometimes, tilted to the side. I don't know why he's not speaking.

"You want me to leave?"

"Not sure," he says. "Did you come to apologize?"

He looks up at me, the blue eyes dulled in the dim light from the lamp on his desk, the only light he has on in the room. I've been in his bedroom before but not often. He doesn't have a TV so we always hung out at my house, or his garage for our band. I step closer to the bed.

"Apologize for what?"

I try to say it like I'm not upset but it's hard to say those words without sounding upset. And I don't know what he's talking about. He edges forward in the recliner, folding the book in his hands.

"Well, let me see. I'm pretty sure I remember asking you to help me run away and then I came by the house and you weren't there. And I spent the last three months in fucking prison so, I don't know, yes. Maybe you could apologize for that."

"I waited for you. I waited all day and then I ran over to your house and no one was home so I just thought—I thought you left." It doesn't sound as unimpeachable when I say it out loud. "When I came back from my run, I found your note."

He picks up the book again, flipping through the pages to find the page he was on. I edge back to the bed, the mattress where he sleeps.

"I can't believe you fucking showed up here, Cyrus," he says, looking into my eyes. "You have no idea what I've been through up there—it's not even Harrisburg. It's out in the middle of fucking nowhere way past Harrisburg and there's no escape. Believe me, we plotted an escape, but there's not even a major highway within miles so even if we could have gotten out of the locked dorm rooms past the armed security—seriously they have armed security, I'm not joking."

He stands up and starts to pace the small space, eyes darting between the carpeting and my face. His hair is longer than usual, like he hasn't cut it since he left, and he doesn't notice the way it falls into his eyes.

"I wrote you," I say. "I explained how I waited and—"

He stares at me like he doesn't know what I'm saying.

"Didn't you get my letters?"

"No, I didn't get any fucking letters," he says. "Are you kidding me?"

He stops at his desk, staring at me like I'm a stranger, or an alien, and I want to run out the door and escape to a place where he doesn't hate me like he hates me right now. It's been three months but it feels like forever.

"I didn't know how to contact you," I say. "Your phone—"

"Yeah, no, they didn't even let me bring the phone with me," he says, pacing still. His room is small—bed and desk and recliner all squeezed together so the carpeting is only a few square feet in between. "It was here, in this house, while I was one hundred miles away in these mosquito-infested woods pretending I cared about Jesus and the Bible because they don't let you do anything—not even eat—unless you recite what you learned about Jesus that day."

"Wow," I say. I don't know what to say. I let my hand touch his sheets where he sleeps, unmade with the blankets rolled up at the base.

"Yeah. But I have my phone now. And I can see things have been happening in Dallastown since I've been gone," he says. "And I think you should leave."

"What?"

"You know, I was going to call you this morning," he

says, stepping closer to me. "I saw you texted yesterday and I was like 'maybe I'll hear him out even though he abandoned me when I needed his help the most' but then—" He shakes his head and breathes out. I want to reach out. He's close enough to touch.

"But what?" I say. "I'm sorry, Jeff, I did wait for you. I went to the bank and I had six hundred dollars in my wallet and I was going to go with you. I packed up my bags and looked up train schedules to Manhattan and I was going to run away with you, Jeff. But you never showed."

"I did show," he says, inching closer. "We went to church and then we went to fucking Bible study at someone else's house instead of mine for some reason and I could have escaped from there, I could have run away right then and there but I thought about you. I thought how you promised to help me and I had no money anyway, so I waited until I came home, packed a bag and snuck out the back door to sprint to your house and—"

"Jeff—I waited—I swear."

His face is broken, like his cheeks are cracked and his eyes are sunken in. His hair is devoid of blond now, thick and disheveled, drifting down his cheeks.

"Sure."

"I swear," I say. "I'm so sorry."

I reach out—I need to reach out—but he backs off, slapping my hand away. The last time I saw him, or the last time before the last time, we were kissing in Mindy's backseat. He backs into his desk as I climb off the mattress.

"Jeff, please."

I step closer because I'm not in control of my legs or I'm ignoring the signals of him recoiling. I need to make this all go away. I don't know what's happening.

"Get the fuck away from me," he says, reaching out with both hands and pushing me hard, back against his bed.

I fall onto the covers where he sleeps, pushing off and stepping forward again. I don't see him forming a fist, or it doesn't register in my mind so muddled by whatever the fuck is happening. I don't see him winding up.

He connects with my jaw and my knees give out. I fall to the floor as he shouts.

"Get the fuck away from me, faggot!"

TWENTY MONTHS LATER

TWENTY-THREE

DAD'S GOT HIS TIE on today, tight around his neck—the too wide blue-and-white speckled silk that signals Big Meeting Day, an event that's happened more often since his promotion. He keeps apologizing that he can't fly to Los Angeles with me, but I stopped listening. I'm too upset.

"I called the airline and they told me I can transfer the ticket free of charge so I was thinking—is there another friend you'd want to invite?" He takes the Raisin Bran and almond milk I left on the counter and puts them away. "Is Sharane available?"

"She's leaving tomorrow. I told you."

"Right," Dad says. "Right."

I get that the new position means he's busier, and I get that the bump in pay allows him to afford my school and Angela's, but Mom would have come with me. She never would have missed it.

"What about Devin? Or Regina?"

"Devin leaves for Penn State on Friday and I haven't seen Regina all summer." I swirl my spoon around the bowl to mix the dry flakes with the milk. I hate biting into the crunchy bits. "I don't know if you noticed."

"I noticed you mope around this house all summer," Dad says, packing up his backpack with the laptop from the dining room table, where he works almost every night.

"Funny," I say.

I spent my third straight summer working at the high school, this time with a promotion to Special Projects Czar—my term, not an official title, since I was charged with assigning tasks to sophomores and juniors working there for the first time. Angela was doing her residency at Penn State, and Mindy was away too, for five weeks in Manhattan at a United Nations program for gifted students. I spent most of the summer alone.

"I asked Donna, but it's her shift this weekend and it was too late to switch," he says. "She told me to apologize."

"She doesn't need to apologize."

I set my spoon down to focus all my ire on him. He zippers up the backpack and returns to the kitchen. Oblivious.

"Well, I'm apologizing again, Cyrus," he calls out through the opening between the rooms. "There's no other option."

I visited Mom's gravesite yesterday, the grass around her headstone brown and trampled with the weather stuck on scorching all August. We talked—or I talked and she listened, like she always listens. I told her how anxious I was about college, or the move across the country, that I don't know how to get around campus or how to buy books or how to share a dorm room with someone who's going to snore, or bitch that I snore even though I don't snore, I don't think. She would have made a list, the way she always made lists—for all the supplies I needed and whatever clothes I should buy, sitting across this table with the pen and long pad, jotting down notes while I ate my cereal, her bushy brown hair drifting into her eyes.

"What about Jeff?" Dad says, loading the backpack with the power bars that serve as his lunch on meeting days, when a client comes in or he has to visit the satellite office in Philly. I forget which it was today.

"Did you really just suggest that?"

"Yes." He returns from the kitchen, backpack zippered and set on the table across from me. "Listen, Cyrus, I know you two had a falling out—"

"He called me a 'faggot' and punched me in the face. Then he stopped talking to me completely."

My jaw still clicks between the bone and the back teeth on my right side, if I open my mouth too wide eating a hoagie or a cheesesteak.

"I know what happened. And I wish you wouldn't use that word," Dad says. "But you said you talked to him. The other night at Sheetz?"

"Just by coincidence. We weren't hanging out or anything."

"I know you weren't hanging out," Dad says, clutching the chair like he's debating whether or not to pull it out and take a seat. "But you said it was nice."

"I said he was being nice. I was surprised." I was shocked when I saw him—how different he looked, the way he'd gotten taller, his hair longer and more disheveled, the tan not as bright as I remembered. At first glance, I didn't recognize him. We hadn't talked in twenty months.

"Do you hate him?"

"Huh?"

"I mean, do you still feel animosity toward him, that you can't let go of?" He attempts to adjust his tie but he pulls the fabric too loose and skews the silk to the right. "You said he offered to drive you home. That maybe it was his olive branch to you."

"I did not say 'olive branch'," I say. "I wouldn't use those words."

I scoop another spoonful of the Raisin Bran, the flakes now soggy in the bowl.

"What I mean is—" Dad pulls out the empty chair and takes a seat. "I know what you went through losing Jeff. Believe me, I was right here watching how devastated you were. When he first left for school and when he came back that Christmas—" He folds his hands on the table and tries to check his watch without me noticing. "The thing is, Cyrus, I've lost some friends in the past—close friends—and every once in a while, I think about them, wonder how they're doing. And it's okay to move on and find new people to spend time with but it's much harder to make friends later in life. It really is. I don't want that for you. And I don't want that for Jeff."

"Well, talk to Jeff then," I say. "I'm not the one who ended it."

"It's not my place to talk to him, Cy," Dad says, reaching across the table. I keep my fingers clutched around the spoon. "You'll have to."

"No shit," I say. "I'm not an idiot."

"You don't get to talk to me like that, Cyrus." Dad pulls back. "I know you're upset I'm not going away with you and I'm upset too, but we talked about this. My company hosts this conference every year and we lost two team members to a competitor last week and I'm the one person who can fill in. They need me."

"So do I," I say.

He glances at his watch again, biting his lower lip.

"I know, Cyrus, I know. But I'll be there for parents' weekend, which is only—what—a couple weeks from now?"

"I guess," I say. I push the soggy bowl away.

"And I was thinking, you know, this might be an opportunity to—I don't know—" He stands up, lifting the backpack. I don't look up. "Did I ever tell you about my friend from college—Dan Preston—the one who came out to me senior year? Actually, he came out to a bunch of us when we were away on spring break and the word spread around the campus and—well, things were a lot harder back then, being gay and coming out."

"It's still hard," I say. "In Dallastown at least."

Mindy and Sharane and I went to Philly Pride this summer—not willingly, on my part, but Mindy insisted I meet the "Philly gays" before I fled to California for college, and it was fine, I mean it was overwhelming and wild and insanely hypersexual but a couple kids from the cross-country team posted some vile shit on Sharane's Facebook page when she posted pictures of us in front of the parade. Mindy cursed them out before Sharane took the posts down.

"I know, Cyrus. I'm not trying to diminish what you've gone through at all. I just—what I was saying was that I tried to reach out to Dan, after we graduated, and he didn't return any of my e-mails. This was before cell phones so all I had was a number for his parents and I left a couple messages but he never got back to me. I think he lumped me in with all the people who made his life difficult at the end of senior year and that wasn't me—you know that wasn't me, but—" He folds his hands together like a child.

"I wish I'd done more to support him. Before he came out. And after."

"And this has what to do with me and Jeff?"

Dad shakes his head, biting his lips.

"I'm just saying maybe give him a call," he says. "Before you leave. Sounds like he's ready to talk to you now."

"I don't know," I say. He should have been ready a long time ago. "Maybe."

"Okay. Well, I have to go," Dad says, walking away from the table, through the living room toward the door. "But I'll take off on Friday and help you pack, okay?"

I get up with my bowl and stumble into the kitchen, ignoring the goodbye wave he throws away as he rushes to his car because the Earth would stop spinning if he were ever late for anything work-related.

I don't hate Jeff anymore. I did for a while. A long time. Not anymore. I would forgive him, I think, if he apologized. Even now.

But he has my number. There's no fucking way I'm reaching out first.

TWENTY-FOUR

"HAPPY BIRTHDAY Shaaaaa-rane, happy birthday to you."

"It's not my birthday," Sharane says.

"I know." Mindy sets the cake and candles in front of Sharane on the sofa. "But what were we supposed to sing?"

I step into the back room off the kitchen, the enclosed porch that's been outfitted with a proper sofa and a big screen television since last I was here, at graduation. I glance at my hand, pink frosting on my knuckle.

"Good luck Sharane, good luck at Princeton," Mindy sings, off-tune and trilling. "Wait, that almost rhymes. This could be a song."

"That is not a song," Devin says from the seat next to Sharane. The candles are still lit. "Is this why you ended the band?"

"Mindy's singing?" I say. "It didn't help."

Mindy throws an elbow that I manage to dodge as I take a seat on the high-backed chair we brought in from the kitchen, set apart from the girls.

"When did you last play?" Sharane says, as if she's lamenting the musical brilliance of the ill-begotten band

Mindy and I formed without Jeff. The wax drips onto the frosting.

"I have no idea," Mindy says, sliding onto the other side of Sharane. "Last summer?"

We gave it a go as a duo in the spring, after Jeff returned to Harrisburg. I wrote a few songs and Mindy and I alternated singing brief verses in aural blasts that were more punk than hardcore, the tracks dependent on synthesized guitar from her keyboards, no Jeff to broaden the sound. We enlisted a guitar player last summer, when it became clear that Jeff and I weren't going to become friends again, but Mindy's choir buddy was more into jam band musings than actual music and we never meshed as a unit. It just wasn't the same.

"Are you going to blow those out?" Devin says, the wax forming puddles at the base of the candles, ruining my pink lettering.

"Right." Sharane laughs as she blows the candles out. "Thank you guys, this is awesome."

"No worries," Mindy says. "I can't believe you're leaving in the morning."

"Are you excited?" Devin says, slicing into the cake with an oversized butcher's knife more appropriate for Hong Kong action flicks than the task at hand.

"I'm nervous," Sharane says. "But excited too. And I'm going to miss you guys."

"Awww," Mindy and Devin remark in unison and the three of them form a wide embrace on the couch.

"Cyrus, get your ass over here!" Mindy shouts.

We're all leaving all over the country over the next week. I'm trying not to think about it.

"I got you a going away present," Mindy says.

"You did not need to get me anything," Sharane says. "This party is enough."

I didn't get her anything. Devin slices me a piece of cake.

"It's nothing," Mindy says, handing her a boxy present in blue and gold wrapping paper, tight around the corners with a yellow bow.

"It's everything," Sharane says and they hug again.

Sharane is leaving for New Jersey tomorrow and Devin's off to Penn State at the end of the week. Mindy starts next week at Columbia, as Ivy League as Princeton, because she and Sharane studied way harder than me. Not that I'm going to a terrible school—Loyola Marymount ranks in the top seventy universities in the country, which is decent enough as long as you ignore the multiple California schools that rejected me.

Sharane pulls out the gift, one of those rectangular desk decorations with a thick backing, wood-carved with the words: there are FRIENDS, there is family, and then there are FRIENDS WHO ARE FAMILY. The hugging resumes and Sharane starts to cry. I take a massive bite of cake.

"Oh my god, Cyrus, I forgot to warn you," Sharane says. "Courtney is coming over tonight."

"Oh." I lick the frosting off my lips. "Do you know when?"

"I'm not sure," she says. "My uncle is stopping by to say goodbye."

"Wait, Courtney?" Devin says, her stringy brown hair brushing against the frosting when she turns. "Is that the boy who went to that religious school?"

"Oh god no, that's Jeff," Mindy says. "But we don't talk about Jeff."

"Right, he's like Voldemort." Devin laughs.

"I saw him," I say, shifting in the hard-backed chair. "At Sheetz."

"When was this?" Mindy asks. "And how come I wasn't consulted?"

"A few days ago," I say. "And I don't know."

"How was he?" Sharane says.

She was the last of us who kept in contact with him but sometime last summer he stopped returning her texts as well, dropping off the face of the earth.

"He just got home."

I set my empty plate on the table, the television playing a commercial to my left, one of those screaming car ads that are beyond annoying and I don't know how boomers watch regular TV.

"He had to go on a mission to West Virginia, knocking on doors to convert heathens to Jesus or whatever."

"Like the Mormons?" Devin says.

"I guess." He didn't share any details. "He's been back for just a couple weeks."

"What did he say to you?" Mindy reaches over and touches my knee. "I mean, how was it?"

"It was fine," I say, blinking a bunch to clear my head. "He looked different, like his hair was longer and he has a mustache now, or the wispy starts of one, but it was strange. I didn't recognize him at first."

"Didn't you go out with him, Sharane?" Devin asks.

I love Devin but she's stupid annoying with the way she sticks the second vowel in Sharane's name, an extended up-tick that's grating. Sharane shakes her head, glancing at me.

"We were friends," she says. "He was a good guy, he just—he had some issues."

"Why are you using past tense, it's not like he's dead," Devin says. "Wait—is he?"

"Oh my god, Devin, how did you get into Penn State?" Mindy says and I hear some commotion in the kitchen. Sharane gets up. Devin grabs her glass and follows her out of the room.

"Are you okay?" Mindy whispers, replacing her hand on my knee.

"Yeah," I say. I tried a bunch of times to get in touch with Jeff in the spring after he hit me but he never responded. No hint of an apology. I had to get over him. I am over him. That's what I keep telling myself.

"Did you guys make any plans to talk again?"

"Well, he offered to drive me home because it started to rain and I had my bike but I told him I was fine. I didn't know how the bike would fit in his car."

"And that's how you left it?"

I hear voices in the distance, a clattering of chattering all at once in my brain. Courtney inches into view. We dated—two full dates and an abbreviated third, during which he told me I was obsessed with someone else so he couldn't see me anymore.

"What?"

"I asked how you left it with Jeff," Mindy says. "Are you okay?"

I nod a bunch of times. "He told me I could call him, or maybe 'to' call him." Courtney waves, a slight wave with just the wrist.

"But I'm not going to."

"Oh," she says. "Does he know you're going away?"

I shake my head. I wanted to tell him but— "We didn't talk very long."

"Are you still pissed?" Mindy says, ignoring Devin's high-pitched cackle from the kitchen. "I mean, it's okay if you are. What he did was—well, if not unforgiveable no one could fault you if you didn't."

"No, I have," I say. "Forgiven him." It wasn't the punch or what he called me that night. It was the after. "But I still don't know why he stopped talking to me."

"You could ask him," Mindy says, squeezing my kneecap. "I mean, maybe you should ask him. Some kind of closure before we leave?"

"Maybe," I say.

Mindy's coming to California with me—"OMG YES! I HAVE TO MEET CODY," she said via text when I brought up the idea of her joining Dad and me when I move into Loyola. Except Dad's no longer coming.

"Listen, Cyrus, I've held longer grudges for way less than what he did to you," Mindy says. "I didn't talk to Regina for three months last fall because she told Rafael I liked him. But the point is—" She brushes her hair behind her neck. "You were obsessed with Jeff and I hate to say it but you've never gotten over him and I think it would help you get a fresh start in Cali if you got some closure, you know. I always thought what happened between the two of you didn't make any sense."

"I know," I say.

I still don't know why he would hit me. I didn't wait for him, yes, but I tried to wait. He wouldn't listen.

"Speaking of closure," Mindy says.

Courtney steps into the room. He's a year younger than us so he's still in high school this fall. Like Cody.

"Hi Courtney," Mindy says. "My rude friend here also says 'Hi'."

She lifts my arm to form a wave and Courtney laughs. Sharane returns to the room with Devin, a different cake in her hands because Courtney's father brought one over and now everyone's discussing the "Freshman Fifteen" as they slice off the pieces and hand them out again, a fresh serving on each plate.

"Please call him," Mindy whispers in my ear, rubbing my knee. "Then we can analyze what he said on the plane ride to L.A.!"

She laughs and I catch Courtney watching us. I smile at him because we don't have any animosity, I don't think. He's the only boy I ever dated and he broke up with me because I was obsessed with Jeff even though I swore I wasn't.

But sometimes I still think about Jeff.

Sometimes it's all I think about.

TWENTY-FIVE

I'VE BEEN TO CALIFORNIA THREE TIMES.

The first was when I met Cody, two years ago. The second time was last summer, when Dad, Angela, and me spent ten days out there as a family—hitting Disneyland and Universal, which I preferred to Disney because of Harry Potter World and Butter Beer even though Angela declared it all to be "lame," like she does with most things. A couple of days we didn't have anything planned, so Dad let me spend it on my own, with Cody in Manhattan Beach, the sun and the surf and skateboarding on his brother's borrowed board, laid back and relaxed and more fun than I'd had since Jeff was gone. That's when I started looking at schools in California, because I wanted to be out there, sitting on the sand watching Cody in his wetsuit, the breeze from the ocean keeping the sun from baking me like the humid sweatshop of central P.A. I couldn't wait to get out of here—for years, I wanted to leave—and I spent spring break visiting Loyola because it was the only school that accepted me and I decided right there and then to attend, after a week on the beach with Cody.

I've spent all summer worried I made a mistake.

"What's up?"

Jeff's garage door is open and he's seated on a low wooden chair facing the opening, guitar in his hands.

"Hey," I say. I didn't intend to stop by but I didn't know what to say if I called him and I'm exhausted from running and his garage door was open. "I didn't know you were playing again."

"Yeah," he says. "I've been trying."

He's grown taller than me—or he was always taller but he's grown a few inches, and his face is fuller, rounder maybe, a thickness that extends down his neck to his shoulders, more muscular than I remember.

"You're allowed to play in here now?"

"Yeah, it's cool," he says. "Roland doesn't bitch about that stuff anymore."

The garage is rearranged, the side to the left of Jeff no longer clear for a vehicle, the space replaced by a long homemade table cluttered with tools and stacks of Bibles, sports equipment in bags on the floor and hanging from the rafters. The woodworking shelves have shifted closer to the entrance, abutted by a bench with stacks of free weights, a set of dumbbells and one of those rowing machines in the corner, where my drum kit used to be.

"You still drumming?" Jeff asks me.

"Yeah," I say. "A little."

I haven't, just a few times this summer in the basement, burning off some energy. I haven't done much of anything.

"And you're still running," he says. "That's cool."

"Not really."

It's too hot in Dallastown to be running. It's been too hot all summer to do much of anything, but the double shot of cake and the never ending stress of this move across the country, away from everyone I've ever known—now all alone, or at least without a parental figure to take care of things, unless you count Mindy, who will help, but she has to leave after the weekend and I'm not moving in until Monday so I strapped on my Sauconys and took off into the blazing heat.

"I'm in unfathomable pain but I'm trying not to show it," I say. The sweat pours down my face. He threads one of the guitar strings through the post and laughs, a small laugh. It's nice to hear him laugh.

"Thanks," I say. "Um, for offering to drive me home the other day."

"No worries," Jeff says. "You don't have a car?"

His mid-2000s Ford Mustang is parked in the driveway.

"No," I say. "I never got my license."

"Why not?"

"It's a long story," I say.

I failed the road test the first time and the second time I missed the exam because I overslept. Depressed about Jeff. Sharane told me he was home for Easter so I stopped over the house, thinking he might still want to speak to me, or at least apologize for the punch in the face, but he told me through the screen door to stop coming over or trying to message him. I stopped trying after that.

"You want a towel?" he says.

"Sure."

He stands up from the chair and moves to the table with the stacks of Bibles, returning with a fluffy white towel and handing it to me.

"It should be clean," he says.

"Thank you."

I wipe the sweat off my face with the back of the towel. I must look crazy to show up like this. I want to ask him what I need to ask him, about why he stopped talking to me and why our friendship fell apart, or why he hit me, why he hated me. But I can't speak. He steps back to the chair, lifting the guitar.

"So, what's up, man?" he says. "When are you leaving for school again?"

I don't remember mentioning school at Sheetz but our conversation was such a blur I must be misremembering.

"This weekend."

"I see," he says, pursing his lips, the sun through the opening reflecting in his eyes. "And where are you heading?"

"Loyola Marymount. In SoCal," I say, like I'm a local. Or pretending to be.

"Right," he says. "California, huh? That's awesome."

"Yeah." I try to gauge his reaction. His hair is shaggy, like he hasn't bothered to style it, and it keeps falling into his eyes. "Well, I had a question for you and I know it's kind of a random request—I'm not sure that's the right word."

"What's that?" Jeff says, like he didn't hear me.

"Um, yeah, see the thing is my dad was supposed to come with me to get me set up at college but he has some stupid work conference in Philly this weekend so he can't go." I hesitate, wiping more sweat from my skin. Jeff's watching me. "Dad said you could use his ticket if you wanted to get a free trip to California. I know you always talked about getting as far away from Dallastown as possible."

"Right," he says.

"Dad suggested I ask you specifically," I say, dabbing the towel against the back of my neck, where the sweat is gathered around my T-shirt. "So I think we can use his credit card. Weed is legal out there, isn't it?"

He laughs, a bigger laugh.

"I don't smoke anymore, Cy," he says, looking up. "But I mean, you could."

"Oh. I was just saying."

Jeff returns to his guitar, cutting off the excess string, and there's this silence again. This awkward between us.

"Mindy's going too," I say. "So it won't just be the two of us."

I'm not sure why I said that.

"She's cool with me going?" he says.

I feel a sneeze coming on, from the dust in the garage or the stress of the conversation. I hold it in.

"Yeah," I say. "She's good."

When I told her that he punched me, I had to physically restrain her from driving to his house and stabbing him in the throat. But it's been a long time. She told me to call him so I assume she's over it.

"I'll have to ask my mom," Jeff says, setting down the guitar. "When are you leaving?"

"Saturday morning." I scrunch my face. "Like 6 a.m."

"Okay," he says, meeting my eyes. "I'll ask her."

"Okay," I say. That's not the response I expected and I'm not sure what to do with it. "I'll umm, well, my number hasn't changed."

He pulls his hand through his hair, brushing the shaggy strands from his face.

"Yeah, well, I have to head to church soon. I'm working there now, can you believe that?" He stands up. "Landscaping and maintenance and shit like that. It's a job."

"Okay," I say. I don't know what to say. He climbs the concrete step and opens the door into the house.

"I'll let you know," he says.

"Okay," I repeat and he disappears inside with a weird wonderful smile. Like it used to be.

I walk out of the garage where we used to play, my drum kit in the space occupied by the rowing machine, Jeff next to me, his sweaty skin shimmering in the fluorescents. I forget sometimes how much I miss playing drums with him. Our band.

We never settled on a name.

TWENTY-SIX

DAD DROVE US to Philadelphia International. His conference was in Philly anyway and he said he'd be stopping by Starbucks to get "fuel" for a full day of "meet and greets" with potential clients or existing clients—he made the distinction but I stopped listening. Jeff was next to me in the back seat.

I've been thinking about what to say to him, how to even begin a conversation, because I'd like to repair the friendship, if he wants to repair the friendship. Mindy said not to expect an apology—and definitely not to ask for one—that I have to be okay with letting the past stay in the past and I think I am. I never expected him to come.

"I have to pee," Mindy says after we clear security.

"But our flight—"

"I am NOT sitting on a five-hour flight while having to pee and have you seen those bathrooms on airplanes?" Mindy says. "My ass does not fit."

"Your ass is fine," I say. Because her ass is fine.

"Don't lie to me, Cyrus," she says. "And the thought of hovering over that tiny seat every penis with poor aim on the plane has pissed onto—" she shudders. "Gross. Oh, there it is!"

She slams her suitcase into my wrist and sprints ahead of us for the bathroom. Jeff laughs.

"Dude," Jeff says. "Mindy has not changed a bit."

"No. If anything, she's gotten worse. Once she got accepted into Columbia, she stopped censoring herself."

"Her mom must be proud," Jeff says as we step under an awning across from the bathrooms, the crush of people rushing past us despite the butt-crack of early.

"Well, she isn't so blunt in front of her mother," I say.

"Huh?"

"Wait—were you being sarcastic?"

"No." Jeff shakes his head. "I meant she must be proud that Mindy got into Columbia."

"Oh. Yeah." I drop my backpack onto her suitcase. "She is."

Jeff dips his head, his long hair parted in the middle and pulled back behind his ears, combed and straightened and exposing his face. Dad hugged me at the curb when he dropped us off, which felt strange because we don't really hug, but he apologized again and brought up his job again but I told him I didn't mind, I said I'd be fine. Mindy's taking forever in the bathroom.

"You know, I never asked," I say. "Are you going to college this fall?"

"Yeah." He nods. "But just HACC York. Nothing like Columbia."

Harrisburg Community College has a branch in North York and a bunch of kids from Dallastown are going there.

"That's great," I say.

"No, it isn't." He laughs, a forced laugh. "I just—I don't know if I'm ready for college yet. Switching between Dallastown and New Bredford made things—" He hesitates, looking down at me, the way he's grown since last we were friends. "I fell behind."

"Well, maybe you can catch up at HACC and go away next semester."

"Sure," he says. "Maybe."

I check my watch because I'm concerned about the flight, not because I'm bored with the conversation, but then I'm worried he'll think I'm bored with the conversation so I drop my arm and the time doesn't register in my mind. But I think our flight is boarding soon.

"Girls take a while in the bathroom," Jeff says. "My girlfriend, she would be in there for hours. I'd be like what the hell is taking so long and there was always some excuse, but I don't know. That's not why we broke up."

There's too much in that statement to focus on any one aspect and my mind kind of blanked after I heard "girlfriend." But who was she and how long were they were dating and why did they break up?

"Why did you break up?" I say, jumping at the opening.

"She—" He sighs and turns away. "It's a long story."

I wonder if he figured out he likes boys more than girls because I've been wanting to know that since I last saw him, maybe more than why he stopped speaking to me, because I don't know how into me he ever was or why we stopped being friends, and I don't know what to say.

"Oh my god, the freaking line!" Mindy shouts across the walkway, cutting off a family of four to get to us. "How are there so many people here this early?"

"No clue," I say.

"Well, let's go, let's go, what are you waiting for?" She yanks the suitcase from my hands. "Didn't you hear the announcement?"

"What announcement?"

She stares at me dumbfounded, then looks to Jeff.

"I can't," she says. "You two haven't changed a bit. They moved our gate, we have to go!"

She pulls on my arm and then we're fast walking, me and Jeff and our luggage trailing Mindy and her luggage down the crowded walkway between terminals because the new gate is like a full fucking mile away. I hate the airport.

"Jeff," Mindy says, slowing her gait to walk beside him. I lag behind. "I thought maybe we should have a chat before the trip, just so we're clear on the weekend."

"O—kay."

They veer around a passenger planted in the middle of the aisle and I almost slam into him. Asshole.

"Here's the thing." Her regular voice is loud enough I can hear her from behind, but I think she's shouting for my benefit. "We haven't hung out in what—two years—and you look good, I mean, I'm still waiting for a compliment on how I look." She stops at the side of the walkway, placing her free arm on his. "But either way, we do need to talk about the elephant in the room. And by elephant, I mean the dog at the side of the road that my car hit and you— well, thank god you stopped because otherwise we would not be talking, but I always wanted to know what you were thinking that night and we never got to discuss because you punched Cyrus the next time he saw you and I was ready to go to your house and do to you what you wanted to do to that dog, but you'd already gone back to school so I'm bringing it all up now."

Mindy talks fast when she's defending my honor, apparently.

"Yeah," Jeff says, facing her. "I honestly don't know what I was thinking."

"It wasn't that long ago, Jeff," Mindy says.

"I know, I know." I step around Mindy to see his reaction but some angry white dude barrels past along the walkway, knocking into me. "But I had a lot of time at school to think and I guess I made up all these excuses in my head to try to excuse the things I did. But I think that's the answer. I was so stuck inside my mind, I wasn't thinking clearly. That night with the dog and then when I came home, with Cyrus—" He glances at me, dipping his head. "I was angry all the time."

An announcement about taking packages from strangers crackles over the speakers and Jeff waits for it to end.

"And now?" Mindy says.

"I'm not as angry anymore," he says. "I've been working on it. A lot."

"Okay," Mindy says. She reaches out for his hand. "We all make mistakes, you know. I stopped driving altogether because of what happened to the dog that night. But I'm glad you're on a path. And you do look good—" She squeezes his arm. "Have you been working out?"

He pulls back like a reflex as another stream of passengers push their way around us.

"Don't worry, I'm not hitting on you." She laughs. "I've been down that road with Cyrus and we all know how well that went."

"You still haven't dropped that?" I say.

"Never!" she says, releasing Jeff to slap me on the side. Jeff smiles.

"Oh shit, we need to go!" Mindy grabs my arm and now we're sprinting, me and Jeff and my luggage trailing Mindy and her luggage, running for the plane that will take me three thousand miles away from everyone I've ever known.

But Jeff is here and Mindy is here, leading us both. I follow.

TWENTY-SEVEN

CALIFORNIA IS MY FAVORITE place. Not that I've been many places—it's the only place I've visited west of Chicago, where we went a single time to accompany Mom at a women's studies conference because Dad was somewhere else, traveling for work, and they weren't ready to leave Angela and me home alone, afraid we'd burn down the house or get hurt somehow or that Angela would forget to feed me. I don't remember much about the trip, except that the hotel was old and cramped—two small beds for the three of us—and I curled up next to Mom and slept beneath her breasts, her silent snores putting me to sleep.

But I love California—the bright sunshine that greets you every time you escape the airport doors, bolder and crisper than the sun in Pennsylvania. Everyone is dressed better too, punker and blacker than anyone in Dallastown. And the people are gorgeous. I mean Jeff is beautiful but Cody is straight out of a Hollywood teen magazine and there were thirty-seven boys on my campus visit to LMU as beautiful as him, the floppy-haired boys with their surf-style shirts and perfect golden tans. As soon as we climb off the plane, I feel it. California feels perfect to me.

"This fucking sucks," Jeff says.

We forgot to bring sandals so when we removed our socks and sneakers at the base of the stairs, the sand burned through our soles, and now we're sprinting, sinking into the sand with every step, the pain so intense I think my toes are actually burning, the charred remains sloughing off as ash until we make it closer to the water, where the grains are packed tighter, and I collapse on the sand near a massive rainbow umbrella.

Mindy refused to come to the beach. Her exact words were: "I only agreed to come to California on the explicit instructions that at no point was my pale Korean ass stepping onto sand."

She's doing some light reading from her Chemistry text at a coffee shop nearby to try to get ahead at Columbia. I didn't even get my books for college yet. I'm not sure where to get them.

"Cool," Jeff says as we spread out our towels, nodding at the family beneath the rainbow umbrella.

It's two men and their children, sunbathing next to us, and even though I've been out here a few times now, I'm still amazed at how openly gay California is—the polar opposite of Dallastown. I try not to notice, because it shouldn't be worth notice. But it is to me.

"You going in?" Jeff asks, pulling off his shirt in the sun.

"In a bit."

If I stand right now he'd notice the parts of my body noticing the parts of his body, the muscles filling out his chest and his neck, the waist as thin as it used to be. He tilts his head with a sideways smile then he jogs toward the water, pausing a second before diving in.

The beach is crowded but not Jersey Shore crowded and there aren't any other swimmers in the water near Jeff.

The surfers are closer to the pier but distant, waiting for their waves in groups of two or three. Cody might be with them, because he surfs most days and he didn't respond to my texts when we landed. It's tough to tell, though, the way they all look the same at this distance—black wet-suited bodies with legs spread across their boards or hunched against the water. Waiting.

"Oh my god, the water is perfect," Jeff says, running up to my towel on the sand, the water dripping onto my feet. "I can actually see my legs."

"I know," I say. "There's no comparison to the Atlantic. It's so much cleaner."

"Well, everything's cleaner than New Jersey," he says, taking a seat beside me.

Jeff came completely unprepared for California, neglecting to pack a beach towel or even a bathing suit in addition to the sandals, so we stopped at a shop a block from the Strand and he changed in the dressing room. His towel is bright orange with a golden yellow sun, California in cursive in sky blue lettering, matching his shorts. He looks good.

"You should go in," he says, squinting at me. He pulls his hair behind his ears.

"I will," I say.

I don't take off my shirt at the beach, not since I hit puberty, my skinny white chest too susceptible to burns. Or embarrassment. I wish I were as confident as Jeff, his wet shorts sagging just beneath his hips.

"Little help!" someone calls and I turn to see a volleyball rolling toward me. I reach out when it comes to a stop and toss the ball in the general direction of a tall, shirtless dude running in my direction.

Manhattan Beach has a bunch of volleyball courts set up next to the Strand and they host international tournaments sometimes. The winners have their names engraved on diamond plates embedded into the central pier jutting out into the ocean.

"What do you think of him?" Jeff says, pulling up the edges of the towel to wipe his ears.

"Who?"

"You know, volleyball stud dude," Jeff says, brushing the sticking strands from his eyes. "Is he your type?"

"Huh?"

"Like, are you into these Cali beach guys?" The sun is right above us with no clouds to block the rays and Jeff leans back on his elbows, his bare chest exposed to me. "Is that why you're going to school out here?"

"No," I say, elongating the 'o' because I'm not sure what he means or why he's asking but buff volleyball dude is of no interest to me.

"So, he's not your type or you didn't come out here for that reason?"

"Um, he's not my type," I say.

"I see," Jeff says. "So, why did you come out here? I mean, I Googled your school and it's a good school and all it just seems so random, you know. There's a Loyola in Maryland that's way the fuck closer." He laughs to himself. "Is it because of Cody? I mean, you don't have to answer."

Cody's not the reason. He's part of the reason, maybe, but he had a boyfriend last fall when I sent in my applications so he wasn't the only reason. We're friends— long distance friends—although when I visited Loyola on spring break—my third time to L.A.—I spent most of the week with Cody. We were at his father's place in Hermosa

Beach on my last night there, in the small back bedroom he shared with his brother, and we kissed, then we almost more than kissed, and I sent in my acceptance letter as soon as I got back to Dallastown.

"No, it's a valid question." I dig into the sand with my hands. "I guess—you know how we always used to talk about leaving Dallastown?"

"Of course. Dallastown Sucks My Balls."

"Exactly," I say. "And I think that's why I came out here. Every time I visit California, it feels different. The opposite."

"No rainbow umbrellas in Dallastown?" Jeff says, pointing to the family next to us. The boys are building castles in the sand as their sister runs circles around them, their fathers engrossed in their books. Oblivious.

"Definitely," I say, letting the sticky sand run through my fingers. "And Mindy was leaving and Sharane was leaving and you and I—" I wait while he nods, the sun on his face glowing against his skin. "There wasn't much left for me."

"Well, your dad," he says, "and Angela."

"Do not bring her into this."

He laughs. This is nice.

"But yeah, my dad still has work out here so he can visit a bunch."

"And Cody?"

The volleyball crew screams as another ball approaches. The buff dude with no shirt jogs all the way up to my blanket. He apologizes when I toss him the ball again and he waits, turning to Jeff, but Jeff is focused on me so he runs away.

"I don't know," I say. "We're supposed to meet later for dinner. Is that okay?"

"Sure," Jeff says, staring out into the water. I follow his eyes to a group of surfers climbing onto their boards, an impressive wave approaching. "Are you two together?"

"No," I say, shaking my head. "We kind of stopped talking for a bit and then we started up again, but just as friends."

"And now?"

"Just friends," I say.

Most of the surfers crash out as soon as they start but one lonely figure catches the crest of the wave, floating beneath, sideways from the pier. The ocean carries him all the way into the shallows and he bounces off, spinning around to go out again.

"And do you think you'll come back?" Jeff says, falling back off his elbows to lie flat on the blanket.

"Come back?"

"To Dallastown," he says. "After college."

"Oh," I say. "Maybe."

"Sure," Jeff says, closing his eyes. His hair has dried a bit and the wind off the water blows it sideways.

"What about you?" I say. "You always wanted to get out of Dallastown."

"Yeah. I just—" He leans up onto his elbows again, his chest protruding a bit. I wonder how often he works out, with the weight benches in his garage, near where my drum kit used to sit. "I guess I'm not sure where I want to go."

"You talked about Brooklyn," I say. "Before."

"I know." He laughs. "I was going to run away to Brooklyn."

He was. And I was going to go with him. If I had waited longer that Sunday, he would have come and we would have gone. I don't know why I didn't wait.

"It's just confusing," Jeff says.

"What is?"

"Life?" He laughs. "I don't know, everything."

A flock of seagulls swoop down around the children next to us, and the little girl screams. Jeff turns back to watch, the water now dry on his skin.

"You know, in order to graduate, we had to go on a mission and I got sent to West Virginia. Like I told you. And I kind of thought it was ridiculous at first but we weren't preaching or anything, we were just offering charity—you know, as a way to get people to join the church of, but it was pretty jarring." He holds his hand over his eyes to block out the sun. "The meth problem there and the lives destroyed, you know. It was kind of hard to see."

"I'm sorry," I say. "I didn't know."

"No, it's okay. But it helped, you know, with my dad. We've been talking a lot since I got back."

"Really?"

"Yeah. I mean, he sounds like he's sober, so I'm trying to be supportive, but—" A massive wave rolls onto the beach, close to our towels. "I don't know if I should trust him again."

"I'm sorry," I repeat, because I don't know what else to say. I didn't think we'd be talking like this and maybe it's okay that so much time has passed, maybe it's been good for us. I've missed this.

"Little help, buddy!"

The volleyball rolls onto my blanket this time, smacking me in the shin. Buff dude steps right up between us.

"Hey, we could use two more if you guys want to join," he says. "Someone who could freaking keep their serves in the vicinity of the court."

He laughs but Jeff just stares.

"Nah, we're good," Jeff says. The dude looks up and down Jeff's body before jogging away.

"I'm sorry—did you want to play?" Jeff says.

"Oh god no," I say and he laughs, like the way we used to be. Our shorthand disdain for everyone who isn't us.

"What were we talking about?" Jeff says.

"Whether or not I thought that guy was hot," I say and he laughs again, full-throated this time, leaning back onto his blanket. I missed this so much.

"Jeff, can I ask you something?" The wind and the waves have this hollowed out echoing when I speak. "Why did you come out here?"

"You asked me to," he says.

"Right," I say. "Right."

The seagulls are swarming around the rainbow umbrella and the children shout and spin about the blanket.

"You didn't want me to come?"

"No, I did. I'm just surprised, is all. We haven't hung out in—"

"Forever." He dips his head and the dried blonde strands get caught in the breeze, spreading out like electricity.

"I guess I wanted to make it up to you," he says.

"For what?"

"For—you know, what happened." He sets his eyes toward the sky, the seagulls squawking ten or twenty feet up. "Like I said to Mindy, I was out of my mind at the time and I called you something I never should have called you and I'm sorry, Cyrus. I should have told you that a long time ago."

I blink with the sun so bright, using my arm as a shield, but I can't find his eyes. And I don't know what to say. It's been so long and there's so much to say and I think he might have missed me as much as I've missed him.

"Cyrus Marion Dunn!"

I turn to spot Cody walking up to our towels, wetsuit unzipped down to his waist.

"Um, hello!" he says, because he's standing there dripping and I didn't move, so I jump up to hug him, his skin wet and cold as he kisses my cheek.

"Hi," I say and spot Jeff standing beside me. "Cody, this is Jeff."

"Jeff? The Jeff?"

"I'm *a* Jeff."

Cody laughs as they shake hands. Cody turns back to me.

"Dude, I can't believe you're here. Did you come straight from the airport?"

His hair is missing—shaved super tight on the top and sides, all the wavy curls gone.

"We dropped off our stuff at the hotel first, but yeah," I say, staring at his head.

"Aww, you wanted to see me," Cody says, reaching out for my elbow.

His skin is darker than Jeff's, a deeper shade of golden, and he looks back to where his surfboard is set, flat on the beach next to a friend who looks older than him, older than me. He introduced me to some of his surf buddies this spring and they were all in their early twenties with names like Gator or Razor or Brock. I couldn't tell them apart.

"What do you think?" Cody says, brushing his hand along his scalp where his hair used to be.

"It's short," I say, glancing at Jeff. "Why is it so short?"

"You hate it."

I shake my head. I don't hate it but it's different, a thin layer of stubble where the yellow waves used to be.

"Yeah, I told my barber I wanted it shorter because the hair kept getting into my eyes when I surfed but he speaks Spanish way better than me so something got lost in translation."

"It looks good," I say. "You look good."

Cody's smile erupts from his tanned cheeks and I try to catch Jeff's expression to my left but I'm not smooth at all, pretending to be searching out the surfers in the distance, paddling in the ocean's wake. The seagulls swarm overhead, forming a line of their own.

"How do you like Manhattan Beach?" Cody says to Jeff. "Is this your first time here?"

"First time anywhere," Jeff says. He's standing closer to the ocean, watching Cody and me.

"Well, welcome to California," Cody says and an awkward silence comes between us, the seagulls squawking above. It's gotten hotter the longer we've been out here and I feel the sweat forming on my skin. I feel the sudden urge to jump into the ocean.

"Oh so listen, I know we were supposed to grab dinner later," Cody says. "But I have to take my brother to soccer practice. Any way we could reschedule? Tomorrow?"

"Oh," I say, glancing at Jeff, his feet pressed into the sand. "Maybe."

"No, but wait, tonight—tonight!" Cody gets all excited again. "I'm at my dad's place in Hermosa." He points over my shoulder across the beach to the houses in the distance. "I'm having a few friends over if you guys want to come, it'd be great."

"You're having a party?" Jeff asks.

"Just a couple friends," he says. "But you can see the sunset over the ocean from my dad's rooftop. You want to come?"

"If you want?" I ask Jeff.

"Sure," he says with a shrug.

"Okay, perfect," Cody says. "I'll text you the address."

"Okay," I say.

"All right, I need to get one last run in before I go get my brother soooooo—"

I nod and he almost misses as he kisses me on the cheek, laughing again then running back to his board on the sand, the wetsuit tight around his waist.

"I'm going back in," Jeff says, turning away from me. He sprints down the beach for the water.

The family with the rainbow umbrella gathers their things next to me—coolers and bags and sand castle tools, the umbrella not as enormous all bundled up. They trudge up the sand toward the volleyball courts as I return to my spot on the blanket, the heat bearing down on my back.

I take off my shirt and head toward the water, cautious at first at the frigid blast on my feet but pushing forward, the ocean rising or the sand sinking with each step, up to my waist until I grit my teeth and dive in. The waves splash at my face when I emerge, white crested peaks that dissolve into foamy puddles around me. I sink back down and swim out underwater to find Jeff, bobbing my head when I reach where he's wading.

Jeff splashes at me, his neck above the water, clear blue skies behind him. I glance back toward the pier to see if I can see Cody but he's blended in with the other surfers in the distance. I splash back at Jeff and he smiles at me. The water is amazing.

TWENTY-EIGHT

CODY'S PARTY HAS WEED. Like a lot of weed.

And alcohol. Like a lot of alcohol.

His friends brought the supplies, 12-packs of beer and seltzer and several bottles of flavored vodka, Jello shots, and this green glass bong adorned with mini surfboards up and down the sides. Mindy is wasted, or wasted for Mindy. We're seated on a ripped vinyl couch with the stuffing coming out, itching at my skin. I need to stop drinking.

"Um, so like—" she says, her neck on the cushion, staring at the sky.

"Yes," I say. "I think so."

Cody's father lives in a duplex in Hermosa Beach that has a huge rooftop deck with a distant view of the ocean, but his father's out tonight, on a date I think, which was enough source of contention between him and Cody's mother that he allowed the party to happen without too many questions.

"I didn't finish my sentence," Mindy says.

"Oh."

The rooftop deck has two levels, this lower portion near the stairs where Mindy and I are seated across from a short set of wooden steps up to a larger outdoor bar guarded by a huge purple umbrella blocking our view of the upper portion. Several strings of multi-colored Christmas lights hang on metal spikes between the two spaces, casting an orange glow on Mindy's face. Cody and Jeff were at the bar with the bong when I left for the bathroom, and when I came back I found her, planted on the couch, head turned to the sky.

"How are we getting the hotel?" she says. "That was the question. I think."

"Right," I say. "I have no clue."

One of Cody's friends, this tall girl with a red streak dyed into her hair, showed up wearing a T-shirt emblazoned with the logo for Brand New, a band too mainstream for Jeff and me, so he laughed at the sight and she smacked him across the cheek. We were multiple Jello shots in so Jeff didn't care and she passed the bong to him.

"You were there when Jeff said he didn't smoke anymore, right?" I say.

Mindy's eyes are focused on the stars above us, forming intricate patterns in the darkened sky, like a map of alien planets.

"Did you say something?" she says. I laugh. Jeff told me he stopped smoking because they drug-tested him at the Christian school and when he came back to Dallastown last summer, he no longer had any interest.

"Why are there so many stars?" Mindy says. "There aren't this many in Pennsylvania."

"I think it's the same everywhere."

I doubt myself even as I say it because I don't know much about astronomy beyond the planets in our solar system or that our galaxy is called the Milky Way, which always confused me as a kid because I didn't understand why they named something so important after a candy bar. I think I spot the Big Dipper among the cluster of brighter stars, out over the ocean, bending a bit like they're moving a bit, or maybe we are. I close my eyes.

"This is good music," Mindy says. "Do you know who it is?"

"The War on Drugs," I say. Cody's iPhone is connected to the speakers on the rooftop and he's got great taste in music. It matches mine exactly.

"Well, they are losing," she says.

"What?"

"The war on drugs." She spins her eyes from the sky as I open mine. "Everyone here is fucking high."

I laugh. "Should we join them?"

"I don't do drugs," she says. "You know that."

"You also don't drink that often and I saw you chugging High Noon less than an hour ago."

"Don't confuse me with facts, Cyrus."

Cody and I went to the Griffith Observatory this spring, when I was out here visiting Loyola, before we ended up in his bedroom downstairs, in a cramped twin bed across from his brother's, skateboards and wake boards and Cody's surfboard taking up all the space on the carpeting. I think Cody wanted more to happen than the kissing but I didn't want to ruin it, reconnecting like we did, or to put extra pressure on the decision to move out here, if something did happen between us. But I think I kind of regret it. I'm turning eighteen in two weeks and it feels late.

"Cyrus, can I ask you a question?" Mindy says.

"Sure."

"What's up with Jeff?"

"Huh?"

"You know." She reaches for my arm. "He doesn't talk to you for forever and all of a sudden he decides to come with us. What's up with that?"

I laugh. When she says it like that it does sound ridiculous. "I asked him the same thing on the beach."

"And what did he say?"

She's dressed in shorts and a long-sleeved shirt, an odd choice for the weather, but she says even a double dose of SPF60 doesn't protect her skin from the wrath of the sun, which sounds like a sci-fi fantasy on Netflix.

"He said he came because I asked him to."

"I see." The music ebbs and fades in the background of our conversation, laughter from the upper deck tumbling down the stairs. "You know, I hate to say it, but I'm starting to feel sorry for Jeff."

"You are?"

"Yeah, you know. He seems so different. More mature, which is good, but also muted. Like his whole personality has faded." I know what she means but I want her to say it. "And it's crazy, you know. You're moving to California and I'm going to Columbia and Sharane is already at Princeton."

She folds her legs beneath her on the couch, so her feet touch my hip. She leans her head against my shoulder.

"After this trip," she says. "Jeff's just going back."

She closes her eyes on my shoulder and I don't last long before I close mine too. Thinking of Jeff.

"Cyrus!"

I wake up to find Jeff and Cody stumbling down the stairs, one arm above the other arm, around each other's necks. I blink to think. Or to see.

"What are you doing down here?" Cody says. The even layer of stubble on his head looks blond in the rooftop lights. It brightens his eyes.

"Cy, have you tried Cody's weed?" Jeff says. "It's so mellow."

"I told you, man," Cody says, his arm stuck around Jeff's neck, clinging to it. "California weed is the best weed. There's no comparison."

"Absolutely," Jeff says, ducking out from under Cody's grip and squeezing onto the couch beside me. Mindy is asleep on my other side.

"Is she okay?" Cody says.

I'm not sure how long we were sleeping or why the stars disappeared from the sky.

"She doesn't usually drink this much," I say, touching her arm to make sure she's still alive and she turns sideways, her knees bent, the long sleeve shirt bunched around her neck. I think she's snoring.

"Mindy Won blackout drunk is not something I thought I'd see in this lifetime," Jeff says. Cody laughs even though he's barely talked to her all night. Or me.

"Jeff wants to go to the concert tomorrow," Cody says.

"What concert?"

"Oh shit—I didn't tell you," Cody says. "Japandroids are playing at Huntington Beach. My friend Laura is going. It's free."

"Japandroids? No way." I turn to Jeff. His smile keeps changing colors in the Christmas lights spread about the deck.

"You want to go?" Cody says.

"Are you fucking kidding me?" Mindy says, sitting up in her seat. "The droids from Canada that were made in Japan? Oh, we are going."

Cody and Jeff laugh at the same time.

"Awesome," Cody says. "Well, I'll check with Laura but I'm pretty sure they're on late so you could come by here and I'll drive us down. It's like half an hour away."

I nod a bunch of times because the only concert I've ever seen was Joyce Manor with Jeff, unless you count the two shows Sharane and Mindy dragged me to, for forgettable pop bands in downtown Harrisburg last summer. Which don't count. And my campus is only a few miles from the places in downtown L.A. where all the hardcore bands play. I can't wait.

"Who's Laura?" Mindy says.

"Oh, she's my friend," Cody says. "We met this summer surfing. She's up by the bar." He points to the purple umbrella hanging over the walkway and blocking our view. The rest of his friends at the party are surfers he's befriended or girls from his school.

"Is she the girl with the hair?" Mindy says, pulling on her hair.

"She has hair," Cody says and Mindy reaches out to slap him but she doesn't move from the couch. "And yes, she dyed a red streak that looks ridiculous but she doesn't listen to me."

"Your hair looks ridiculous," Mindy says.

Cody laughs, shifting his leg back onto the stairs.

"Yeah. I was telling Cyrus the barber cut it too short."

"I think it looks good," Jeff says and I think I strain my neck spinning so quick between Cody and Jeff, wondering what else they were doing on the rooftop besides smoking. I get kind of crazy when Jeff talks about boys. Apparently. "Just, it's hardcore, you know."

"Cool," Cody says.

"You should get a tattoo," Mindy says, leaning over me and squeezing closer to Jeff.

"I've been thinking of it," Cody says. "Maybe a surfboard?" He looks at me and I don't think I react but he adds, "No, that's lame."

"I almost got a tattoo this summer in Manhattan," Mindy says. "We went to the shop and went through all the options in the booklets but what I wanted was pretty specific so I needed to have it drawn first and that seemed like too much effort."

"A tattoo of what?" Cody asks, stepping over to her. The stars are back in the sky, the cloud cover clearing as fast as it came.

"Well, I know this is might sound ridiculous, but I've always been a huge Naruto fan and now I'm a Boruto fan and long story short, it's the symbol on their forehead protectors."

Cody glances at me because he's not into anime, not that I am really, but I watch with Mindy at her house sometimes. Her mother thinks that it's "witchcraft," the way the characters shoot lightning and fly across the sky, but she stopped trying to fight it because "your friend Mindy never listens to me."

I hear a flash bang and an explosion of noise before fireworks shoot straight up to the sky, a blast of rocket-fueled light, yellows and reds and purples and blues exploding out from the center, thirty feet above us, spreading out in slow motion before fading in a cloud of smoke.

Cody spins for the stairs. "Fuck! I told them not to set off fireworks from the rooftop!" He rushes up to the upper deck as another comet crack precedes two more flashes, shorter bursts of white sparks that dissipate quicker.

"Cody's a good guy," Jeff says, leaning into me on the couch.

"Thanks," I say, even though it's a weird thing to say.

"I wish I could stay out here," Jeff says. "This place is amazing."

"Why don't you?"

"Huh?"

"I mean—" I glance to my right to see if Mindy is listening but her eyes are closed again. "You don't have to fly back on Monday if you don't want to. You said you didn't start school until Thursday or Friday, right?"

Other voices are shouting from the rooftop and Jeff's eyes are alight in the glowing bulbs.

"I do have work on Tuesday," Jeff says. "And where would I stay?"

"I don't know," I say. "My dorm?"

"I'm sure your roommate would love that."

"He seemed cool when we met on FaceTime," I say. "He probably wouldn't mind."

Jeff bites his lower lip, scratching the side of his head beneath the baseball cap he donned tonight, the shaggy hair slipping out the sides.

"You really want to show up with some other dude on your first week of school?"

"You're not some other dude," I say. Possibly out loud, but I can't hear myself with the fireworks going off again, followed by a rush of people down the wooden steps coming straight at us. A huge plume of smoke rises from the rooftop.

Laura with the red-dyed streak screams "Fire!" and grabs my hand, pulling me up from the couch. I release to reach back for Mindy, shaking her awake, and Jeff helps me lift her off the cushions. The momentum carries us down the stairs to the fire escape, all the way down to the street.

Everyone who isn't Jeff or Mindy or me evacuates to their cars, escaping the party without ramifications. Cody's still upstairs, putting out the fire I think, as Mindy bends down to take a seat, slumping on the sidewalk at the curb. We've been awake for at least twenty-four hours when you consider the time zone change, and my legs start to shake as Jeff calls for an Uber on my phone.

"I'm so sorry," Cody says when he emerges from the house. "I told my asshole friends not to fuck with fireworks up there."

"What happened?" Jeff says.

"One of the bar stools did not survive."

"Are you in trouble?" I say.

Cody shakes his head. "Probably."

"I'm sorry."

"It's okay, it's not your fault." He steps closer to me on the sidewalk. "I'm just glad you came."

"To the party?" I say. "Or to California?"

"Both." He steps forward and kisses me. Right on the lips in front of Jeff. And he follows with a hug, short and quick but sweet.

"The Uber's here," Jeff announces and I turn away from Cody but I don't see any cars where Jeff is pointing, just the empty street a few blocks from the beach. We help Mindy off the curb.

"Well, thanks for coming," Cody says. "And assuming my dad doesn't notice that his rooftop deck was on fire— Japandroids tomorrow?"

I look to Jeff but he's walking up the street to the Uber and I'm holding onto Mindy, her body limp in my arms.

"Do you need help cleaning up?" I say.

"It's fine," Cody says, checking his watch. "I have a feeling Dad's not coming home."

We hug again—or he hugs me, because I'm holding onto Mindy, and I shake her awake as he pulls away.

"Text me when you get to the hotel, okay?" he says.

I tell him I will as our fingers release, but then I climb into the backseat with Jeff and his knee touches mine the whole ride back to the hotel.

TWENTY-NINE

"STAY STILL," JEFF SAYS.

We purchased aloe in the hotel lobby—for severe burns, the package said, and every touch is by turns soothing and excruciating. Crimson red circles my ankles and feet. I yank away from him, the pain too much to take.

"You're impossible," he says, standing up and stepping over to the wall of windows at the edge of our room, tossing the minty gel onto the mattress.

"I know. But it hurts," I say, elongating the vowel in a mincing whine.

The sunburn didn't really hurt, at least in the part of the day when I was still sober, but after the Uber ride home and getting Mindy to her room, I took off my shoes and socks and noticed the awful shade of red on the tops of both feet. The pain came in waves.

"You know what might help?" Jeff says, rooting through his backpack set on a plush green sofa by the wall of windows. This hotel is Dad's go-to-place when he's flying home from LAX because you can see downtown L.A. in the distance, the sparkling lights this late at night.

"Cody's friend gave me this," Jeff says, pulling a joint out of the front pocket. "I was going to save it for later, or maybe fly it back home but I bet it will help with the sunburn."

He takes a seat on the mattress across from me. The room has two queen beds easily more comfortable than any of our beds at home and a 60-inch flat-screen on the near wall, the green felt lounger in the corner. The shades are open but I can only see the sky from where I'm lying, not the city, my feet stretched out in extreme pain.

"I thought you didn't smoke anymore."

"I don't," Jeff says, twirling the ends between his fingers. "But she gave it to me—that girl Laura—" He scratches at the back of his neck and laughs. "I think I've lost my tolerance."

"Do you like her?"

"What?"

"Nothing," I say, pushing up from the mattress, so that my legs drop off the side. "You want to smoke it?"

He nods and we head to the bathroom to avoid breaking hotel rules about smoking, turning on the fan and running the shower at high heat to create enough steam to mask the scent.

Jeff sits on the toilet—lid down—and I hop onto the counter next to the sink, crimson feet dangling off the edge.

"Umm…" He holds out the joint and indicates without speaking that he doesn't have anything to light it with but I don't either—neither of us smokes anymore. He offers to run to the lobby to where we bought the aloe but I decline.

"We don't need to smoke," I say. "This is cool just hanging."

"But your feet," he says.

"The aloe's working, I think," I say. "Thank you for forcing it on me."

He smiles. The recessed lights in the ceiling highlight his tanned skin.

"Thanks for inviting me," Jeff says. "I needed a vacation. More than I realized."

"It was my dad's idea," I say.

"You mentioned that."

"Yeah. I mean, we hadn't talked or hung out in so long I didn't—"

"Think of me." He smiles again.

"Maybe." I smile back. "But my dad laid on all this stuff about losing his closest friends when he was young and I—"

Jeff nods as the steam escapes from the shower stall, up to the ceiling tiles. I think to shut off the faucet now that we don't need it anymore but I don't want to move. This is nice, sitting here with Jeff.

"It sucks what happened to us," he says, after a while. His eyes are a little dulled and his cheeks aren't quite the same, the whiskers filling the space where his dimples used to be, the lines drawn sharper, less rounded. "What the fuck happened to us?" He laughs, like he's just throwing it out there but I wonder if he thinks about it. As much as I think about it.

"Well, you did call me a 'faggot' and punch me in the face."

I deadpan it as best as I can to put it out there without animosity, my teeth clenched and the pain in my feet slipping up my legs to my knees.

"I know, I know." He drops his head to the floor. "That was unforgiveable."

"No," I say. "It wasn't. I would have forgiven you."

He looks up at me, his hair a tangled mess that he pulls back from his face. He left his hat in the other room.

"What do you mean?"

I clutch the edge of the counter, my tongue pushing out from the side of my teeth, needing to speak. Mindy told me not to press.

"If you apologized back then. Or even talked me again. I kept texting." The steam fills the room with a gauzy haze. "You never responded."

"I know," Jeff says. "It's pretty hard to come back from calling your best friend the F word when he's gay."

The steady stream on the white brick walls of the shower get louder and the overhead fan is too weak to clear the vapor, the humidity choking me.

"But I would have forgiven you. I was reaching out back then because I didn't want to lose you as a friend," I say and maybe it's the sunburn or the exhaustion or the fact that I can't actually see his face through the haze but I don't hold back, like I normally do. "I thought we could still be more than friends, Jeff. I still wanted to. You know that."

"Yeah, right," he says. "Don't humor me."

"What?"

"Nothing." He stands up and steps across the tiled floor for the shower.

"What are you talking about, Jeff?"

"Just that you're not innocent in all of this, Cy. You're as much responsible for the end of our friendship as me."

"How?"

"Oh come on, Cy, don't play dumb."

"I'm not," I say. I'm not. I let go of the counter I've been clutching and feel my fingers forming fists. "What are you talking about?"

"You know what I'm talking about."

Jeff opens and closes the shower door in quick repetition. The steam floats in a plume above my head.

"I have no idea what you're talking about," I say, jumping off the counter on my sunburned feet. Maybe I haven't forgiven him yet.

"You don't know anything you might have done before the whole punching incident—and it was a glancing blow, not a hard punch—" He shakes his head and turns back to the shower. "But I'm not defending that. I can't defend that. And I said I was sorry. But you should be too."

"Sorry for what?"

The steam is spreading water down my skin. I don't know what's happening.

"Two words, Cyrus. Two words." He spins from the shower to face me. "Court. Knee."

"Courtney?"

"Yeah, your boyfriend. Ring a bell?"

"Boyfriend? We went out for like a week," I say, noticing the mirror to register my reaction but it's clouded in the billowing mist. "And that was after you punched me."

Jeff steps back into the shower and the spray wets his face.

"Forget it."

I don't know what he's talking about but if he thinks me dating Courtney after he punched me in the face and cut off all contact is me breaking up the friendship, I—

"Please," I say.

He turns around again. Close to me. The water rolls down his cheeks.

"Cy, when I saw you that Christmas, after I got sent away to that Christian prison and I thought you hadn't waited for me—I didn't know you had written me and I sure as fuck didn't think you'd waited for me because when I came home that Christmas and turned on my phone for the first time in months, what do you think I saw at the top of my Insta feed?" He breathes out before he speaks. "You kissing Courtney."

I blink. I think I blink. I don't speak.

"So yeah. I get how you 'waited' for me," he says with the air quotes, "and you had a plan to help me run away and all. But as soon as I was gone you sure as hell didn't wait for me."

Sharane caught us kissing and ended up posting the picture by accident with a bunch of photos from the party. She took it down as soon as she realized. I guess it was too late.

"It wasn't what it looked like," I say. "We were not dating at the time. I just met him that night."

"That doesn't make it any better."

Jeff steps past me, over to the sink, running his fingers through the water.

"Yes. I'm sorry. I shouldn't have kissed him but I hadn't heard from you since you came back and—" I hesitate, waiting for him to turn. He doesn't turn. I can't see his face in the stream-shrouded glass. "I thought you hated me, the way I wrote all those letters and you never responded."

"I never got your letters, Cy. You know that. Don't you know what it was like—to go from a normal life hanging with you and our band and a concert you convinced me to go to that I never should have gone to and all of a sudden I'm in freaking religious classes with counseling half the damn day and the other half is hard freaking labor with no Internet at all, all because I went to a Joyce Manor concert and you kissed me in the backseat—"

"You kissed me back—"

"I know," he says. "I know. But then Mindy hit a dog and I got sent away."

"Jeff."

I reach out for his shoulder but he shakes free and I see his face. Crying.

"I had to freaking fake it, Cy." The snot is bubbling from his nose, the heat from the shower pouring moisture down our faces. "Pretend I loved Jesus and accept him as my Lord and Savior, just to survive, you know. And after a while I accepted it, it was easier that way. But it fucks you up, you know." He rubs his eyes with the palm of his hand and backs toward the shower again. "Makes you doubt everything you've ever known. And I hated myself, Cy. I really hated myself. And I guess I took it out on you."

I listen because I need to listen, as he leans into the shower again, turning the faucet off. I stand by the sink and wait. The silence is deafening.

"I'm sorry I called you the F word, Cy, that crossed a line and I can't take it back. But it killed me, seeing you kissing that kid. After everything."

"I'm sorry," I say. "I'm so sorry, Jeff."

"It's too late," Jeff says, the tears and the sweat mixing together on his face. "I couldn't take any more pain."

THIRTY

WE CALLED MY DAD when we woke up, to see if he could get Jeff's plane ticket changed. He wanted to go home. Today.

It was too expensive to change last minute so the best he could offer was earlier tomorrow, on the same flight as Mindy. Jeff said that was fine but then he stopped speaking so now neither of us is speaking and I never should have invited him out here this weekend. I don't know what Dad was thinking.

Mindy took charge of the agenda today—heavy on tourist destinations—because she wasn't about spending the rest of the trip with the two of us arguing without some kind of distraction. I told her what happened—as best I could remember because we were getting along so well all day and at Cody's party and then all the past came up again and now we're not speaking. I don't know what I was thinking.

"I'm going in," Mindy says in front of the Cartier store, the sunlight reflecting off the wall of glass at the entrance. We've been window-shopping on Rodeo Drive, watching all the tall women with short expensive handbags spinning in and out of shops from our spots on the sidewalk. We have yet to venture inside.

"Really?" I say.

"Yeah, my mom always wanted a Cartier bracelet," Mindy says. "Back in Korea that was one of her dreams—coming to America and getting enough money to buy a Cartier bracelet." I look at her strange. "I know, I know, it's an immigrant cliché, but I just want to look. She'd kill me if I didn't take a look."

"Will they even let you in?"

Multiple muscled security guards are gathered inside the wall of glass.

"Why the hell not?" she says.

"I'm not sure you're allowed to just browse in a store like that," I say. "Dressed like this."

"Speak for yourself," Mindy says, spreading her arms wide. She's wearing a white T-shirt with gold leaf imprints over her breasts and khaki shorts, SPF60 covering every inch of exposed skin. "I look good."

Jeff laughs, for the first time today.

"See, Jeff agrees," she says. "You coming with?"

"Sure," Jeff says.

"This is a bad idea," I say. Because this is a bad idea. Mindy glares at me.

"Well listen, Mr. Grumpy Negative Man. I am on Rodeo Drive in Beverly Hills and we've been walking around for an hour without going into a single store and I am not missing out on the opportunity to get a picture of myself inside Cartier, possibly wearing a bracelet. For my mother." She pauses like she's finished but picks up again before I speak. "And you may not be aware of this, Cyrus, because you are not fully aware of women in general." She rolls her eyes beneath her oversized sunglasses—I can tell by her tone. "But some women enjoy the look of expensive jewelry. That's the whole reason a store like this exists. So go ahead and wait out here in the heat while Jeff and I go inside, and if I end up getting arrested for trying on a fucking bracelet, tell my mom I love her!"

She trails off as she opens the massive glass and gold door and waves for Jeff to follow. He shrugs and disappears inside.

Cody texted when we got to Beverly Hills, telling me Japandroids would be on late so we could come over whenever. I tried to ask Mindy when she wanted to meet him but she was asking the Uber driver to drop us off "where all the rich bitches shop."

And Jeff wasn't speaking.

I've been trying not to think of it, why Jeff is still upset about what happened twenty months ago despite how stupid it was—I mean I could have cleared it up with one sentence about how much rum Sharane's uncle put into the coquitos, and it's not like we were exclusive or anything—he emphatically denied any feelings for me after our first kiss that summer. So, I don't get why he expected me to wait for him to come back from that religious school and tell me he had feelings for me all along, when he specifically wasn't responding to my letters, which I know now he never got them so I can't blame him for that, but the thing is I was waiting for him. Coquitos aside, I was waiting for him. And I would have forgiven him, even after he cut off all contact with me. But he woke up this morning and told me he wanted to leave.

It's killing me.

Get your ass in here right now.

Mindy's text gets me moving, through the huge glass doors with the security guards eyeing my board shorts and

Billabong shirt, so I dip my head and slip over to where she and Jeff are huddled with a salesperson around a small glass table, shiny gold and diamonds on multiple levels of shelves locked inside.

"Cyrus!" Mindy says. "This is Cyrus."

The woman behind the counter smiles. She has straight blonde hair tied up in a ponytail and doesn't look much older than us.

"Hi Cyrus," she says. "I'm Jessica."

"Jess—do you mind if I call you Jess?" Mindy says. "She lives in Manhattan Beach and her brother goes to the high school there."

"Mira Costa," Jessica says. "Mindy says you have a friend who goes there?"

"Yes. Cody Martin."

"Hmm, sounds familiar. One of my brother's friends is a Cody. But it's a common name in Manhattan Beach."

She lets out a nervous laugh. I glance at Jeff, watching the security guard closest to us.

"Jess was going to let me try on one of the bracelets," Mindy says. "But they need to call security and her manager over before they can open the case, so I'm just looking."

"Well, that's for the ones up here," Jessica says, pointing to the collection on the top shelf closest to the glass, the diamonds sparkling under the bright lights of the store. "You could try on one of these if you want."

She points to a lower shelf with bracelets that aren't as nice, I guess, or just don't have as many diamonds.

Mindy is right—I don't pay much attention to what women are into, like jewelry and stuff, which may be strange for a gay guy but I'm not that much into what gay guys are into. Except other gay guys, I guess.

"How much is that one?" Mindy says, pointing to a silver bracelet at the corner of the bottom shelf.

"Oh, let me see," Jessica says, opening the case with a key attached to a lanyard around her neck. She pulls out the bracelet carefully, unwrapping and finding the price tag on the underside. "It's $999."

"That's not bad," Mindy says. Like she has that kind of money.

"Do you want to try it on?"

"Sure," she says, nodding a bunch of times and sticking out her arm. "Cyrus, take a picture."

"I'm sorry, Mindy, we don't allow pictures," Jessica says.

"Really?"

Mindy sticks out her lower lip. The security guard Jeff is watching takes a step closer.

"I'm sorry," she says.

"It's okay," Mindy says. "I guess I'll have to verbally describe my experience to my poor old mother. Who doesn't hear very well."

Jessica grits her teeth as she turns Mindy's wrist over, placing the bracelet on. Mindy's mom hears fine. Her daughter is insane.

"Hey, Jeff, take a look," she says, showing off the bracelet. It's silver and stringy with gold woven through. "Jeff!"

He shifts his focus from the security guard.

"Um, can we please have you not start a fight like at the Food Bank?" Mindy says. "I'm pretty certain the security guards here are packing."

Jessica's eyes grow wide and she forces another laugh.

"Just kidding," Mindy says. "But you need take this off me before I attempt an escape and go down in a hail of bullets on Rodeo Drive."

Jessica laughs for real this time and Mindy looks at me.

"Cyrus, please," Mindy says. "I'm using my best material right now. Can you lighten up?"

"I'm sorry," I say.

"They're usually more fun than this, Jess," Mindy says. "But they're kind of having a moment today."

Jessica puts the bracelet back into the case and locks it, returning the key to its place beneath her blouse.

"And here's what's ridiculous—they aren't speaking to each other because of shit that happened two years ago. Back me up here, Jess. That's insane, right?"

"It does sound insane," she says.

"See—I knew we'd be friends."

Mindy reaches across the counter but Jess pulls back, again with her teeth clenched. The security guard coughs behind us.

"Sorry, my bad," Mindy says.

"Maybe we should get going," I say.

"Not until you guys make up. I told you up I am not spending the rest of this gorgeous day in L.A. with you two idiots fighting."

I look to Jeff and he looks back but nobody speaks.

"Wow," Mindy says, sunglasses off now. "Okay, Jess, I'm going to have to get your opinion on this."

There aren't any other customers in the store, so I guess it's okay she's spending so much time with us even though we're clearly not buying anything.

"These boys were the best of friends a couple years back and then they kissed in the backseat of my car and I got into an accident—which was really tragic and people got injured. Namely me," she says, pointing to her ribs and wincing, the way she does anytime she's looking for sympathy from me. "But I don't blame anyone but myself and no one needs to be blamed for anything that happened after, except they stopped being friends and they both want the other to admit they were the cause for the end of the friendship when it's obvious to anyone who's paying attention that they're in love with each other and neither of them wants to admit it."

My face turns red in the bright lights of the store and I look from Jeff to the security guard. He can shoot me now.

"Isn't it obvious, Jess?"

She contemplates, looking back and forth between us.

"I can see that."

"Of course," Mindy says. "But that's some long-term shit that isn't going to resolve itself today—which we have all agreed!" She turns to me, glaring. "And we all start college this week and won't even see each other again until Thanksgiving, which sucks so hard I don't even need an apology for you guys acting like jerks on my very first trip to Beverly Hills, as long as you stop right now and agree to get along."

She looks at us both at the same time somehow.

"Please." She reaches out for me and I nod so she looks to Jeff.

"Both of you."

He nods too.

"Perfect," Mindy says. "And Jess, I know you don't have your phone but I need your Insta handle because I am going to stalk you and become your friend for real because I think I'm kind of done with men."

Jessica laughs.

"Even the gay ones are a freaking pain in the ass."

I glance at Jeff again and he hasn't run away, even after Mindy outed him in front of Jessica. Maybe he is gay which

THE BEST HARDCORE BAND IN PA   253

is confusing to me, because he mentioned dating some girl before our flight and I guess I have a bunch of questions for him but I can't ask anything that might ruin it again and I don't want to ruin it for Mindy.

"So, no to the bracelets then?" Jessica asks.

"Oh, god no, Jess," Mindy says. "These prices are ridiculous. But when I get my law degree, I'll be back here, okay?"

"Okay," Jessica says, with a wide white smile.

"You guys okay?" Mindy says, squeezing my hand and whispering. Jeff walks ahead.

I want to say yes, I need to say yes. But it's not up to me.

It's hard not to think what could have happened with Jeff if I hadn't kissed Courtney.

THIRTY-ONE

"GO GO GO!"

Jeff darts behind me from the sidewalk to the street, impatient with the gaggle of tourists choking our pathways, so I follow him through the middle of traffic with cars shooting fumes into our faces as we take on the streets of L.A. on powered wheeled scooters. It's amazing.

We went to the Walk of Fame after Rodeo Drive but it was pretty disappointing. We didn't know most of the celebrities, so I was Googling while Mindy and Jeff were making fun of the randomness, like someone you'd heard of then three in a row from ancient television, and yes, we passed Donald J. Abomination To Society and Mindy had to keep Jeff from pulling out his dick to take a piss while I recorded it for Instagram. Then Jeff found the scooters.

"I think it's this way!" he shouts as he turns down a side street.

We're riding at full speed—or Jeff is. I'm keeping a thick grip on the handles of this motorized death trap Jeff keeps swinging in and out of traffic. Mindy passed on the scooters as emphatically as one can decline, but she also needed to pee and refused at the restaurant where we ate lunch—"Did you see the bathrooms? No of course you didn't, because boys do not give one second's thought to what girls have to deal with on a daily basis." She took an Uber to the nearest Starbucks and texted the address.

"Watch the fuck out!" I hear someone scream as Jeff escapes a collision with an irate SUV driver cursing at top speed. He swerves in between the parked cars and the curb then back into traffic and I follow, further behind, lifting my hand to apologize as Jeff crosses the block onto the shaded sidewalk of an unnamed side street, coming to a stop.

"I'm lost," he says as I catch up to him. His hair is a feathered mess from the wind, the stray strands attached to his forehead with sweat. He whips out his phone because we've already passed at least four Starbucks and none of them are the address Mindy texted.

"Okay," he says, pointing. "It looks like if we keep going along this street, we'll hit La Cienega and then we make a right and it should be right there."

The maps are spinning as he spins the phone in his hand so it's tough to see but I nod. Things have been good between us since the Cartier store, like last night is forgotten. Jeff says he needs to pee too.

"Let's go."

He jumps off the sidewalk into the street and there's more honking from the cars because none of these streets are made for these kind of scooters, but you're not supposed to ride them on the sidewalks so it's unclear who allowed this mode of transport when all the drivers are pissed off at our presence and the traffic out here is insane. Starbucks appears like a green golden goddess in the distance but we have a massive highway to traverse to get there so we wait at the light. Jeff tamps down his hair, sticking up in multiple directions, and smiles, that sweet perfect smile.

"What's up with all the rainbow flags?" he says, pointing at the banners attached to all the streetlights and signposts around us.

"I think we're in WeHo."

"We who?"

"WeHo. West Hollywood."

"I know what it is," he says, then, "Oh."

We make our way across the highway, parking the scooters on the sidewalk, and Jeff makes a beeline to the bathroom as I spot Mindy with her coffee on the opposite side. I place an order for Jeff and myself and take a seat across from her by the windows.

"This was not the closest Starbucks."

"No," Mindy says.

"Is there a reason you gave this address then?"

"I asked the Uber driver to take me to the Starbucks in WeHo," she says. "Because I'm not going to L.A. with two gay guys and not come through."

I look over my shoulder for Jeff but there's a line four deep at the bathroom.

"Do you really think Jeff is gay?"

"Of course," she says, sipping on her flat white. "You don't?"

"I mean, maybe," I say. I pull on my T-shirt to keep the sweat from pooling around my stomach. "But he hasn't said anything."

"Jesus, Cyrus. He told you the whole reason you got into a fight two years ago was because he saw you and Courtney kissing." She stares at me until I blink, but I don't want to speak. I want her to say it first. "Don't you think that means he's into you? And don't you think if he's into you, he's probably into other guys?"

"But he had a girlfriend," I say. "Last year."

"Well, you and I went on a date once too," she says. "Sometimes it takes a while for people to come out, you know."

"Or maybe he's bi?" I say.

"Sure. Sure," she says, glancing past me to make sure Jeff's not coming. "But here's the thing, Cyrus, it doesn't matter, right? Whether he had feelings for you and whether you had feelings for him, I mean it's a shame you couldn't connect and I do think that time away helped him, but that's all in the past and you have to let it go."

"But what if I can't?" I say. Because what if I can't.

"Cyrus." Mindy sighs, cupping her hands around her coffee on the table between us. "You decided to go to school all the way across the country at least in part to be close to Cody and now you're sitting here pining over Jeff, and the last freaking thing you're going to do is move across the country for the boy you've been talking to long-distance and then turn around and do the long-distance thing with a boy from Dallastown. That's not what we are going to do."

I laugh. When she says it like that it does sound ridiculous. Except.

"Order for Serious. Caramel Macchiatos," the barista calls out.

"I think that's you," Mindy says.

"What?"

"I got 'em," Jeff says, out of the bathroom and over to the counter for our drinks. I don't know if he was close enough to hear anything.

"We're putting a pin in this," Mindy says, lifting her fingers like she's putting a pin into corkboard. "We'll discuss later, okay?"

Jeff sets down our drinks on the wobbly black table and Mindy shifts in her seat so he can slide in beside her.

"You still like Caramel Macchiatos, right?" I say to Jeff, trying to avoid Mindy's glare.

"Of course," Jeff says. "Did you get iced with an extra shot of espresso?"

"Of course."

"You know me well," Jeff says.

"Oh my god, get a room," Mindy says and Jeff looks at her strange. "Just kidding!" She smiles.

I can feel the sweat pooling at the back of my neck, not just from the scooter ride.

"Cool shirt, dude."

A tall guy with a flock of pink hair comments on Jeff's attire—the Fucked Up T-shirt with two of the letters blacked out because I guess you can't curse on clothing you wear in public. I've heard of the band—they're like "hard core" hardcore, lots of screaming at insane volumes that makes Japandroids seem tame. I didn't know Jeff was into them.

"Thanks," Jeff says.

"They played here, when was it?" Pink Hair asks his friend.

"I don't know your bands," the friend says and steps over to the coffee line. Pink Hair shakes his head and steps closer to us.

"Last fall, at the Teragram, right? Did you guys go?"

"We're not from here," Jeff says, sipping at his iced macchiato. The chatty guy looks older than us, like early 20s, with spiky pink hair and the remnants of a beard, regular-colored not fluorescent.

"Where are you from?" he asks.

Jeff looks at me confused, like why is this guy talking to us.

"Pennsylvania," Mindy says.

"Oh yeah? Which part?"

None of us responds because people don't just walk up to strangers and talk to them in Pennsylvania.

"I grew up there," Pink Hair continues. "Outside Philly. In Bensalem."

"That's cool," Mindy says. "We're from Dallastown."

"Where's that?" Pink Hair says.

"In between Lancaster and Harrisburg," Jeff says.

"Oh, okay." He looks between Jeff and me. "And what brings you out here?"

His friend comes back after ordering their drinks, his plain grey Tee stretched tight against his chest, which is the theme of most of the guys in the Starbucks, now that I'm noticing.

"Cyrus is starting college tomorrow," Jeff says.

"Oh yeah?" Pink Hair turns to me. "Where at? Brad went to USC."

"Um, Loyola," I say, a little embarrassed because USC was my number one choice but I didn't get in.

"Awesome," this Brad says, sipping on a maroon-colored drink that isn't coffee. "I think our neighbor's daughter goes there."

"Who?" Pink Hair says and they drift into a conversation about whether or not their neighbor has a daughter of college age.

"So, are there any gay bars around here you'd recommend?" Mindy asks. She just asks it.

"Excuse me?" Brad says.

"I'm sorry, I meant no offense but—"

"Oh honey, no offense is taken," Brad says. "We're actually going to Gym Bar after this. You guys want to come?"

"Sure," Mindy says. Pink Hair laughs.

"We're not twenty-one," I say. Because we're not twenty-one.

"It's three o'clock in the afternoon, sweetie," Brad says. "Ain't nobody carding."

"For real?" Mindy says and she turns to me all excited because it's been a goal of hers to go to a gay bar with me. At the start of the summer, we borrowed Sharane's car and trekked down to Philly for an under-18 dance party in the Gayborhood, only to find out the club had closed. We wandered through the streets watching guys and girls stumbling in and out of bars and kissing on the sidewalks, all sloppy and drunk. It was kind of fun.

"Absolutely," Brad says. "And what is your name, darling?"

"I'm Mindy," she says. "And this is Cyrus and Jeff."

"And none of you have ever been to WeHo?" Pink Hair says.

We shake our heads.

"Interesting. Well, I'm Oliver and this is Brad," Pink Hair says. "And if you guys want to see the real sights in California, you're more than welcome to join us."

"You want to go?" Mindy says, to me I think, but I look to Jeff. I don't know if he's gay or he's bi or none of the above but I don't want to force him to do something he isn't ready for yet. He shrugs, which I take as a yes. Brad laughs.

"We are fully corrupting minors," he says.

"Are you guys at least eighteen?" Oliver asks. "I don't want to literally be corrupting minors."

"Of course," Mindy says, and I nod because I'm turning in two weeks and I don't want to be the youngest person who ever came through WeHo.

"Excellent," Brad says with his too-tight shirt and pressed white shorts. They head for the door with their drinks and we follow.

"Are you okay with this?" I ask Jeff, pulling him back to me. He shrugs again.

"You sure?" I say, maybe more for myself. Like Mindy, I've wanted to try going inside a gay bar, but only when I was more prepared or better dressed and at least not covered in sweat from a scooter ride through the streets.

"We could go for a little," Jeff says, sucking down the rest of the macchiato.

He steps forward in the bright sun of the sidewalk, trailing Mindy and the local strangers, laughing ahead of us. I follow.

THIRTY-TWO

"Oliver has a friend."

"I know. His name is Brad," Mindy says. "We met him."

"No, another friend," I say, returning to my seat on the patio.

"I'm pretty sure Oliver is friends with everyone here."

"Relax," I say. She smiles.

The patio is pretty empty, just another two tables besides us, the crowd inside hiding from the sun. We're several shots in—or Mindy is, and I brought us water after peeing in a bathroom that appeared to be a converted closet—a couple urinals and one nasty toilet, no stall attached. I wasn't sure whether I was supposed to lock the door but I was afraid to touch the lock so I peed as quick as I could and used my elbows for the faucet in the sink.

"Well anyway, Oliver's friend—I forget his name—"

"The one passing out the Jager shots?"

"Yes! Yes, him," I say.

"I've had four."

"Wait—what?" I must have miscounted.

"Well, I figure when in WeHo might as well… be a ho?" She laughs to herself. "I'm not sure where I was going with that joke but I'm not at all sober."

"I'm not sure how you're still standing."

"We're sitting, Cyrus," she says, pointing to her elevated stool. "How many have you had?"

My feet are dangling at our patio table and my mind is spinning with everything I've witnessed this afternoon. I left Jeff at the bar with Brad, surrounded by chiseled muscle dudes in ridiculously tight shirts, some of them dancing but the rest of them clustered in clusters of man-flesh and it's a lot, all at once. None of the guys are my type—they're too old or too muscular or both—but it's my first time inside a gay bar and I haven't exploded yet, so I'm taking it as a good sign.

"What about Oliver's friend?" Mindy says. "The shot guy."

"Right," I say, shielding my eyes from the sun over Mindy's head. "He asked if Jeff and I were dating."

"Uh huh." Mindy sets down her water and contemplates.

"What?" I say.

"We talked about this!" she says. "You are out here because of Cody, right? I mean, you didn't randomly choose a school nobody's heard of just to be close to the beach. I didn't even know you liked the beach." I laugh but she's not laughing. "Cyrus, you like him and he definitely likes you. I assume. I didn't really talk to him last night. That was my bad. I'm drinking too much. I need to stop."

I peek inside the bar to see if I can see Jeff, but with the sun so bright outside, I can't see anything.

"Oh my god, you're not even listening to me," Mindy says, super loud. "You are obsessed with Jeff, you know that, right?"

"That's what Courtney said when he broke up with me."

"Exactly," she says. The shot guy cruises past us with a tray of purple-colored Jagermeister, stopping at the neighboring table. Mindy stares him down before turning back. "I mean, I get it, you and Jeff have a history and you haven't actually dated Cody but you've known him for what—two years now—and he kissed you on the lips last night after the party. I think I remember that. Was I dreaming?"

"No." I shake my head.

"So go for it, Cyrus," she says. "He's out and he likes you and he's not all conflicted like Jeff—no offense, but—" She sighs. "I don't know. Do what you want."

I decided to apply to schools out here because of that summer trip with Dad and Angela and Cody, on the beach in Manhattan Beach. And I decided to come to Loyola after we kissed in his bedroom at his father's house in Hermosa. But I wanted to leave Dallastown—not just because of the excessive heat in August and the ridiculous winter snow, not just because everyone is judgmental in central PA, if you aren't into Jesus and you happen to like boys, the opposite of here, the opposite of this. But Jeff and I always talked about leaving and I wanted to leave with him. Then Jeff and me stopped being Jeff and me and it wasn't the same anymore, it was worse than before. Mindy is the best friend I could ever ask for, and Sharane and I became good friends but it wasn't the same once he left. I needed to leave.

"Wow. You are literally watching Jeff right now."

He's dancing at the edge of the room to a Madonna song, which is not something I thought I'd ever see, but if he's dancing inside a gay bar and he's admitted he had feelings for me—real feelings, not just drunken kisses, then maybe he's ready to come out. Maybe he already has. He smiles through the opening at me, his shaggy hair flopping around his face.

"It's fine. You're ignoring all of my advice, so I will stop offering and also this Jager guy needs to stop talking to those assholes and come back to me."

Lady Gaga comes on over the speakers and Jeff is still dancing, surrounded by muscled men, looking out onto the patio at me.

"Cyrus."

"Huh?"

"Jesus Christ, I'm getting another shot," she says and gets up from her stool.

"Wait—" I say, grabbing her arm. "Maybe you should calm down."

"Excuse me? You did not just tell me to calm down, did you?"

"No," I say. "I mean, not like that."

She frowns like she's mad—mad for real—and I look to Jeff for help but he's disappeared back into the dark of the bar.

"I meant you've had a lot of shots," I say. "Maybe hold off before another one."

"Okay, Dad," she says. "I don't actually have a dad because he was way too chicken shit to come to this country, thus abandoning my mother and me but that's a story for another time."

She tells that story all the time.

"I know I'm not your dad," I say. "But I want to make sure you're okay. You drank a lot last night and you're drinking again and I've never seen you drink this much before."

"Well Cyrus, you are more perceptive than expected," she says, which sounds offensive but maybe I didn't hear it right. "But I'm okay. I'm just—I'm a little stressed."

"About what?"

"Ugh." She sits back down on the stool, sipping at the water. "I'm starting college in two days—you are too, by the way—so I have concerns beyond which boy you'll hook up with this weekend."

"Oh my god."

"Sorry," she says. "Just—"

She points to two guys at the table next to us making out in broad daylight.

"Get a room!" I shout. Really, really low. Mindy laughs.

"But seriously, you have nothing to worry about. You're Mindy, you're awesome. You know you're awesome. You were the valedictorian of our class."

"Well, let me let you in on a little secret, Cyrus," Mindy says, leaning forward on the circular surface, thick black laminate stained with beer glass rings and Jagermeister. "The awesome is sometimes an illusion. You don't realize how much work it took to become valedictorian. Like, you know how you coasted through AP History by teaming on projects with me?"

"You noticed?" I say.

"Yes," she says. "And it's fine, Cyrus. I was happy to carry you, but someone had to do the work. That's why I didn't go out and party like Regina or Devin or some of our other friends. No offense to them, but it was hard fucking work. And it doesn't always come naturally to me. I'm not some super genius in math, for instance, but I get by because I work hard. And I'm afraid college is going to be too hard for me."

"Would you stop?" I say, reaching out for her arm. "You'll be fine."

"I know I'll be 'fine,'" she says. "I'm not going to fail out or anything, but what if I'm not at the top of my class? That's not something I'm prepared for. Sharane said she already has homework and a major project to do for psychology, which she was spending all day today doing instead of partying at gay bars like we are. And she's at Princeton, which no offense—Columbia is going to be much harder."

"It is?"

The Jager guy is back with more shots but I give him the nod to brush him away. I think that's what I did. I've never been to a bar before.

"I mean, Princeton is probably not any easier coursework-wise, it's just that I'll be in Manhattan and I'll want to go to all kinds of shows and clubs and I'll want to explore all the things I did this summer, but if I do all that I won't be number one in my class."

She dips her head and finishes off her water. She never talks about herself like this.

"First of all, I feel like you've left out some major details on what exactly happened in Manhattan this summer," I say. "Was there a boy involved?"

"What happens in Manhattan stays in Manhattan, Cyrus," she says, spinning her head around as the Jager guy walks away. "But what were you saying?"

"I was going to say that you don't have to be an overachiever at Columbia," I say. "You could just be an... achiever."

"Oh my god, Cyrus." She's up and out of her seat, waving the Jager guy back to us. "That is definitely the lamest thing you've ever said."

"I know. But I'm serious. You can do this. You're the one person in the world I have no doubt about. And you should have fun. It's nice to see you letting go this weekend. With your mother three thousand miles away."

"Do not bring her into it," Mindy says.

The sun isn't as bright anymore and I wonder how long we've been here. At a gay bar. My head has stopped spinning.

"I'm sure she doesn't care if you're not top of your class at Columbia," I say. "She just wants you to be happy."

"You have met my mom, right?" Another table grabs the Jager dude, the patio super crowded all of a sudden. "Happy is about seventeenth on the list of things she wants for me. Bringing home a nice Korean boy from a family she approves of is number one. But being the best at school—no matter what level of school—is a strong number two."

"Well, so what?" I say. "She's just your mother. If you disappoint her, she'll still love you. I'm sure my dad isn't happy I came out to school so far away but he's letting us use his credit card all weekend, so he can't be that upset."

Mindy dips her head.

"You need to call him."

"What?"

"You need to call him," Mindy says.

"I did," I say. "This morning."

We changed Jeff's flight to tomorrow morning, same as Mindy's. It's too soon, way too soon.

"No, I meant when you're out here. You need to call him. Like a lot."

"I will."

"No. Now I'm being serious, Cyrus." She grabs my hand on the stained black laminate. "Your dad pulled me aside when we were waiting for Jeff and he asked me to watch out for you this weekend. He's worried about you, Cyrus. So far from home."

I know he's worried. And I probably shouldn't have been so mad at him for not coming out here this weekend. If he were here, then Jeff wouldn't be here. So maybe Mindy's right.

"Okay, enough of this depressing talk," Mindy says. "We're in the middle of a gay bar in WeHo and I'm getting another shot."

She leaps over to Jager guy like a long-jumping Olympian as Jeff emerges from the bar. Brad and Oliver come crashing in behind. Laughing.

"What do you think of Gym Bar?" Oliver with the pink hair says, taking a seat.

"It's cool," I say. Jeff grabs Mindy's seat, next to me.

"This is one of the more casual bars on the strip," Oliver says. "You won't find many drag queens or leather freaks here, not even on a Saturday. But we can head to The Abbey later if that's your scene."

"Oh," Jeff says. "I think we have to leave soon."

"You are not leaving," Brad says. "Where do you have to go that's better than this?"

"We have a concert," I say.

"Oh my god," Brad says. "Baby gays are so precious."

I'm not sure what he means but it wouldn't be fair to Cody to back out at the last instant unless—I guess I could invite him here. He said he'd been to WeHo on College Night once or twice but it wasn't his scene.

"All right, we need to know," Oliver says. "You boys are boyfriends or just friends? And if not boyfriends then why not, which one of you is pretending to be straight?"

"Well this one here—Cyrus, right?" Brad says. "He's been glued to his seat the whole time so my guess is probably gay, but a closet case? I can't tell about—what's your name again?"

"Jeff," Jeff says.

"Right." Brad looks him over, up and down his face to his chest. "I can't get a read."

"We're friends," Jeff says. Answering for me. "We were in a band back in Pennsylvania."

"What kind of band?" Oliver says.

"Hardcore," Jeff says, pointing to his Fucked Up T-shirt.

"Hardcore reggae?" Brad says, laughing to himself. He's kind of a dick. Mindy returns to the table with several shots on a round metal tray.

"And you, my dear?" Brad says. "Lesbian, bi, or cis? Oh, never mind, you're all kinds of awesome."

"Oh, I know."

"So how long are you guys in California?" Oliver says.

"We're leaving tomorrow. Jeff and me," Mindy says.

"Oh, fuck that," Brad says. "Mondays is trivia night at Blazing Saddles. You can't stay one more day?"

"I recognize those words as English but they do not make sense together," Mindy says.

Oliver laughs but Brad sees someone he knows and steps away from the table. I think we need to meet Cody soon.

"Are you two boyfriends?" Jeff says. He just says it.

"Noooooooo," Oliver says, shaking his head dramatically. "We're just friends."

He scratches at his face, the stubble on his cheeks.

"We dated for a bit but it didn't take."

The music is louder now, blasting over speakers at the edges of the bar, the crowd getting bigger the longer we've been here.

"We probably need to leave," I say, checking my watch.

"Wow," Oliver says. "You can't stay for one more round?"

He reaches for the last shot—I'm not sure how we got down to one shot but Mindy is smiling and Jeff seems wasted and I don't know why I stopped drinking.

"You want it?" Oliver asks me, reaching out for my hand but I pull back on instinct.

"Sorry," he says, a little cross-eyed, and I signal to Jeff and Mindy we need to leave but they're both too drunk to notice. Oliver gets up when Brad calls for him.

"Let's go," I say, louder this time. "I think Oliver was hitting on me."

Mindy and Jeff laugh together.

"Dude, everyone in here is hitting on everyone else," Mindy says. "Well—except me."

"I think you're the wrong gender," Jeff says.

"You 'think'?"

Jeff laughs. I'm not sure what's happening.

"What about the concert?" I say.

"Ugh, I don't feel like going to a concert right now," Mindy says, staring up at the sky from the patio. She mentions it's spinning.

"What do you guys want to do?" I say. Maybe Jeff wants to stay.

"What time is it?" Mindy says.

My watch says five but that doesn't seem right.

"Five?" Mindy says. "How the fuck is it not later than that? Is this jet lag?"

"It's five shots is what it is," I say.

"All right, Dad," Mindy says. Jeff laughs again. The Lady Gaga-Madonna-Beyoncé mix is blaring over the speakers and the chiseled muscled hunks have moved outside, next to me.

"Do you really want to go?" Jeff says.

This bar is 100% not my scene, even if I'm 100% gay, but if Jeff doesn't want to leave, I'm okay with staying. I just don't know what to tell Cody.

"Whatever you guys want," I say. "I'm okay with staying."

It's my last day with Jeff. I have all year with Cody.

"Is there a ladies' room in a gay bar?" Mindy asks.

She lifts her hand to her mouth and then we're running, carrying Mindy through the throng of chiseled muscle guys down the hall to find the ladies' room. Just in time.

She pukes for a while. Jeff and I wait, not speaking because it's too loud to hear anything and I can't actually think. Mindy is laughing when she emerges.

"If only my mom could see me now," she says.

"Are you okay?" Jeff asks. He reaches behind me and touches my back.

"She'll be fine," I say. "She's Mindy. She's an… achiever."

She clings to me, her arms wrapping around my waist. Smiling.

"You want to stay here?" I ask Jeff.

"We can go," he says, his hand still on my back.

"So let's go," Mindy says, pushing me into Jeff and releasing.

I keep holding on.

THIRTY-THREE

THIS IS INSANE. Legit insane. We are on the beach watching Japandroids on the stage and in the distance you can hear the waves, crashing in on repeat.

Their set started super late and I didn't have the energy to do more than stand and watch, but Cody grabbed hold of Jeff, and Jeff had a hold on me as we crashed into the mosh pit—up and down slamming into shirtless teens in the sand, all this violent thrashing for the last twenty minutes, so swift and harsh that the rest of the crowd dispersed, escaping the widening space where our bodies are bouncing into strangers, the stars above our heads like glittering lights inside a concert hall. It's amazing.

A slam-punch to my side knocks me off-balance, stumbling but spinning back upright to spot Jeff throwing elbows in front of me, clearing out space so that Cody can get lifted, up and off the sand above lanky kids' hands, extending their arms to keep him off the sand, the crowd deciding en masse to stop thrashing long enough to propel Cody all the way to the stage. The drums explode and the chorus rages, the sun setting so long ago we're bathed in moonlight above the stage lights, the crowd singing along to their most popular song around me. Younger Us.

Cody attempts to swing over the bouncers to join the band on the platform but some massive dude reaches out to collect him, tossing him back into the masses. Jeff starts laughing so I start laughing then I'm slammed into again, forward and sideways, falling to the sand this time but it's soft not rough, and a pair of hands grab hold of me. Jeff picks me up.

"This is incredible," Jeff says at the close of the song. "Fucking 'Younger Us'."

"I know," I say. I know.

Mindy took a pass on the concert so I offered to go back to the hotel to make sure she returned safe but she said she'd be fine, said the vomiting sobered her up "right quick" and she just wanted to sleep.

I didn't protest. I wanted to see Japandroids with Jeff.

And Cody.

The next song begins and before I can even process which track it is, the mosh pit activates, the adrenaline rush like the crush of hands and arms and shirtless bodies slamming into me, collapsing at first then exploding out and accelerating, like a wave. Crashing in on repeat.

Some skinny kid slams into me, knocking me sideways into another skinny dude in board shorts and no shirt— there's definitely a theme among the concertgoers in the pit—and I lose my balance, slipping on the sand again. I'm wearing my running shoes, but the soles are worn down and don't grip the surface like they do the solid ground. Someone grabs hold of me to pull me back upright and at first I think it's Jeff but then I see Cody, wild eyes and shaved head, sun-yellow tank clinging to his skin. I hold on.

"Where's Jeff?" he says as the Japandroids' singer banters about Huntington Beach or California or America maybe, the drummer punctuating with bass attacks between tracks. Japandroids only has the two band members, drummer and lead guitarist. Like Jeff and me.

"I don't see him," I say, standing on my toes to see over the crowd.

"There he is."

Cody points as Jeff waves from the other side of the pit, closer to the stage, but then "Heavenward Grand Prix" explodes from the speakers and the crowd swallows us whole.

Cody is dancing beside me, pushing up into me, his rhythm matching mine. We're almost the same height and we love the exact same music, although we don't look the same—which would be weird if I was attracted to someone who looked like me, but we've had this connection since we met at the ice cream shop two years ago and now we're here, together, on the beach watching Japandroids perform on a stage. It's amazing.

"Oh my god, I need water," Cody says at the close of the song, his sweaty hand grabbing hold of my hand and pulling me out from the pit. He's been drinking since we got here—purple-colored punch out of clear plastic bottles, spiked with alcohol that smells like the turpentine Dad applies to the deck behind our house. I took one sip and handed it back to him.

Cody yanks harder because I'm trapped among a flurry of bodies, craning my neck to find Jeff but I've got perspiration in my eyes and the bodies are so close together, I can't really see. We clear the crowd into an open space on the sand.

"You're hilarious," Cody says, leading me toward the row of food trucks lined up on the asphalt next to the beach. "You can't miss a minute of the band."

I haven't eaten since lunch but I don't think I'm hungry, or my mind's too obsessed with the band and Jeff, or Cody next to me, his skin shimmering in the lights from the makeshift stage.

"What are you getting?" Cody latches onto my elbow. "They have these churros that they deep-fry in magical oil to make them crunchy and light at the same time and they don't overdo it with sugar like everywhere else."

His smile extends to the corners of his eyes and the thin layer of hair on his head looks yellow in the moonlight, matching his shirt.

"Jeff!" he shouts and I look beside me and now they're both beside me.

"You guys left me in the pit to die," Jeff says, breathing heavy.

"I'm sorry," Cody says, releasing my arm. "We were starving. But Cy was looking for you, so it's all my fault. You hungry?"

"Yeah," Jeff says, turning to me. "What are you getting?"

"I don't know." I can't think.

"I do know we need more of that punch," Jeff says. "Have you seen the guy?"

There are several guys walking around with coolers of purple-flavored liquor because apparently in California you can smoke weed and drink on the beach without showing I.D. I'm so glad I moved here. I think.

"What do you want, Cy?" Cody asks, his wallet open and credit card out. I still have Dad's card so I offer to pay but Cody refuses.

"Just the churros," I say. "Jeff?"

"It's on me," Cody says, turning back.

"I'm good," Jeff says.

"You sure, dude?" Cody says and Jeff nods his head. I look at him strange. I thought he said he was hungry.

"Just the churros," Cody says to the food truck guy and a couple minutes later we're seated on the half-wall between the beach and the promenade, Cody scarfing tacos while I'm chomping on churros—more amazing than even Cody described—and the band is still playing.

"When are you leaving?" Cody asks Jeff.

"What?"

"Sorry, I meant—are you still in town tomorrow?" Cody says. "Our school doesn't start until Tuesday so if you guys wanted to come to Manhattan Beach, I think my friends and I are hanging out all day."

"I'm flying home first thing," Jeff says.

"No," he says. "You should stay."

"That's what I told him," I say but I wish I hadn't said it, the way he's looking at me. I cough on the churro.

"Can you change your flight?" Cody asks.

"He has to get home for work," I say.

"Oh yeah, where do you work?"

"Some church back in Pennsylvania," Jeff says. "I do their lawns and maintenance and stuff. It sucks but it pays pretty well."

"Ohmygod, that's so crazy," Cody says. "My uncle handles the maintenance for the whole Catholic diocese around Redondo Beach. Hey—if you lived out here, I bet he could hook you up with a job."

"Huh," Jeff says, turning his eyes to the stage. Japandroids are playing "Adrenaline Nightshift," which has a killer drum solo so I want to get back into the pit but Cody's trying to convince Jeff to stay in California longer and I don't want to interrupt.

"But I'm serious," Cody says. "You could stay a couple more days—call in sick or something. You can't just spend two days on your first trip to SoCal."

I don't know why Cody wants Jeff to stay when he knows our history unless Cody's no longer interested in me and maybe that's why we haven't hung out as much this weekend, maybe it's him not me. Or maybe it's Jeff.

"Maybe," Jeff says, pointing to the guys with the drinks. "You want more?"

Cody nods and Jeff reaches into his wallet and makes the deal right out in the open before Cody and I can warn him about the security guards looming. They make a move toward him.

"Run!" Cody shouts and he's moving before I'm moving, grabbing hold of Jeff and yanking him back toward the concert, in the slippery sand where my shoes can't get a grip but I'm running, in deep drifting chunks of beach behind Jeff and Cody, the security guards gaining on me, about to tackle me and take me to the ground when Jeff reaches back, grabbing my T-shirt at the side, the threads sticking this time so I stick to his side, diving in behind Cody into the pit. We throw ourselves into the crowd, disappearing into flailing arms and crashing bodies, the security guards repelled by all the people circling around us, the drum kit bursting from the stage and the lead singer screaming from the front as this skinny dude with no shirt slams into me and I slip on the sand with no grip on my soles again but Jeff holds me up.

He won't let go.

THIRTY-FOUR

CODY'S WASTED. I don't know what they put into that purple drink but whatever it was, it was way too much and he's done. I've never seen him like this. He can barely walk so Jeff and I have an arm on each side, holding him up the entire way from the beach across the highway, down the street to the parking garage. No way he can drive.

"Do you know what color his car is?"

"Blue. No black. Dark blue?" Jeff says.

He's drunk too. I have no idea how we're getting home.

The beach was a mass exodus when Japandroids finished their set but Cody had to pee so I helped him into a Porta-Potty with its rancid stench hitting me in the chest, a full day of fetid feces at the base of the toilet, baking in the heat. I held my breath as I pulled his pants down because his arms weren't functioning and his eyes weren't functioning, and I've never seen Cody without his pants on—or anyone ever—but there was nothing sexual about it, the rotted scent of shit overwhelming my senses.

We find Cody's BMW on the next level.

"You have to drive," Jeff says.

I don't have a license but he can't drive and Cody's eyes have been closed ever since we left the Porta-Potty.

"You okay?" Jeff says after we slide Cody into the backseat and he climbs into the front next to me.

"I never passed my driver's test and I haven't practiced in forever but other than that, perfect."

Jeff laughs and leans over to check on Cody—stirring a bit in the backseat. He slurs a sentence or two that isn't English or Spanish then he slumps sideways into the rear window behind the driver's seat.

I look at the mirrors to check for any vehicles I might hit in my first attempt to drive in two years but it's empty in the garage so at least I won't kill anyone in here—it's just I can't get the gearshift to move, like it's jammed into place, and I start to panic, worse than I'm already panicking, because Jeff's eyes are closed.

"Jeff." I tap him on the shoulder.

"Huh?"

"How the hell do I get it into drive?"

He blinks and shakes his head, like he's been asleep for half the night.

"We are never getting home," he says.

He turns on the car's stereo—connected to Cody's Bluetooth—and a post-rock track rings out from the speakers. I watch Jeff's head bob along to the sound, forgetting about the car and whether I might get stopped for driving without a license by the California State Police. Jeff closes his eyes and I don't mind.

Waiting for him.

"Press the brakes before you shift, my friend," Jeff says. "And turn on the lights. The cops will definitely notice us without lights."

I'm slow with the gas and heavy with the brake so there's a little lurching at first—a whole lot of lurching—

but once we clear the garage it's two turns to the Pacific Coast Highway and then it's a straight ride for a while, along the Pacific Ocean.

The road is empty because it's after midnight on a Sunday and we have our windows down with the water in the distance, the breeze from the beach touching the tips of my face. I try not to look, to keep my focus on the highway, but it's hard not to look, the white-tipped waves crashing onto the shore to my left. Jeff falls asleep to my right.

I can't make out the beach in the dark, or the vastness of the ocean, just the tips of the waves in the moonlight. I slow down, even slower than I've been driving, to try to savor this moment, at the edge of the world on the highway next to the ocean, the love of my life in the car with me. And Cody.

Cody took me to Huntington one night when I visited this spring, his surfboard attached to the rack on the roof of his BMW. I watched from the beach as he surfed for a while and we ate at this restaurant right off the promenade where tonight's concert took place, my first time eating raw seafood—something called ceviche. But that night we ended up in his bedroom at his father's house, making out, and I don't know if it was the fear his brother might interrupt or the fear of revealing my skinny body to another person's body, the fear of complications when I went away the next day or the fear that Cody was too experienced for me— he'd had a boyfriend for almost a year—but I made us stop touching after a lot of touching, and when he drove me to the airport the next day, it felt awkward—awkward enough that I didn't call him when I got back to Pennsylvania. For almost a week. He's asleep in the backseat, snoring on the leather banquet.

The wind presses against my cheeks, each mile a little cooler and the ocean more distant the further we drive, away from Huntington Beach. I want to close my eyes—I'm so tired I need to close my eyes—but I blink a thousand times, sticking my face out the window to snap me awake, the scent of the salt and the sand, like the smell of Jeff's shampoo, banging through my brain. Jeff's asleep in the passenger's seat.

His eyes pop open as we pass into Seal Beach, the BMW slowing at the first red light I've encountered since we left Huntington. The GPS tells me to turn right, away from the ocean.

"I get why you wanted to come out here," he says. "It's so peaceful."

The headlights are diffused in the dark on the roadway.

"What do you think about staying?" I say. "Like, seriously."

"I should," Jeff says, slipping into that sideways smile.

"Really?" I glance through the rearview to make sure Cody's still asleep. "I mean, that could have been us tonight, up on the stage. Guitar and drums, spinning riffs like that. Except they didn't play 'Lucifer's Symphony'."

"That would have been insane," he says.

I wait, wanting the wait to be over. Sometimes I think I've spent the last two years waiting for him.

"You know what sucks, Cy?" I glance at him as I drive, away from the coastline. "We never came up with a name."

"I know." I laugh. "I know."

"And Dallastown Sucks My Balls would not work out here."

"Then we'll get a new name," I say, contemplating. "West Coast Dallastown? Or no, West Coast Hardcore."

Jeff shakes his head.

"Huntington Beach Sucks My Balls?" I say.

"There we go," Jeff says. Laughing.

We pull onto 405 North toward Los Angeles, fifteen minutes from Manhattan Beach according to the GPS. Cody's mother is pretty chill but I'm not sure what she'll say when we pull up to her house with her passed-out son in the backseat.

"I wrote some songs, you know," I say.

The freeway is filled with more cars than the drive so far but it's not that frightening. I'm almost calm, with Jeff next to me on his last night in California.

"That's awesome," he says. "Did you record any? I would love to hear them."

I shake my head. Mindy and I did an aborted recording of one of my tracks—one of the few that didn't focus on Jeff—but we didn't get it right. The recording had a hiss that sprung up every time she switched from keyboards to bass so we deleted the track and never got around to trying it again.

"I was listening to our recording the other day," Jeff says. "Our song."

"And God Died?"

He laughs. "Yeah, I mean I don't know if that was the name, but yeah."

"How did it—how did it sound?" I missed this.

Not just Jeff but the band, our songs. My purpose.

"I mean, good," he says as I weave around a slow-moving pickup in the right lane, checking the mirrors thirty-eight times before veering left because I don't think I've ever passed someone on the highway before. "I hadn't listened to it—since we recorded it maybe, I don't know. But it sounded good."

"I'd love to hear it again," I say.

"Yeah," Jeff says. "I was planning to create an mp3, actually. But you know what's crazy—" He turns to face me but I keep my focus on the freeway with my hands on the wheel super tight, like the car might switch lanes on its own if I don't grip tight enough. "I had the recording playing—pretty loud—and I was playing along to see if I could remember. Roland walked right past the open garage to get to his car and he didn't say anything. Didn't even notice. Can you believe that shit?"

I shake my head. "Really?"

"Yeah," Jeff says. "And I got upset, you know, like the way I used to get upset at him." He laughs. "I was thrashing around the garage for a while, lifting my weights, tempted to throw one of the dumbbells right into his fucking woodworking table, the piles of stupid Bibles to brainwash other teens. I'd get kicked out of his house for real then. For good."

"Wow," I say. Out loud, I think. I can hear him breathing heavier now and I look back to Cody again, eyes still closed. "I thought you said it was better between you and the stepfuck?"

"Stepfuck." He smiles. "You're the only one who calls him that."

I'm back in the right lane, hugging the shoulder so no cars are near me, still nervous about driving at night without a license in California.

"But no, things have been better because I made them better. I stopped fighting with him. I was away at that school so long, dealing with my—I don't know, rage—I wouldn't let it get to me anymore. I couldn't let him get to me anymore, not just the way he tried to control my life but the way he ruled my emotions, the anger I felt all the time. I couldn't do it anymore. I stopped fighting."

He dips his head and I want to look but I'm too afraid to divert my eyes, a steady stream of cars passing by me on the left.

"So, yeah." He sighs. "It's frustrating as fuck that Roland didn't seem to care about the song that got them talking about New Bredford in the first place."

"Goddamn stepfuck," I say and Jeff laughs. I don't want him to leave.

"What time do we have to get up for the flights?" he says.

"Six," I say. "Maybe earlier."

"Shit," Jeff says, looking at the clock on the center console of Cody's BMW. "That's way too soon."

"Well, if someone hadn't made my dad switch his flight this morning."

I say it like a joke because I want us to be joking and I just wish we could have one more day.

"Yeah," Jeff says. "That was kind of dumb."

"We should stay up until the flights," I say. "No sense in sleeping now."

Mindy and Sharane and I attempted an all-nighter once, studying for midterms, but Sharane passed out on the living room couch as Mindy puked orange bursts of Red Bull in the downstairs bathroom. I don't remember when I fell asleep but I know Dad woke me when he woke up for work and I bombed my midterm, with how tired I was. It was fun, though. Despite the grade.

"What do you think?"

"Sure," he says, that sideways smile in the freeway lights.

I'm not sure how we'll get home after dropping off Cody but I pull onto the exit ramp toward his house near the sun-tipped beaches of southern California, as far away from Dallastown as possible in the continental United States.

If Jeff and I were still friends I never would have come out here without him, though. I didn't want to wait.

THIRTY-FIVE

"ARE YOU AWAKE?"

"Uhnnnhn."

I toss a pillow across the beds because Jeff fell asleep again—or maybe I did, catching myself nodding off in a deafening movie explosion.

"Sorry, yes, mmmawake," he says. I think. He didn't use enough syllables. "Time's it?"

"I'm afraid to look," I say, propped up on the mattress with a mixture of fluffy and firm pillows—the hotel provides both—but I can't see past Jeff's body, wrapped up in his blankets with the air conditioner blasting, the alarm clock next to his bed. "Maybe five?"

Jeff rolls over to his left, scratching at his eyes.

"It's three-thirty," he says. "Fuck."

We got Cody home, which was more difficult than expected because we were trying to get him inside without waking his mother but he was dead asleep and difficult to move, so Jeff splashed a bottle of water on his face. Cody didn't mind. He let us keep the car to get to the hotel.

Then he kissed me. On the lips in front of his house. In front of Jeff. Rough and dry with stale alcohol breath, holding me tight until the lights went on inside.

"Is there any water left?"

"There's Fiji in the fridge," I say. "I think the hotel charges, but we spent twenty bucks on a movie neither of us is watching, so I don't think Dad will mind."

I jump over to the mini fridge, extracting the water from the plastic lock that signals the expense of the bottles.

"He's going to kill you when he gets that credit card bill," Jeff says.

"Most likely," I say.

I hear him coughing in between swallows, finding the nightstand after three tries with the Fiji. I still have my contacts in so I can see Jeff in the light from the television screen but my eyes are so dry his face is a blur.

"Do you have any aspirin?" he says, rolling over to me. "I feel like someone is slamming one of those spikes you bury in the sand to hold up the volleyball net into the side of my skull." He makes the motion of hammering a spike into his head. "Repeatedly."

"I have Advil somewhere," I say, up and off the mattress again, sorting through my luggage. Dad was helping me pack the night before we left but it was hectic or I was so frantic—not knowing what I'd need for school or what could fit on a plane. Dad tried to be the parent who remembers everything and takes cares of the little things, after Mom died.

I know he tried.

"Hurry," Jeff says, face down on the mattress now. "I'm dying."

I find the bottle buried within one of the side pockets of my backpack.

"Thank you," Jeff says, holding onto my hand as I hand him the pills, his fingers on my skin.

"Do you want some Red Bull?" I say.

"Oh, hell no," Jeff says. "Do you want me to vomit?"

"Yes." I laugh. "I mean, no. But we are making it through this all-nighter. We only have three hours to go before we leave for the airport."

"Three hours?" Jeff says, face up on his pile of pillows now. "What if I nap for two of them? Real quick, you won't even notice."

"Naps are not allowed! That's not an all-nighter," I say, taking a seat at the edge of his mattress with the cans of Red Bull from the lobby. "Plus, if you fall asleep then I'll fall asleep and we won't wake up for your flights."

"So?" Jeff turns to me. "I thought you wanted me to stay."

"Well, I do. Wait—do you want to stay?" I blink through the blur, the contacts clearing a bit. The movie's still loud on the television—an action film in the "driving cars ridiculously fast" tradition—and I do a quick scan for the remote but I can't find it.

"I mean, if you're asking me if I want to go to the airport in three freaking hours to fly back to Roland's house on no sleep," he says. "That does not sound particularly appealing."

He slurs at first then repeats. "Particularly."

"It's that bad?"

"Huh?"

"At home. With the stepfuck?" I say.

"Yeah." Jeff scratches at his chin. The stubble is longer than this morning and I wonder how often he has to shave now. I shave less than once a week. "I mean, he's mellowed. Or like I told you earlier, I have. I don't drink and I don't do drugs and I mean, I guess that's good and all—but…"

He shakes his head, staring out the wall of windows, the lights of the city in the distance, like stars.

"Cy, there's something you don't know about—" He pushes up on the pillows, meeting my face with his eyes, red marring the white. "I didn't get sent away for drugs."

"You didn't?"

He pulls the blankets up to his chest again, up to his neck. The lights are less blurred the more I keep blinking and the volume of the cars on the television is deafening.

"It doesn't matter now," he says. "Never mind."

"Jeff, of course it matters." I inch closer on the bed. "You can talk to me."

He shakes his head again, sinking beneath the covers. "It's whatever," he says, his voice muffled beneath the quilts. I can only see his hair, fluffier than earlier, still disheveled. "It's better now—it really is—not having to fight him and Mom over everything. There's no fucking way I would have been allowed to go to California two years ago."

"But you're eighteen," I say. "It should be different now."

"I guess," he says. "I mean, I can legally leave."

"You could stay out here as long as you wanted," I say. "You don't need anyone's permission anymore."

"Yeah," he says, biting on his lip. He lifts up on the pillows, looking past me out the wall of windows. "I do have to work tomorrow, or—what day is it?"

"No fucking clue," I say. He laughs.

I missed this. I missed this more than I ever thought I'd admit. And if he could stay the rest of this week he'd fall in love with this place and he could move out here and we could start up the band again, like we never stopped playing. And he could tell me why he got sent to New Bredford, if it wasn't the drugs. I don't want to press.

"You know, there is something that could keep us awake," Jeff says. "Other than the Red Bull."

"What's that?"

"It's a secret," he says, motioning for me to lean closer, then he whispers, beneath the blanket, and as I lean in, he yanks me down into him, rolling over and climbing on top of me, punching me. I blink to breathe.

He pins my arms above my head and I try to wriggle free, my legs kicking up to toss him off but he spreads out and lets his body collapse on top of me, laughing—both of us are laughing—his teeth bright in the light from the screen. We're wrestling.

I can't believe we're fucking wrestling.

He shifts his full weight on top of me, holding me down, shifting up my body inch by inch until his face is in front of my face. His eyes on my eyes. His hair drifts down around his cheeks and touches my skin, at the chin. My arms are pinned.

They say waiting is just like wanting because you always want the wait to be over.

He leans in and kisses me.

Hard and rough like pent-up aggression mixed with sleep breath, then he pulls back all abrupt. Waiting.

For a split second I think about telling him to stop. That I kissed Cody tonight and it felt great like it should have felt great, but I'm half asleep and wide awake and Jeff is on top of me, my arms pinned to my waist. And I want to kiss him again—I've always wanted to kiss him again—so I pull my arms free and pull him closer to me.

And then we're kissing.

Hard and rough on my lips, but different this time. More sexual. And then we're rubbing and touching until our shirts are off—Jeff pulling off his and then pulling off mine and now our chests are touching, bare skin to bare skin, in a way we've never been.

Then for a moment—a brief perfect moment—Jeff pulls back, like we're moving too fast because we are moving too fast and I'm afraid it won't last. I blink, clearing my eyes and trying to clear my mind because I can't think—or I don't want to think—so I reach out for him, squeezing his waist and his butt, his flesh.

He pushes into me, under my chin, kissing my neck, down my chest to my nipples. Tiny rapid kisses that turn to licks at my stomach and my head starts to spin. I breathe him in.

Jeff lifts up, brushing the hair from his face and tucking it behind his ears. Waiting.

He reaches for my shorts and I reach down to help him, quick and awkward and confused like a dream, kicking the fabric off my feet.

He rolls over and pulls me on top of him.

I close my eyes and let him take the lead. Like it used to be. It's everything.

THIRTY-SIX

I FELL ASLEEP. My alarm went off and jolted me awake, next to Jeff on his mattress, his arm around my waist. I turn off the buzzer and slide down next to him, sideways on his pillow. The sunrise on his cheeks.

"Did you hit the snooze?" he says through the pillow-case.

"Yeah," I say, but I don't know for sure. It's too early for the alarm to be going off and my head feels like it's expanded to three times its normal size. It keeps pressing.

"Ten more minutes," Jeff says.

I hear him snoring immediately, soft and quiet with little peaks and half-snorts like he's breathing in too fast and needs to spit it out. The covers are curled between my feet and the end of the bed, and I climb down to pull them up, over Jeff and me, his tight muscled body so close to my body. We've never slept in the same bed before.

My phone buzzes again—way sooner than ten minutes—and I wait, as long as it takes, before I reach out. I don't want this to end.

It's Mindy. ALL CAPS ON MY SCREEN.

She needs to get to the airport. Now.

Like right now.

I put on my clothes in a rush—fishing my boxer briefs and T-shirt off the floor, shoes in my hands, eyes so dry the contacts seem painted on and I really need to piss but there's no time to piss, so I open and close the door as quiet as I can, out into the hallway and down the hotel stairs to Mindy's room, shoving my feet into the sneakers after I knock. I'm bent over tying the laces when she opens the door.

"What the fuck, Cyrus?" Her bags are packed, in her hand. "Are you ready?"

I blink a few hundred times because I'm not sure I can see. I'm not sure I'm awake. She pushes me aside as she drags her luggage toward the elevator, the hotel door slamming shut in my face.

"I have a car," I say, as we wait for the elevator to arrive.

"We'll talk on the ride, then. Ass."

Mindy has to drive because my lenses are fused to my retinas and everything outside is a bright-shaded haze of colors and shapes, yellows and oranges and puffy dark blues. Plus, I don't have a license. I should get a license.

"I almost left you," Mindy says after the valet hands her the keys and we climb into Cody's BMW. "I had the Uber set to come but I texted one last time. What the fuck, Cyrus?"

I try to squint to focus. It's not helping.

"If I miss this fucking flight, I miss the train to Penn Station and I will literally miss my first day of college," she says. "Do you want that on your head?"

"I'm sorry," I manage. I don't know what else to say. She pulls out into traffic faster than I drove on the highway last night but I don't dare bring it up.

"And where the fuck is Jeff?"

"He's asleep."

"I thought he was on my flight."

"He is but—"

"He's asleep?" She swerves across three empty lanes to make a turn at the light. "That's helpful, Cyrus."

"I'm sorry," I say, all sheepish in my head. "Last night was—"

"Oh, I'm sure it was," she says, slamming on the brakes as the light switches to red before she can turn. "Fuck, I hate driving."

"I drove last night."

"You drove where?" she says.

"To the hotel. From Huntington Beach." My mouth feels as dry as my eyes and I wish I had some water. There's an empty bottle in the backseat, the one Jeff splashed onto Cody to get him to wake.

"Without a license?" Mindy says. "Jesus fucking Christ, Cyrus. First of all, that was stupid as shit. If you get caught driving without a license as a minor—which you are still, I'm pretty sure—you can't get a license for another three years. At least in P.A. And you still haven't told me why you weren't answering this morning or what happened last night, which is getting more annoying every second, so spill."

"There's a lot to spill. How much time do we have?"

"Seven minutes," she says, checking her GPS as we move again. "Give me the abridged version."

I'm not sure there is an abridged version and I don't think Jeff would want me to tell anyone but I need to tell someone. It won't feel real unless I tell someone. The next traffic light turns from yellow to red but the colors are too bright, messing with my head.

"Jeff and I had sex," I say, rubbing at my eyes until the shapes come into shape.

"Okay, so wait—" Mindy says. "Wow."

She swings around a slower vehicle and slams on Cody's brakes again.

"First of all, I hate that I'm using 'first of all' so much. And I can't believe I'm cursing this much. But there is no fucking way we can discuss this in seven minutes. And what the hell is wrong with you, Cyrus?"

I start to laugh but she's not laughing. She's pissed for real.

"I'm sorry," I say. I keep apologizing and I'm not sure what for. Except everything.

"I mean—listen, you can have sex with whomever you want. As long as you were safe and used protection," she says. I dip my head. "But what the hell were you thinking?"

"I don't know," I say because I thought she'd be excited for me, the way I was excited, waking up next to Jeff. I never had sex before. And it was Jeff! Naked on the bed. She reaches out for my hand across the center console.

"Cyrus, are you sure that was a good idea?"

"I don't know," I say. I'm not so sure anymore.

"Listen, I like Jeff—or I used to like Jeff and then he punched you in the face because it's obvious now he was in the closet but I get it, that was a long time ago and he's seemed super chill this weekend, more mature. But what about Cody? What about what I told you? You came all the way out to California for a boy you like and now you're messing around with Jeff. We're in the kid's car, for Christ's sake."

She's never been this upset with me. It's unsettling.

"I didn't come out here for Cody," I say.

"Oh yeah?" she says. "Well, that's good, I guess. But that brings me to another series of questions about why you did come out here. Why you are leaving the best friend you will ever have, alone on the East Coast at some school where she does not fit in—I repeat not—and is freaked the fucked out about heading to tonight."

"You spent all summer in Manhattan," I say.

"I know," she says, "but this is different. That was forced camaraderie amongst a group of high school overachievers with poor social skills. I mean, I pretty much ran the place after the first week. But this is college, Cyrus. It's every woman for herself and it's not some sunny, breezy California school. It's harsh Northeast winters all the way at the tip of Manhattan and my roommate's going to hate me and my boyfriend's going to cheat on me and I'll be walking home in the snow crying over the breakup and slip and fall on the ice and no one's going to pick me up."

She squeezes my fingers.

"You won't be there to pick me up."

She's about to cry so I'm about to cry and it hits me all at once—Mindy is leaving me. In less than five minutes. And this whole weekend I've been obsessed with Jeff, not Mindy or Cody—the people who've stuck by me the past two years. Even now, all I can think about is Jeff in our room, naked under the covers. I'm a horrible person.

"I'm a horrible person," I say.

"You're not a horrible person."

"I am. I shouldn't have had sex with Jeff. And I shouldn't have let Cody or anyone else believe I was coming out here for him because I already cheated on him the first weekend."

"You didn't cheat on him if you weren't dating," she says.

"That's just semantics. He kissed me tonight. Last night." I don't know what day it is and time feels like a construct created to cloud my brain so I'd only make poor decisions this weekend. "And then I—then we—then Jeff."

She sighs.

"I know, Cyrus. Then Jeff. You've been obsessed with him since the day we met."

I wipe up the moisture leaking from my eyes, the contacts itching as the tears swim to the surface.

"I never told you this but way back when we were doing that history project in tenth grade—" she says. "You remember the one about Gettysburg with the clay sculptures you moved one arm at a time?"

"Of course," I say. "How could I forget?"

"Well, I remember every time you got a text from Jeff— and you got a lot of texts from Jeff—you'd stop working and get lost in the response. And I didn't even realize at the time you were gay, because I was completely oblivious even though it was super obvious. But I was like—wow, they are really good friends. And then when you told me you were gay and Jeff knew, that's when I knew, before I ever saw you kiss. And I know how devastated you were when the friendship ended." She pauses at the light, the signs ahead for LAX. "How you didn't recover."

The sun dips behind the first clouds I've seen out here all weekend and the tears have cleared my contacts enough that I can see without blinking.

"You're in love with him, Cyrus. You've always been in love with him. That doesn't make you a horrible person."

The car moves again, easing into the rush hour traffic despite the butt-crack of early, Mindy focused on the road and me at the same time.

"Well, I never told you this," I say, "but since we're spilling—that day Jeff went away to the Christian school, I packed a bag and took money out of the bank and I was going to run away with him, to help him run away. And I told myself it would only be a week or two before I came back to Dallastown, but a part of me—a big, big part of me—wanted it to be forever. Jeff and me in Brooklyn, sharing an apartment with our band and maybe he'd fall in love with me like I was in love with him." I laugh. "It sounds stupid when I say it loud."

"It doesn't sound stupid."

The tears come again and I don't wipe the moisture from my face this time.

"And it's not about attraction or lust or whatever—I'm attracted to Cody too. It's that I needed Jeff, the way he made me feel. That emptiness I felt for two whole years after my mom died—that was so hard, Mindy. It was every day. And I did all the steps my therapist advised, to focus on the pleasure every time I felt the pain but there wasn't any pleasure, so everything was waiting. All of it was waiting."

"And then came Jeff," she says.

We pull off the exit ramp into the endless line of cars fighting to get to the airport.

"And then came Jeff," I say.

It takes a while to get to the first terminal and it takes even longer for her to merge into the passing lanes—assholes at LAX refuse to give an inch—but we're quiet the whole time, neither of us sure what else we should say. She pulls along the curb at her terminal.

"Wait—how are you getting the car back to the hotel?"

"I'm driving it?"

"I'm not okay with that. Maybe I should find parking and then you can Uber back?"

"But how do I get Cody's car back to him?"

"I don't know," she says, glancing down at the clock on the console.

"Do you have to go?"

"Yeah," she says. "Yeah."

"It's okay," I say. "It's like two miles away."

She nods because there isn't any time and then she reaches out to hug me. When I pull back, she pulls me closer, over the console into the driver's seat.

"I'm sorry I yelled at you for—" She pauses. "This morning. And listen, I wish we had more time to talk about all of this but we will—FaceTime works in both Manhattan and Manhattan Beach—and Cyrus, you're a good person. You're a great friend and you're a good person. You're doing the best that you can."

I see an officer approaching, waving at Mindy to move her car but she doesn't notice.

"You're not supposed to have this shit figured out. We're all figuring this out. I'm freaking out about Columbia and whether or not I made a mistake going to school in Manhattan and now I have a five-hour flight to think about it and get super stressed again. We're all doing the best we can, Cyrus. But I'm glad I got to spend this last weekend with you."

The officer taps on the window, startling Mindy, who's apologetic as she climbs out of the car. I wipe off my eyes and meet her by the trunk.

"You know, you never told me whether you had a boyfriend in Manhattan or not," I say. "I feel like you're hiding something."

"I'll give you a call when I land." She leaves her hand on my wrist as we pull out her bags at the same time. "We'll talk."

The officer is onto the next car, waving at them to move, and between the shouting and the honking and the stench of the car fumes gathering in a putrid swale around us, it's not the time for sentimentality but I reach out and hug her again. For as long as I can.

"I love you, Cyrus," she says, grabbing her bags and jumping onto the curb in through the airport doors before I can speak. I'm going to miss her more than I want to admit. I miss her already.

THIRTY-SEVEN

"WILL CODY MIND that I'm driving his car?" Jeff says from the driver's seat of Cody's car.

"Let's not mention it."

"Does he know that you don't have a license?" he says.

"Let's not mention it."

Jeff laughs.

"No, it's cool. He said we could keep the car today to help with the move-in. He's surfing anyway."

"Nice," Jeff says.

I thought about Cody the whole drive back from the airport, whether I should be honest with him about Jeff—what we did, how I feel about him—but when I returned to the hotel room, I saw Jeff's bare chest, exposed on the mattress with his eyes closed and skin bright in the sunlight streaming through the wall of windows. I couldn't focus on anything else.

"Does he know I'm still here?" Jeff says, heavy with the brakes, the traffic insane the five miles between the hotel and my school.

"I told him you missed your flight."

I texted Dad about the flight and he said to call the airline for a new ticket, once we figured out which flight

"Jeff would be awake for." He sounded upset, which is fair, but he was at the conference this morning so he hasn't texted since and I guess he hasn't checked his credit card yet.

"Turn up here," I say, pointing at the LMU flags on all the signposts ahead.

"That was quick," Jeff says.

Loyola's a ten-minute ride from LAX—twenty with traffic, and there's always traffic—so we wind out our way through the curving streets toward Del Ray North, on the "bluff," they say, where I'm rooming this semester. My roommate and I have been in touch this weekend—his name is Chet and he's been here since Saturday and the rest of the floor has already moved in.

"I guess this is it," Jeff says as we park in the lot behind the dorm. "You excited?"

"I think so," I say. I think so.

We haven't talked about last night. I didn't know what to say and I'm on no sleep, my brain cluttered with everything Mindy said or what I should say to Cody or the fact I'm moving into my college dorm room today. And the hotel lobby's coffee was nowhere near strong enough.

"Do you know what floor you're on?"

Jeff eyes my suitcases in the trunk.

"Third," I say. "But there's an elevator, I think."

"There better be." He smiles and the blue sky frames his face. After his shower, he spent forever in the bathroom styling his hair, pulled back behind his ears, cleaner and softer than the rest of the weekend.

We head around the building to the front and the entrance is open, which is fortunate because I don't have a key. I think I'm supposed to stop somewhere to get my move-in materials but I'm not sure where, the way my brain isn't functioning, which doesn't bode well for my ability to manage being away on my own. I just declared a major last week—Business Administration with a minor in English, which I originally had reversed until Dad informed me that most English majors end up as teachers. I don't want to be a teacher.

The elevator door opens at my floor and Jeff nearly slams my suitcase into some girl's leg.

"Do you mind?" she says, backing up in the hallway. She has green-and-brown hair—mixed together like it's supposed to go together—and a nose ring spanning both nostrils at the center of her pale face.

"Sorry," Jeff says.

"No worries. You boys moving in?"

"He is," Jeff says, halfway in and out of the opening.

"Cool. I'm Dorea and I'm basically in charge of this floor, which some may argue with, namely Chet—wait, are you Chet's roommate?" She talks way too fast for me to follow but Jeff nods. "Well, this might be a problem, because Chet and I are embroiled in an immortal struggle for dominance of the floor and since his fragile male ego cannot fathom having a female in charge of him—like most men—we are not getting along. And I say 'most' because I'm just meeting you, so I shouldn't generalize. Are you Cyrus?"

"Wow," Jeff says.

"You're sweet," Dorea says, rubbing his arm. The elevator door dings in its attempt to close but she reaches out to stop it.

"I'm Cyrus and this is Jeff," I say, exiting the elevator with my other suitcase.

"Interesting." She closes one eye, green-and-brown like her hair, and looks me over. "Chet mentioned his roommate flew in from the East Coast and arrived on Saturday, but it's currently Monday and you are just now moving in."

Jeff laughs.

"We got delayed," I say.

"I don't know what that means." She shakes her head and steps past us into the elevator as it beeps again. "But you're Chet's roommate, which is strike one, and you waited two whole days to meet me, which is strike two. You'll need to step up your game, young Cyrus. I'm in 304, which is right across the hall from you and Chet, so if you feel the need to purchase a peace offering, I accept cash and gift cards in lieu of a present. Sound good?"

The elevator doors close as she waves goodbye.

"That was awesome," Jeff says. "I feel like she was the embodiment of Mindy, somehow with more attitude."

We head down the hallway to find my room, laughing.

I don't want him to leave.

Chet is shorter than me, and plumper, and Indian, which is a lot of adjectives but he's a lot of personality, like Dorea. He's been in and out of the room while Jeff and I unpack.

"We're going to Pizza Hut if you want to join us," Chet says, snaking his head through the door.

"Oh." I look to Jeff. "Do you want to?"

"I could eat," he says. I could too. Despite the massive credit card bill awaiting my father, I don't remember eating much all weekend.

"It's the next building over," Chet says, grabbing his keys from the dresser. "I have to round up some people on the floor but I'll meet you over there, okay?"

Chet gave us the lowdown on the 3rd floor of Del Ray North. One side of the hall is for boys, the other side is for girls, we're all first-year, and we share bathrooms at the end of the hall—separate for boys and girls except you're allowed to use either, depending on your own identity, which is not on-brand for a Catholic university but this is California, so I think that takes precedence. I wasn't exactly excited to attend a school founded by Catholics, but they made it clear there's no religion requirement or church attendance or anything. And it's the only school in the state that accepted me.

"Where are the hangers?" Jeff says at the closet, a pile of my shirts in his hand. We've been unpacking into the dresser they provided but it's already full.

"There aren't any?"

"There's two," Jeff says, pulling open the folding doors to reveal two lonely hangers swinging from the bar.

"Go see what's on Chet's side."

The room is identical on each side, twin beds flanking each wall, dresser at the foot of the bed across from the closet, desk at the other end by the window. There's a small refrigerator below the window that Chet said was here when he got here and his parents are bringing a television down when they visit on parents' weekend. My dad is coming too.

"Lots of hangers," Jeff says, opening Chet's closet to reveal a massive collection of clothes on hangers and the shelves above them, a wide assortment of shoes on the floor. He's way more into fashion than me. But so are most humans.

"You think he took yours?" Jeff says.

"I don't know," I say. "That would be weird."

"It would," Jeff says. "You want me to kick his ass for you?"

"No," I say. "We should maybe ask him first."

"You're going to ask him?"

"Probably not," I say. Jeff laughs.

Chet asked about my sexuality in one of our text exchanges this summer, but all casual—like "You're gay, right?" and a "Cool" when I said "Yes," because I don't hide it on social media anymore, not since Philly Pride. After Sharane took her posts down, I decided to post my own, the three of us draped in rainbow flags in front of a parked Snoopy float that some kid on the street took for me. I don't know why Snoopy—why he was there or why that was my official coming out post on Instagram. But it wasn't as big a deal as I used to worry it would be. Everyone I cared about already knew.

"So what time are the flights again?" Jeff says, checking his phone as he sits on my bed. "We should head to the airport after the pizza, maybe?"

"You're leaving?"

The window is open and I think I can smell the ocean in the breeze. The campus is two miles from the beach.

"I mean, you have a lot of unpacking to do and you have to get the car back to Cody and didn't Chet say there was some kind of orientation thing tonight?"

"Yeah," I say. I set up my laptop on my desk but I don't have any books yet. Chet's desk is filled with them. "But I'm pretty sure it's lame."

"Don't be ridiculous," Jeff says, crossing then uncrossing his legs and leaning forward over his knees. He shaved this morning with the hotel razor in the bathroom, nicking himself beneath his skin but it's healed enough you can hardly tell. "It's the start of college. Maybe there's a pep rally or something?"

"I don't think they do that in college," I say, stepping closer to the bed.

"Either way. You don't have to entertain me all day."

"I'm not. I mean, you could just come with. Pretend you're a student. And you could crash here tonight. You said you could call out of work tomorrow, right?"

"Cy." He looks across to Chet's bed. "You know I can't stay here. Where would I sleep?"

"Well—" I nod toward my bed, which makes Jeff laugh. An uncomfortable laugh.

"I'm not sure Chet would be okay with that," Jeff says.

"Fuck Chet. He stole my hangers."

Jeff laughs again.

"I was really hoping you'd stay," I say, taking a seat on the bare mattress beside him. "I mean, we haven't even talked about last night."

"I know," Jeff says, shifting away on the bed a couple inches. "And maybe that's for the best."

"What do you mean?"

"I just don't know if it would help." He looks past me out the open window, the ocean beckoning. "I think it's better if we preserve it. The memory of it."

I look at him strange because he's acting strange—like he wants to escape all of a sudden, forget last night even happened.

"What are you saying, Jeff? Didn't you like it?"

"No," he says. "I mean, yes." Clouds outside shift shadows into the room, across his face. "I mean, I enjoyed it. Very much."

"Okay," I say, edging closer to him again.

"It's just, you know, we weren't talking anymore and we weren't even friends and I realize a lot of that was my fault but I don't want to jeopardize this, what we had this weekend. I'm afraid if we analyze it too much, we would ruin it." The breeze blows the hair into his eyes. "I want to hold onto this when I get back to Dallastown, you know. I need to."

He laughs. It's a nice laugh. But I don't want to let go.

"But you don't need to go back to Dallastown," I say. "You can stay here."

"How?"

He points to Chet's bed again.

"Well," I say, thinking out loud the insane thoughts I've had this weekend. "What if we got a hotel room? I have money in my account—a lot, because it's supposed to last the whole semester, but I can get a job here to replenish my savings and you could too. Cody said his uncle would hire you to do maintenance for the church or whatever, like back home."

Jeff scrunches his face and I try not to break.

"Or, you know, if you're sick of working for a church, we could be dishwashers or bus boys, like you were planning back when you were going to run away to Brooklyn."

I wait, trying to gauge, but his face is blank, eyes blinking like he's thinking, but I can't tell if he's considering what I'm saying or figuring out how to let me down easy. It's killing me.

"But that's a big step and I'm not suggesting you decide all that right now. Just stay out here a few more days and think about it," I say. "We could even check out some bands playing in downtown L.A. or wherever that Oliver guy said Cloud Nothings played."

"Yeah," Jeff says. "Maybe."

"I mean, you can't leave L.A. after just two days. Even Cody said you should stay."

I shouldn't have brought up Cody but I'm panicking and I don't want him to leave. Jeff rubs at his face, the stubble cleared except for the faint whiskers on his lip. One of the two hangers in my closet falls to the floor.

"Let's just meet the guys at the pizza place," Jeff says. "I'm too starved to make any long-term decisions."

"Okay," I say.

"They're probably talking about you already," he says. "Chet must think I'm your boyfriend."

"And if he asks, what would I tell them?"

"We're friends, Cy." He reaches out to take my hand. "Really good friends. And I'm so incredibly sorry for cutting you out the last two years, I—" He sighs, letting go of my head and dropping his head. "I had a lot of shit to get through."

"It's okay," I say and for a second, I think we're about to kiss but then he jumps off the bed and walks to the window.

"I'm really glad we're friends again," I say, because that's more than I expected at the start of the weekend and I don't want to scare him away.

I can't lose him again. I couldn't survive if I lost him again.

After everything.

THIRTY-EIGHT

WE MAKE THE TURN onto Manhattan Beach Boulevard in Cody's BMW, Jeff's iPhone hooked up to the speakers, a track I've never heard before.

"You don't think she's into you?" he says.

"Dorea? No. She must know I'm gay."

"I mean, how?" Jeff says. "Not unless Chet told everyone but that would be a massive dick move and he's not a dick. Even though he stole all your hangers."

Chet bought pizza for the crew—like nine other people who live on our floor and are already the best of friends because everyone moved in over the weekend and had been hanging out except me.

"Well either way, she was hot for your body," Jeff says as we head up the hill past the high school. Cody's school. "And I'm sure you'll reveal your sexuality eventually. Maybe after your second date."

"I didn't know Mindy and I were on a date!"

I slap him on the side as we crest the hill to the bright blue vision of the Pacific Ocean and it swells through my soul—the scent, the sound, the taste—the sand and the ocean and the waves. It's like a rollercoaster almost, right at the peak of the first incline, when your heart seizes and your stomach collapses and your lungs want to scream but you hold it all in. Like a dream.

"That's gorgeous," Jeff says, staring out the same windshield as me.

"I know," I say and we ride down the slope in silence, the singer on the stereo our soundtrack to this moment. I want to stay here forever.

"These guys are good," I say, pointing to the screen, the singer's pained wail over grinding guitars, like a post-rock track mixed with guttural punk.

"Drug Church," Jeff says. "I just discovered them like a month ago."

"Wow. They're pretty great."

"I've been getting into harder shit this summer," he says at the light at the base of the hill, the salty air filtering through the windows. "Bands like Fucked Up and Envy and Drug Church." The guitar and drums echo around the BMW's multi-speaker sound system. "It's tough to know what they're saying with all the screaming but when you read the lyrics it's kind of amazing."

I nod without turning, staring at the ocean, a lighter shade of cerulean underneath the cloudless sky. The percussion crashes over me.

"I mean, it's more hardcore than Joyce Manor, but melodic, you know. I've actually been trying to play some of their stuff on my guitar, but it's really hard. I'm not even close."

He moves forward through the light into downtown Manhattan Beach and I don't speak. He notices.

"What is it?"

"I just wish we were hanging out," I say. "This summer. You could have shared this band with me."

I point at the next intersection, indicating we should turn left. Cody was napping when I texted but he said just to wake him when we get to his house.

"I know," Jeff says. "But at least we're together now."

He reaches for my hand, taking hold of my fingers, and I press my palm against his. He passes the intersection.

"You missed the turn," I say but Jeff keeps driving, his fingers clutching mine as we get closer to the beach, turning into the lot adjacent to the Strand.

"I don't want to go to Cody's just yet," Jeff says, putting the car into park. "I thought we could take a walk on the pier. Just us."

"Okay," I say. I think that's all I say. I might have gasped "Oh my god"—the way he's still holding my hand.

"I don't know when I'll get to see this again," he says, opening the door and pulling away from me. "The ocean."

I stay inside as he climbs out, no room to move while a family on my side struggles to pack their beach gear into their car before piling inside their minivan. I take a breath. I don't know what he said.

But I think Jeff is leaving.

The Manhattan Beach Pier is not like the Boardwalk in Wildwood, where we used to go every summer when we vacationed at Stone Harbor. There aren't any rides and there aren't any games and it's a single pier, not a connected set, but it's more peaceful—more beautiful, no flood of jellyfish beneath your feet like the Atlantic Ocean. A bunch of dudes are playing volleyball in the sand and heavy throngs of sun-bathers are closer to the ocean. Out in the distance, the surfers in wetsuits are waiting for their waves. We don't speak.

We walk side by side with an awkward space between us to the end of the pier, facing the aquarium, an octagonal building with a red clay roof that's been here forever, I think. I lead Jeff counterclockwise around the building because Cody told me it was bad luck to circle past the other way.

I stop at the end of the pier and Jeff stops with me. I don't know what's happening.

"Jeff, what's happening? Are you leaving?"

He takes my hand again and leads me the rest of the way around the aquarium, to a bench facing the ocean. The sunlight glows on his face.

"I'm sorry, Cy, but I booked a flight and it's leaving in a couple hours. I'm going to Uber to the airport."

The words hang in the space between the ocean and the waves and I don't respond because I think I didn't hear him right, the way it doesn't make any sense to me. Why he would leave.

"I bought my own ticket so don't worry about your dad. I'm guessing he'll get a refund."

"What's happening?" I say.

The surfers are beneath us, under the pier and spread out across the water. The sun is bright in Jeff's eyes.

"I'm not going home, though," he says.

I blink a bunch of times, the glow on his skin pressing into my eyes.

"I got a flight to Tampa."

"Florida?"

"Yeah, where my father lives," Jeff says, holding my hand—I'm not sure if he's been holding it the whole time. The lack of sleep might have broken my mind. "You know how we've been talking, and he's going to all the meetings and he got a job in construction now, so he's out of my grandmother's place and he has a place where I can stay. He said I could stay as long as I want."

It gets darker the further out you look into the ocean, from blue to black.

"When did you decide this?'

"I'm not sure," Jeff says. "I've been afraid, you know, to put any weight on it—Dad being sober. But I don't want to go home right now—back to Roland's house—and I don't have a place to stay out here—your kind offer of a hotel room notwithstanding—so I'm hoping, praying—" He shakes his head back and forth as a swarm of seagulls squawk over his shoulder. "Maybe he's changed."

I keep hold of his hand when he tries to let go.

"Why can't you go home?" I say. "And why can't you stay here? The money doesn't matter. Seriously."

"Yeah, I should have told you this a long time ago but—" A pair of surfers catch the same wave at once, but one of them falls a few seconds in while the other one floats above the water, all the way into the shore. "You know how I told you they found the weed under my bed and that's why I was getting sent to New Bredford."

"Yeah," I say. Like it just happened yesterday. I look down at his T-shirt, riding up on the side the way he's sitting, where the bruises once marred his skin.

"He didn't find drugs, Cyrus. He found porn—gay porn. These stupid old magazines I stole from the 7-11 when I was twelve or something, before I even knew you." He laughs, looking out onto the ocean again, and our hands are no longer touching. I'm not sure when he released them. "But I had them hidden still and Roland was looking for drugs I guess and I got super pissed so we did fight, because he called me an abomination, that was the word he used on me while preaching at me, and then Mom started doing her stupid bobbing and weaving, speaking-in-tongues bullshit like she's done ever since she became 'born-again' and I punched his fat fucking face—not because he found the porn but because he'd ruined her, you know. My mom."

A group of teens pass by on skateboards with hip-hop blasting from their speakers, loud and impatient.

"But that's her now, you know. She thinks I'm an abomination too. She wanted me to go to New Bredford even more than him because they all believe that shit, that being gay will send you to Hell or whatever the fuck."

A bubble of spit escapes his mouth as he laughs, an uncomfortable laugh.

"So, I faked it," he says. "Or I did my best to fake it, and then I met Rachel at our church on Easter—like it was a total setup with my mother and her mother but she was really cool and we dated for a while and it worked for a while because she was a true believer too—she wanted to save herself for marriage." The wind blows his hair in and out of his eyes. "But a few months in, she started to want more, you know. She wanted to do everything up to the actual sex so we did some stuff and it really bothered me. It really fucked with me. How much she loved me, and how much I—I couldn't."

He reaches out for my hand, his lips pursed and the tears coming down his cheeks. The skateboard kids round the aquarium on their way back past us, the hip-hop louder from their portable speakers.

"I'm sorry, Jeff," I say. "That's—I had no idea."

He stares out at the ocean, his fingers squeezing mine super hard, hard enough that it hurts. I don't let go.

"So, stay here in L.A. This is the literal opposite of Dallastown. You won't have that here." The seagulls circle again above me. "You'll have me."

I don't know how he doesn't laugh because it was a stupid thing to say but he keeps hold of me.

"You know, Cy, when you came into my garage the other day it was like—I don't know, such a blast from the past—from a different part of my life where we were in a band and we could hang out all the time and I didn't have to—you know, face it. All of it. The fucking—" He hesitates, a few tears escaping his eyes. "The all of it."

I don't know what to say because this is killing me, the way I wish I had known all along and why he never felt he could share this with me and the two years he spent in Jesus school being taught how not to be gay. I should have waited for him. I should have fucking waited for him that day.

"And last night was amazing, Cy. This whole weekend. And I can tell why you like it here so much—it's so chill and the weather's fucking perfect and the gay bars are—well—"

He forces a laugh.

"So stay," I say. I just say it. "Why won't you just stay?"

"I need to see my dad, Cy. I still love my mother, but—I don't know, she's been brainwashed by Roland or that stupid fucking religion and I can't not be gay. Not after this weekend."

I can hear the surfers shouting and the skateboard kids screaming or the children in the aquarium yelling out loud but it all feels distant. He blinks or I'm blinking and I feel like I'm floating now, out over the water, watching us speak.

"This was my first time, Cy. Doing any of this. And I'm not ready for it yet. It's scaring the fuck out of me. Not just being gay or coming out but all of it. College too—I'm not even close to having the background or the classes to go to a school like yours. I mean, in my junior year most of my classes were about religion or counseling—'re-education camp,' we called it—and senior year I was angry at the world. I barely graduated."

I'm shaking my head or my whole body is shaking because he's making sense but it's not making any sense to me. He could just come here. He doesn't have to wait.

"But they have community colleges here too," I say. "I could help you."

"Where would I stay, Cy?" He shakes his head. "A hotel is not practical."

"I told you I have money," I say. "I'll—"

"Cy." He reaches out for my hand again. "I need to give it a try with my dad. He's got a place for me to stay and I want to try to repair my relationship because when I tell my mom I'm gay I might loser her forever and I'm not okay with that. I'm not okay with any of this. I need one parent to love me."

The tears are flowing, but he shakes his head in the wind to stop them, standing up.

"Wait," I say. He breathes out, the sun on his face and the moisture fading, the wind creating massive waves for the surfers to chase. "Don't leave. Please."

Jeff wipes his nose with the back of his hand. The seagulls spin off the side of the pier and crash toward the ocean.

"Cy, you remember lunch with Dorea and Chet and that crazy kid with the orange hair who kept yelling about these secret tunnels Elon Musk is building underneath L.A?" I nod. It just happened. "I mean, dude was legit insane but funny, you know. And everyone was so excited for the first day of college but you weren't, Cy. You weren't there with them. Because of me."

I reach out for his hand and squeeze so hard I think it breaks.

"You came out here for Cody, I think. At least a little bit. And that boy is amazing—he let you drive his freaking BMW all weekend and you don't even have a license." Jeff laughs but he's the only one laughing. "And he really likes you, Cy. The way he talked to me about you, at the party at his dad's house before they almost burned down the place. You need to give him a chance. You can't be stuck on me."

"But I am," I say. It's all I can think to say. "I love you, Jeff."

I can't feel my skin.

"Maybe you did, Cy. And maybe I loved you too. But we spent a world apart the last two years—literally. You were in the real world in shitty ass Dallastown and I was in Christian re-education camp wishing like hell I was back in shitty ass Dallastown. That's how bad it was."

Some tourists pass close to our bench, speaking with a Russian accent. Jeff's still standing, one foot on the wood, knee bent. I'm holding on.

"And now you're out here. With the Loyola crowd and with Cody and his friends and the Gym Bar. You don't care if anyone knows you're gay. But I do, Cy. This is all new to me. I've been hiding all my life."

"You weren't hiding at the Gym Bar," I say. "You had a ball there."

"I know," he says. "But I also hadn't had a drink in like two years so—" The seagulls swarm from beneath the pier, out into the air next to us. "I just need you to enjoy your first experiences at college without worrying about me, you know. Because last night was amazing, Cy. You have no idea how amazing it was for me. But also incredibly confusing, and all day I've been trying to work through it in my mind and I need time. I need time to work through it."

"But I love you," I repeat. He has to know that.

"I love you too, Cy." We're still holding hands, at the tips of our fingers, and he's facing me. "Always."

I think we're about to kiss again, and if we kiss again that might convince him to stay. But his fingers slip from my grip as the waves crash in around me.

"I need to go," he says. "But I swear I'll come back to visit. Soon. And maybe someday we'll live in the same place and start up the band again."

"Someday?"

I'm drowning.

"Yeah," he says. "I'm not saying it won't be soon. I don't know how long my dad will stay sober or how long I'll last in Florida." He laughs. It's a small laugh. "But if it works out, I'll take some classes down there just to catch up and maybe next semester or next year I could join you at Loyola. You and me and Chet and Dorea."

He laughs again, longer this time. I'm still drowning.

I watch as he pulls out his phone to set up the Uber. I want to reach out to stop him but I can't stop him. It's killing me.

"Come on," Jeff says, pulling me off the bench, back toward the aquarium. He leads me around the wrong way this time, stopping at the end of the pier.

"Jeff." The sun isn't as bright as the clouds spread in the distance. "What's happening?"

"Just this," he says. "I want to remember this."

He pulls me in for a kiss.

It's quick—way too quick—but we kiss. At the edge of the pier with the waves crashing under our feet.

At the end of the world.

He pulls away but I reach out for his waist to pull him in for a final embrace.

"I have to go," he says when we separate. "The driver's waiting."

There's nothing I can say to make him stay anymore and I don't think I can speak either way so I just nod and hold onto him as long as I can until he walks away.

They say waiting is just like wanting because all you want is the wait to be over.

He turns and waves halfway down the pier and it's so quick I almost miss when he kicks into a sprint.

My whole life has been waiting for him.

THIRTY-NINE

"I'M SORRY."

"Are you okay? What happened?"

"I'm just—I'm sorry."

"Cyrus, you're scaring me," Dad says. "What happened? Is it your roommate? Is it Jeff?"

Chet's still at the orientation—or the after-party at the student center, free food and drinks and a live band for us freshmen. I told Dorea I wasn't feeling well and I'd meet them back at the dorm and when I got back to the dorm, I couldn't stop crying. I'm hoping that's normal.

I mean, not the nonstop bawling but feeling homesick the first night away at school. Hearing Dad's voice is bringing it all up again.

"No. I just—I miss you," I say, rubbing my eyes at my desk to keep the tear ducts from opening again. There's still the part ingrained in my brain that crying in front of another man—even your father—is not socially acceptable.

"I miss you too, bud," Dad says, and I think it's the first time he's ever called me that. It's weird. "You sure you're okay?"

"No," I say, looking out the darkened window into our parking lot, bordered by trees, the ocean breeze. "No."

"What's wrong, Cyrus? You can tell me."

I don't tell him. I tell my problems to Mindy or Donna or Angela even. Not Dad. Like if I sprained my ankle or needed help on my math homework, then yes, I would go to my dad and he'd be able to help me, but the other stuff— the Jeff stuff.

I need Mom.

"I'm sorry I left, Dad," I say. "I'm sorry I went all the way to the west coast to go to school."

"Oh," he says. "That's okay, son. You don't think I'm upset at your choice of schools, do you?"

"Well Mindy said something about you being worried and—" I shift in my seat, closing my laptop. I have an 8 a.m. class tomorrow that probably requires books but I haven't gotten books yet. "Aren't you?"

"Cyrus, I'm in Ontario all the time, you know that," he says. "So now I can look forward to the trips instead of dreading them because it takes me away from you and your sister. You'll see me all the time."

"Yeah but, you'd rather I went somewhere closer. Drexel."

"No, Cyrus. I mean Drexel is a great school for engineering and the sciences but once you decided against those majors, it didn't make a difference where you went. I let it go."

"I decided against engineering years ago," I say. "You should have let that go a long time ago."

"I know," he says. I think I hear a chuckle under his breath. "But I was holding out hope."

I step over to my mattress, the sheets still in the package from Target, where Cody drove me this afternoon for all the supplies I failed to bring to California. I even got hangers. Chet claims he brought his own from home and I guess I believe him, but I haven't had the energy to put anything else away. I've only been crying.

"So how did the move-in go?" Dad says. "You haven't been responsive with texts today."

"I know," I say.

"What happened?"

"Jeff left," I say.

"Okay," Dad says. "Wasn't he supposed to leave today anyway?"

"Yeah," I say. "Yeah."

I didn't spill the entire complicated history of me and Jeff to Dorea or Chet—not yet—and I couldn't tell Cody why I was upset, even though he kept asking why I wasn't excited or maybe whether I was excited. He picked out the sheets for me, pale blue or off gray, I can't tell in the room's low lights.

"Did—" Dad pauses again or the connection freezes. "What happened this weekend? You were fighting?"

"No. I mean, we were but then—"

I glance across the room to my desk, where Jeff left me a note folded under my laptop, thanking me for this weekend and telling me he'll be back soon. I didn't see it until I got back from orientation. He knew he was leaving before we left for Manhattan Beach.

"We were fighting but then we weren't and things were great again—as good as they've ever been—" I am not sharing any more details than that with my father. "But then he left. He went to see his father in Florida. His real father."

"Oh," Dad says. "What brought that on?"

"I don't know," I say. "I mean, he told me but I'm still processing because I thought he'd stay longer with the way things were better between us but—" I don't know how to process it. "I just miss him. And I miss Mindy and I miss you and I miss home. I wish I were home."

I wish we had FaceTime'd but Dad's not great at FaceTime and his hotel room connections are never good. I'm three thousand miles away.

"It's normal for students to get homesick when they go away for college," Dad says. "I felt the same way. One week in and I asked your grandmother to come pick me up at Drexel. I begged her to come and get all my stuff so I could move back home and commute to school."

"Seriously?"

"Seriously."

"You never told me that."

"Not exactly my proudest moment," he says. "But you'll be okay, Cyrus. You really will. How is your roommate, by the way—what's his name again?"

"It's Chet," I say. "He stole my hangers."

"He stole your hangers?"

I shift on the mattress, scooting back against the wall, trying to open the package with the sheets but they're wrapped too tight so I give up as soon as I start.

"It's a long story," I say. "But he's okay. And there's this girl Dorea on our floor that Jeff thinks is into me."

"Oh yeah?" Dad coughs. "And, uh, is she nice?"

"Yes, but I'm not turning straight now."

"I didn't say that, Cy."

"Sure."

"Cyrus, you know I don't care that you're gay."

"But you'd be happier if I were straight?"

I've never said that to him. I don't know why I just thought of it, but I've thought of it.

"No," he says. "Absolutely not."

"But if I were more into sports or engineering and stuff, we'd have more in common. If I were into girls."

I hear some voices in the hallway and I wonder if Chet is coming back from orientation. I've never shared a room with anyone before. I hope he doesn't snore.

"Cyrus," Dad says, his voice stronger, deeper. "I really hope I've made it clear but in case I haven't, I love you no matter who in the world you happen to love. I just want you to be happy. If dating guys makes you happy, that's great. That's wonderful. And we can talk about that. We can talk about Jeff. You know that, right?"

I take it for granted. I know I take it for granted. His acceptance.

"Yeah," I say. "Thank you."

"You don't need to thank me, Cyrus," he says. "My job as a father is to ensure that you're happy. And it's been hard, Cyrus, being your only parent. Your mother was so much better at this. She's so much better at all of it. But I did my best, Cy. I hope you know I did my best."

It's dark outside but there's a bright light from the parking lot penetrating. We should have gotten window coverings at Target. Maybe Cody could drive me tomorrow after school.

"And it's okay to miss Jeff. It's okay to miss Mindy. But you'll make new friends out there and you'll make new memories and no matter what, I'll be here. I've lived in this house for twenty-five years and I'm not going anywhere. So, if you come back to Dallastown after you finish college or you decide you don't like it out there—after you give it some time—you can always come back. I'm here for you. This home is here for you."

"Okay," I say.

I never really think about it that way. Home. The tears are coming back.

"So how was the rest of the weekend with Jeff?" Dad says. "Are you friends again?"

"I think so," I say. I sniff loud enough for him to hear, wiping my eyes.

"What's wrong, Cyrus?" Dad says. "What happened with Jeff?"

I want to tell him. Not the sex part but the fact that he's been in the closet all these years and his parents sent him to fucking Jesus school to deprogram that out of him, which is so disgusting I want to fly back to Dallastown and punch the stepfuck in his fat horrible face, or maybe have Dad go over there and do it for me. He'd do it for me. He'd do anything for me.

"Was it a mistake to ask him to come?" Dad says. "I'm sorry if I—"

"No," I say, shaking my head so hard I almost fall off the bed. "We—"

He wrote "Love, Jeff" at the bottom of the note he left on my desk.

"I'm in love with him, Dad. I was in love with him back when we were friends and then I was mad at him when we stopped being friends and maybe even hated him even though I still loved him and then this weekend we made up and he came out to me because he's gay—he's always been gay. But his parents don't want him to be and that's why he got sent to that religious school and this was like the first weekend he came out to anyone, maybe even to himself. I don't know. And he likes me. He definitely likes me." I wait but Dad doesn't speak so I plow forward.

"But then he left. And I don't know why he left. I mean, I know he wanted to see his father and I know this is all so fresh and new to him that I think it scared him but he could have waited you know, just one more day. I just wish he were here with me. I wish you were here with me. It's not that I'm homesick, I think, it's everything, Dad. I don't know what to do."

"Cyrus, you remember when you came out? Not to Donna and not to Angela. But to me."

I shake my head but he can't hear me.

"Well, technically you didn't come out to me. You came out to Angela and she told me," Dad says. "But remember when I came into your room and told you that I knew."

I'm shaking my head again. I don't actually remember.

"You were shaking, Cyrus. You were on your bed shaking."

I'm on my bed shaking.

"And you didn't need to be scared. Believe me, I was more scared than you, to say the wrong thing or to make any kind of mistake that would make you think I didn't fully support you." He pauses and I wait. "But that's the thing, Cyrus, it's really hard to come out. Especially in Dallastown, as you mentioned to me. So, give Jeff some time. Let him take some time. And in the meantime, enjoy yourself out there. You only get to do this once, bud. Freshman year. And freshman year two miles from the beach is incredible. I envy you, Cyrus. You have no idea how much I envy you. Your mom and me—we always dreamt of great things for both of you. But Angela is just like me, you know. She's hard-headed and not very emotional and she goes out and gets what she wants and that's great—that has served her well in life."

I think I'm crying again and I don't care if he hears. We never talk like this.

"But you, Cyrus. You feel things the way your mom felt things and you always let things come to you so when they come to you—the good things—you have so much joy, and you've had so much joy so it's been really hard to see you this summer not having that joy anymore and I don't know if it was Jeff or your other friends being away, but you'll find it again. I know you will. You deserve it, Cyrus, you really do."

I pull up the comforter to my chest, the way it's cold through the open window, the breeze from the beach.

"I know you love Jeff and I'm certain he loves you too, Cyrus," Dad says. "But let him come back on his own time. And don't wait. Enjoy Loyola. Enjoy this week. Start living for yourself, Cyrus. Not Jeff. Not me. This is your time for you."

Cody picked out the comforter and it's way too big for this mattress but he said he liked the pattern and he can't wait to see it in my room.

"You going to be okay?" Dad says.

"Yeah," I say. "Thank you."

"You're welcome, son. And any time you need to talk, I'm here."

Some cars pull into the parking lot and I hear more voices in the hallway, loud and impatient. I wipe my eyes.

"Well, it's late here, Cyrus. I don't want to end this if you still want to talk but I do need to get to sleep."

I haven't slept in three days.

"Okay," I say.

"I love you, Cyrus. And I'll be there in a couple weekends for parents' day, okay?"

"Yeah," I say.

"I can't wait," he says.

"I love you too, Dad," I say. I never say it. Not enough.

"Hang in there, Cy. You and Jeff will be okay. The fact that he came out there and you guys had a fight and you're still friends after that means you will be friends for a long time, I think. No matter what happens."

"I hope so," I say. I hope so.

Dad hangs up and I move the phone to the charger, checking my texts. Mindy made it to Manhattan and Cody texted "Good night" from Manhattan Beach but I haven't heard from Jeff. Not yet. He should have landed in Florida hours ago. I turn on the music he was playing for me in Cody's BMW—Drug Church—returning to the unmade bed.

I pull the comforter back over my body, the breeze from the ocean falling over my face. Mom would have loved Manhattan Beach, her toes dipped into the water under a wide rainbow umbrella, breathing it in. I wonder if I shifted my desk to the side whether my drums would fit in here. I wonder if Chet would mind.

They say waiting is just like wanting because you always want to the wait to be over. I'm sick of waiting. I've spent all of my life waiting.

I'll ask Cody to drive me to a music shop and get a used kit, something small maybe, so at least I can play. I don't care if Chet objects—he stole my fucking hangers.

Cody ended his text with a kissing face emoji. Jeff's right about him liking me. And Mindy's right about how awesome he is.

And Dad's right. He's always been right.

I need to start living for me.

THE END.

ACKNOWLEDGEMENTS

TO MIKE, who has been with me from the moment I started this novel, in its initial iterations many years ago, and who has put up with me always saying "I have to write" when he wanted to do something with me and I couldn't, because—well, because of this. You mean the world to me, always. And I couldn't have done this without your support.

To Mom and Dad, for your unwavering support of my writing and your many hours of watching Elie, without which I couldn't have written a portion of this in Manhattan Beach. To Elie, of course, who was sitting by my side at all the places this was written, including right now as I write these acknowledgments.

To the friends who have supported me and my writing, thanks for being there for me for so many years and in some cases, for putting up with early drafts of this, before a pandemic-era re-write. There are too many to name but I'll try: Tanya, Jackie, Laura, Katie, Kat, Alex, Regina, Corrine, Karen, Crystal, Aaron, Rob, Jonathan, Larry, Jill, and the many others who supported my first novel so lovingly (especially Maureen!).

To my wonderful editor Kristy Makansi and the rest of my publishing team at Amphorae (Lisa Miller and Laura

Robinson), thanks for all your help and support in getting this over the finish line in the version everyone is able to read today. To Sarah Elizabeth Schantz, thank you for your amazing notes and edits and knowledge on setting. You were so helpful in making this story better.

To John Darnielle, thank you for writing "The Best Ever Death Metal Band in Denton," one of the best songs ever written and the original inspiration for this story of Cyrus and Jeff. Let's hope this novel makes their band famous.

To Joyce Manor, whose concert videos got me through the first month of the pandemic, when I thought I couldn't possibly make it a month without going to shows, let alone a year. But because of those videos, I decided to revisit a novel that had been filed away for years, refocusing the story on this band out of Torrance with a new second half set in my favorite place in the world.

And finally, to Matt Switsky. We miss you every day, buddy. You were always one of the biggest fans of my writing. Wish you were still here to read it.

ABOUT THE AUTHOR

BILL ELENBARK started writing stories in the empty pages of engineering class notebooks in massive lecture halls at Rutgers University. He earned his MA in Writing at Rowan University where his love for Young Adult stories flourished. He is an avid indie rock music fan who has attended close to 500 shows over the past decade, from the "do it yourself" spaces of Brooklyn to landmark stages in Los Angeles and New York City. He travels all across the country for his day job as an engineer and has lived all over the state of New Jersey. When he's home he spends much of his time commuting to coffee shops in Manhattan and Brooklyn to write. He currently resides with his partner in Jersey City.